THE VOICE

THE VOICE

By

COLM CONNOLLY

SOUVENIR PRESS

ISBN 0 285 62572 1

Printed in Great Britain by
Redwood Burn Limited
Trowbridge, Wiltshire

for
Anna,
Eoin and Ciara

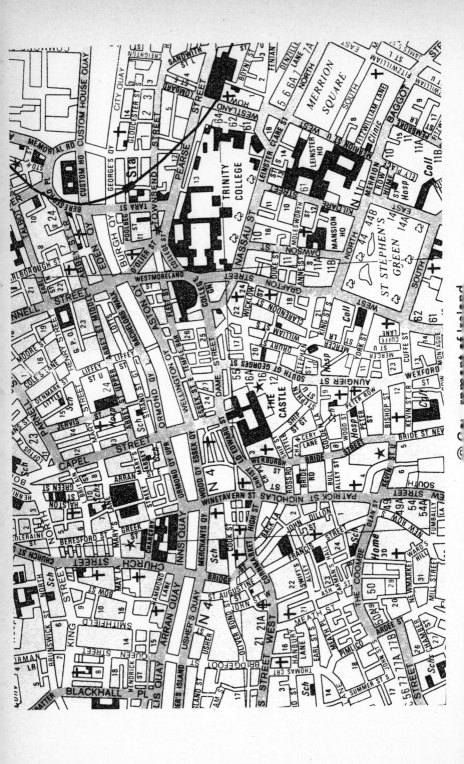

© Government of Ireland

The characters in this book are imaginary. The events, so far, are also imaginary.

To the many people who lent their trust and knowledge, I extend my gratitude.

Colm Connolly

When the elephants fight,
It's the grass that suffers.

Swahili proverb

Contents

Prologue

The children had been warned repeatedly. But now, as always, the warnings and threats were being defiantly ignored.

Football in this part of the suburban Dublin park was strictly forbidden, an area of manicured lawns and cultivated shrubbery. Playing pitches were provided, they had been told time and again by angry park keepers and gardeners, beyond the giant artificial pond. Those pitches, the children complained, were dry and hard, the earth packed and worn bald by generations of studded boots; these lawned areas now, well they were as smooth as a billiards table, and a goalkeeper could make miraculous saving dives without losing inches of knee skin.

Today, in the fertile imagination of young Tommy Gaffney, a hundred thousand fans roared their approval of his skill and speed. At home, millions more watched the television closeups of his ballet of weave and thrust.

The goal, which consisted of two sports jackets lying ten feet apart on the grass, loomed quickly. Now or never, he reckoned. He completed his scoring bid with a searing instep kick which would surely tear a jagged hole in the back of the make-believe net. But he sliced it badly, the plastic ball soaring above the goalkeeper's outstretched arms and incredulous face and dropping into the centre of the dense bushes with their borders of multicoloured shrubs.

The rules of the game were simple and unquestioned on such occasions: he had to find and return the ball.

He shuffled past the grinning goalkeeper, the taunts of the other members of the opposition cutting and stinging his sensibilities, through leaves and thorns, the growth rising along his body like the sea on an outward-wading man, until he disappeared from view.

Inside the jungle it was dark and eerie, the light breaking through the foliage in diffused streaks, the density of the growth baffling the sound of the voices of his companions sitting outside in the sunshine. Tommy crouched, eyes narrowed to penetrate the gloom and the tangle of roots and low branches, his nostrils filled now with the musty smell of age, hands greening from the bark moss. Then he heared the sound.

It was a low moan, broken and agitated. Now he was afraid and lonely. The sound was repeated, louder and protracted but the same. He slid onto his stomach defensively, his fingers sinking into the decayed and brittle leaf flooring, dust lifting reluctantly on the lethargic thermals caused by his movement. There was a slight stirring ahead, heard but not seen, and another moan, shorter. The boy stretched forward, reaching to move aside the ravelment of growth which formed the visual barrier between him and the thing. Black and matted fur, trembling, appeared as the branches and leaves parted. The dog, a labrador, was lying on its side, belly towards the boy, quiet now except for a lone whine beseeching understanding and help.

Tommy Gaffney's tight expression broke and widened into a joyous smile and then changed as rapidly to concern and sympathy as his eyes took in the animal. 'Easy boy,' he said soothingly. 'Good boy. Yer alright now, I'll look after ya.'

He reached further forward, fingers straight and horizontal, to stroke the head of the dog. Instantly, the whining gave way to a growl. The boy's reaching hand stopped, hovering inches from the dribbling nose, and then moved back. The growl ended as the jaws slopped open, nose skin withdrawing and wrinkling to reveal long teeth, chipped and yellowed with age and contrasting with the white, glutinous saliva that covered the tongue and gums and which trailed sluggishly in a steaming waterfall onto the animal's chest and forelegs. The eyes were wide, the whites barely visible, and, strangely, did not appear to follow the boy's hand as it retreated. The dog still growled, breaking off only to make useless efforts to swallow or sever the white stream. The boy did not understand, assuming the growl was one of natural defence against the stranger and not one of weak but open aggression.

The voices of his friends, raised now in impatient cajoling, reached him, competing in ribald humour.

'Get yer finger out, Tommy...shift yer arsehole...stop playin' wi' yerself, ye dirty bugger...'

His own voice, when it came, was soft. 'Come on, boy,' he pleaded with the animal, 'I'll make ya better again. Come on, b...' The last word was squeezed into his cheeks as the yellow teeth snapped together in one savage bite, the animal's head a blur of white and black movement, jaws horizontal for maximum purchase. The big incisors crunched through the boy's gums, uprooting teeth and tearing nerves, the canines sinking deeper until they met through the soft flesh of the tongue.

The dog was up on all fours, legs braced against the weight, growling and whining, jerking his head from side to side; Tommy's arms flailed uselessly against the animal's head and chest, his screams broken and strangled with each powerful pull and with the blood which now flowed into his throat. The other boys, moving towards the noises, stopped in their tracks when the big dog backed into view, dragging their friend by the face. His body, unfeeling now, was limp as it was pulled, stomach downwards, through the dust to the edge of the lawn. After one final shake and growl, the dog released its hold, allowing the mutilated face to fall into the dirt border. It tried to swallow but failed, and instead lowered its face to allow one foreleg to stroke the side of the mouth to help disgorge its tattered trophy.

Only then did the mesmerised onlookers move, the boys scrambling backwards, tripping, screaming and cursing in a terrified rush for the safety of where, none of them knew or cared.

The sounds and movement unsettled the dog momentarily. He felt no fear, only relief with the retreat of sound which signified a respite for his exhausted body. He looked down to the torn child. Small bubbles of blood filled and burst with each laboured breath expelled through the pulped flesh and splintered bone. Had *he* been attacked or did he attack the *boy*?

13

The sequence was a blur in the fever which tormented his brain and taunted him with thirst and hunger and yet made him unable to swallow food or water.

New sounds now penetrated, different from the children's cries, lower and questioning, urgent. The dog moved reluctantly and unsteadily through the dusty gloom, away from the sounds, past his recent refuge and out on the other side of the lawn, towards the open gates and the roadway beyond. A sudden shout made him slow his trembling gait to look back. Three men were running across the lawn in pursuit. Behind, in the distance, the children clustered silent. A woman and another man knelt beside the injured boy.

The dog moved on, his shaking legs defying co-ordination and causing him to stagger and weave drunkenly in his trot. He urged more speed from his tightening muscles, lungs noisily sucking oxygen through pink-tinged saliva which flecked his chest and shoulders with every step.

The last sound he heard was a jarring blare; the last sight was a hazy glimpse of red and silver at his right side.

Two medical experts would confirm the cause of the dog's madness, as they had done after the other animal attacks in the past five days. And, as before, they would be able only to speculate about the origins of the outbreak.

They could not know then, nor would they ever learn, that the savagery which had been unleashed was deliberate, part of a plan activated two months earlier...

Part One

THE GATHERING

Chapter One

The couple lay in the semi-darkness, the light from the bathroom throwing long shadows across their perspiring torsos on the dishevelled double bed.

They watched the exhaled smoke from the cheroot, spiralling slowly and aimlessly. Outside the ground-floor apartment, a car drew into a neighbouring parking bay, tyres hissing on the rain-soaked concrete, headlights playing briefly on the curtains screening the lovers from the rest of suburban London. The slamming of the car door and chink of milk bottles kicked but not displaced from their doorstep perch. A hall door. Then the room returned to the silence of thought.

The bedside telephone jangled, jolting them from their reveries.

'Let it ring,' said the young man, placing a restraining hand on his partner's arm.

'It could be important...'

'You mean, of course...'

'Oh, for God's sake. Not that rubbish again. There *is* no one else!'

The older man shrugged off the hand and lifted the receiver.

'Hello?' he snapped irritably.

The voice in the earpiece was metallic, distorted. 'Mr Charles Casswell?'

'Yes...'

'The former actor?'

'What do you mean, *former* actor? I'm still an actor and...'

'Come, come, Mr Casswell,' the gravelly voice now patronising, 'you haven't worked for the past two years. Since that story about you appeared in the Sunday newspapers.'

'Look, what the hell has that got to do with you? Are you one of those telephone cranks or something?'

The young man beside Casswell propped himself up on one elbow, curiosity tinged with nervousness.

'Relax, Mr Casswell. It's nothing like that at all. Are you alone?'

'Well, no. Not exactly,' Casswell replied awkwardly, thumbing the heavy signet ring on his little finger in a series of semicircles.

'No. I wouldn't have thought so.'

'Look, whoever you are...'

'Easy now, Mr Casswell. I've called to offer you employment. A contract. Three months' work with my little company.'

'How much are you offering?'

The young man sat upright at the words. Casswell seemed not to notice. Nor did he react when the young man left the bed and began to dress, snorting with indignation and hurt pride.

'Did I hear you correctly?' Casswell asked the voice. 'Ten thousand pounds for three months?'

'Exactly, Mr Casswell. I'll be in touch. Goodbye.'

'Look, when...?' The line purred. Casswell replaced the receiver.

'What the hell was all that about?' demanded the young man.

Casswell swung his legs out over the edge of the bed but kept his eyes on the telephone, remembering the words. He ran a hand through his silver hair and then twisted the signet ring around his little finger.

'Well?' asked the young man impatiently, watching the telltale fidgeting. 'Who was that?'

'I've no idea, dear boy. He didn't say.' Still his eyes stayed on the telephone.

'Don't give me that bullshit,' said the young man, slapping one leg to lend emphasis. 'It was someone offering you ten thousand pounds and...'

'He had the strangest voice,' said Casswell, unheeding. 'Distorted. Funny.'

'Well, it obviously turned *you* on,' said the young man sarcastically. 'That and the ten thousand pounds.'

18

'It was a trunk call. I could tell that. But I couldn't make out the accent,' said Casswell, voice still reflecting thoughts. 'And I'm pretty good with accents, too.'

'That's about *all* you're good at, you old bitch,' said the young man, his voice rising, trying to sting, to regain recognition. He stepped quickly to the older man's side and spat the words. 'Well, that's it. You can keep him. And I hope it bloody well falls off, you old...'

The backhand swipe straightened the thin frame and hurled it back across the room to crumple in the corner beside the silent stereo unit. After the initial shock came the pain.

'You lousy old bitch!' the young man screamed through the undamaged side of his mouth. He pulled himself upright and, on all fours, scrambled across the room to peer into the dressing-table mirror. In the gloom and through the mist of the welling tears the action was one of emphasis rather than usefulness. The cheroot burnt a hole in the wool carpet.

'If you've marked me I'll never forgive you,' he moaned.

Casswell didn't hear. He was already in the bathroom, urinating noisily.

Ex-marine Sergeant Carl Stolford couldn't blame the woman. Nor the meagre surroundings, the body well past its prime, the taste of alcohol and nicotine, the pretence of passion, the useless struggle to maintain interest and erection. It was the mirror of the whole, reflecting his present and, more depressingly, his future.

Damn the Pentagon, the Press, the great screwed-up, self-righteous, hypocritical American nation. And especially Lieutenant Russ J. Claymore Jnr, psychopath and congressman's nephew. Where was he now? Bet your scrotum he wasn't stepping between the dog shit on the cracked sidewalk of a Brooklyn Heights district such as Roosevelt Park Avenue. Not for that boy the crumbling four-storey walk-up of the Prospect Park area. Probably patting the scented hair of a young filly after her night's endeavours. The money would help heal the bruises, but it would be the nearest she would come to the Claymore family fortune.

Bastard. Forty-seven women and children in the Vietnamese village dust, along with Lieutenant Claymore's vomit. Stolford

19

had taken the brunt of the attack, if it could be called an attack, and the aftermath, including the ditch mass grave. Then the false report of resistance found at the village. Small arms fire by Vietcong. No casualties on either side. Huts destroyed when the gooks quit firing and retreated. But, unknown to the marine platoon, the gooks were there, watching, and they moved in later with cameras. The photographs reached Saigon and the world's Press within two days. It was too big.

Claymore said he had fallen behind the platoon because of a stomach upset and had ordered Sergeant Stolford to take the men on to clear out any Vietcong they might find in the village. But he denied instructing him to wipe out everyone they found. His orders, he told the provost marshall's investigating officers, had been deliberately misinterpreted. Claymore, already decorated for gallantry, was acquitted. Stolford was dishonourably discharged and pilloried by the Left and Right. Back in the States he was an outcast in his home city of Chicago, so he moved to New York. But what work can be offered to a career marine sergeant? Nineteen years of military life added up to night watchman at a warehouse or a bouncer at a nightclub or a hotel doorman. So when mercenaries were needed in Angola he sunk what was left of his savings into a ticket to London to join 'Colonel' Callan. He was turned back at Heathrow Airport, without official explanation and, with his background, no hope of appeal.

An attempt to divert to Ireland was stopped by the Irish authorities before he could book the flight.

Since then he had worked as a barman in a series of joints. Stubborn pride prevented him changing his name and this inevitably led to confrontations with drunk and not-so-drunk 'true' Americans. Stolford, more than six feet tall, broad-shouldered, and a devotee of unarmed combat, usually won although it hadn't left his face and body unmarked. Last night had seen the end of his latest job and the beginning of a scar running diagonally through the left of his bushy eyebrows. It also brought the sympathy of the gin-soaked divorcee who took him to her apartment in the East 60s for first aid and more.

But even now, as he approached the faded façade of his own apartment building and its sentinels of overflowing trashcans, his step was military, neat black hair unruffled atop his worn and less-than-handsome face, arms swinging in rhythm with his gait. But where now? A thirty-nine year-old soldier in exile from the life he had loved and the only one he had really ever known. The answer was waiting in his mail box in the hallway.

The brown paper package, six inches by four and a half inches and sealed with Sellotape, was unstamped. Who would send him such a package? He had no friends in this part of the country, certainly none who would bear him gifts. So, just what was inside? His brain computed and threw out the answers, all of them unpleasant.

As he stood in the gloom of the hallway, gently squeezing the padded package, the door of the ground-floor apartment opened on its security chain and the voice of the elderly female tenant queried, 'Is that you, Mr Stolford?'

'Yes, Mrs Schliemann.'

Relieved, the woman released the chain and stepped into the doorway. Peering through the scratched lenses of her spectacles at his hands and then at his face, she said unnecessarily, 'Ya got it, alright?'

'Yeah,' he answered. 'Who brought it?'

'Don't know,' she said flatly. 'Leastways, he didn't give a name. Just said he was a friend of yours. Middle-aged, small guy.'

Seeing his frown of frustration, Mrs Schliemann hurried on. 'Wasn't American, though. I could tell that much. European. Anyway, said you'd be glad to have that.'

'Yeah, sure. Thanks, Mrs Schliemann,' said Stolford, smiling reassurance.

'You've been in a fight or somethin', Mr Stolford?' said the woman, peering at his bandaged eyebrow.

'Eh, no, not a fight,' he said unconvincingly. 'Tripped and fell.'

As he began climbing the rickety wooden stairs, he heard her door closing quietly and the chain being slipped into place again. Inside his 'railway' apartment on the third floor he switched on one of the rings on the small electric stove and placed a half-filled kettle on it. He left the package on the plastic-covered kitchen table, curious but very unsure. He sat before it and gently ran his fingers over the paper, searching for some tell-tale sign, a wire perhaps or a piece of metal. Whatever was inside was padded by soft paper or cloth.

When the water had boiled he brought the package to the stove and, holding it by the tips of a pair of scissors and crouching below the eyeline of the stove, moved it slowly backwards and forwards through the steam. Gradually the Sellotape lost its adhesion as the package became waterlogged. Several times he paused to feel the outline of the contents but he could find nothing to confirm his suspicions.

Finally, with the scissors and a penknife, he eased the brown paper away from the inner wrapping of tissue paper. Still wary, he peeled the tissue in strips and then sat back on the kitchen chair, surprised and relieved.

The package contained a cassette tape and two thousand dollars in cash.

Across the Atlantic, five hours earlier, another day in the life of Dublin's Mountjoy Prison had begun as it would end, with the moronic dullness of a routine unquestioned for decades. For the 427 prisoners and those of the 240 staff on duty inside the grey fortress of four wings, today, like yesterday and all the other days before, would offer no surprises or disappointments. This certainly was of comfort to some and depressing to most.

Peter Edward Phelan, former electronics engineer now officially described as one 'who did fraudulently convert', made his way with five other prisoners down to D base in the bowls of the 133-year-old prison. After lunch he would make the journey again, for the last time, to complete his stint in the printing shop. Tomorrow morning he would leave Mountjoy with full remission for good behaviour, and go home to Betty.

The thought brought a smile to his sallow, bespectacled face. Officially he was not due for release until Sunday but, because prisoners are never turned out at weekends, he was leaving three days early. After two years and six months, those three days seemed a lifetime bonus.

Reunion was more important in these last few months that at any time during the two and a half years. She had sold the house and moved into a Dublin Corporation flat at Ballymun on the north side of the city. She had lost her job as a bookkeeper shortly after Peter had begun his sentence. The wife of a convicted fraud was clearly unsuitable, although that was not the official reason for her dismissal. She now worked as a copy-typist in a solicitor's office. Peter was glad they were childless, a feeling not shared by his wife, despite the economic stringency. But what of the future?

Alone in his cell that night he faced the question really honestly for the first time since he began his sentence. Certainly he had planned his future many times before but always in the belief that something would turn up from the outside, a suggestion, an offer. Nothing had. But he had convinced the visiting committee and the prison officials that with both his previous and his new-found skills he would be able to start afresh. What he didn't tell them was that he was unwilling to claw his way back up. He had already lost two and a half years through a gamble, a calculated risk which had left him, for a short time, relatively wealthy. He had enjoyed prosperity, worth even the prison sentence, although he would never admit this to Betty. He felt he had served his apprenticeship and learnt lessons. At twenty-eight years of age he was young enough to try once more. But try what? In the mental sterility of the prison the problem baffled him again. He needed the stimulation of the outside world for the obvious answers which he felt were waiting. Despite this confidence, he lay sleepless until almost one o'clock in the morning.

Six hours later he woke to the usual metallic clinks of the cell locks opening and the prison officers uttering their programmed instructions, voices monotonous, in tones reflecting the boredom of repetition.

Phelan's stomach tightened when he remembered in the haze of waking that today would be the last time he would hear those sounds and smell the gagging stench of sweat and coarse disinfectant unique to prisons. He sat up on the steel bed and swung his legs out over the side. He was already dressed when the officer reached his cell and opened the door.

'Right, son,' said the elderly man, as Phelan folded the last of the bedding.

Gathering the few personal belongings from the small table, Phelan took one last glance around the peeling walls and out through the barred window. He found it difficult to remember that at times this room, even with its peephole door, offered seclusion, privacy, escapism. He would not be caught again.

Downstairs in the 'reception' area, he stripped naked and handed over his denims. A cursory glance from one of the officers at the front and back of his body and then he was handed a cardboard box containing his own clothes, letters and other papers in his possession when he first arrived at the prison.

Phelan shivered slightly as he dressed. The first time he had stood in this barn of a room with its pale grey walls and broken white tiles he had shivered too. Then it was a different kind of fear. How different, he wondered, was this room from the depot site upon which it had been built, a depot for men awaiting deportation.

The elderly officer waited outside the grubby cubicle with the patience of a man with nothing better to do. When Phelan stepped out, the officer smiled wryly.

'Proper dandy now, aren't we,' he said kindly, sensing Phelan's embarrassment.

Upstairs in the office minutes later, Phelan signed for the money he had earned during his months in the printing shop: exactly £42. Then a brief word of caution from one of the deputy governors about repeating mistakes and the initial frustrations of restarting civilian life.

At the main gate the elderly officer smiled encouragement. 'Take it easy, son,' he said warmly.

The younger man on the gate duty completed the entry in his log and then unlocked the small door. As Phelan stepped out into the dullness of the Dublin morning, the officer said with a grin, 'See you soon, lad.'

The time was just after eight o'clock on the Friday that would tear Peter Phelan asunder.

Chapter Two

Charles Casswell stood naked before the bathroom sink and bared his teeth.

The financial outlay had proved worthwhile. The perfectly capped teeth contrasted nicely with the sun-lamp tan of his face. The full-length wall mirror reflected his satisfaction with the recent years struggle to maintain his figure. Mature rather than middle-aged, he felt. It retained the muscular development of his athletic youth. The chest and upper arms were heavy, the stomach surprisingly flat. Looking lower, he smiled. Nothing to worry about there either.

Today he had shed ten of his fifty-three years. He was going to work again. A victim of cruel circumstance, he had told himself repeatedly during the last two years. Others had done the same thing, and were still doing it, but were spared the diligence of moralising Sunday newspapers. It was unfortunate that at the time of the revelations of the 'investigating team of journalists' he had a starring role in a television series as a priest in charge of a home for problem schoolboys.

Since then the contracts had faded to a stony silence. Roles for which he would have been eminently suited went elsewhere. Even provincial rep companies had shut the door. Fellow actors in the dole queue had shunned him or answered his greeting with deliberate indifference. All that would change now. He was on the way back again. He could tackle any role, any dialect, any character.

But the voice on the telephone still baffled him. The tones were similar to those usually given to robots in science fiction movies. Hoarse and mechanical with no rise and fall, no

25

inflections. Why should the caller disguise his voice? Was it someone he knew? A hoax? Too elaborate for that. There were other and easier ways to be cruel to a man down on his luck.

How different things would have been during the last two years if Joan had stayed with him. He knew he wasn't the easiest of men to live with, temperamental, sometimes solitary. But she knew his moods and accepted the lifestyle. It was tougher on the children. Two boys whose father appeared more often on the television than at the breakfast table. Known in millions of homes at home and abroad, except his own. But he could be lonely too. Joan said she understood, even when the gossip columnists placed him at all the best parties and linked his name to those legally linked to others. It was part of the business, he told her. Inevitable and sometimes desirable.

That last hotel suite party had just been novelty born of dulled appetite. The end of location filming for the television series. Soldiers had done it during the war. Why label a man for just one night of bawdy novelty? Would Joan have reacted as she had if the Press hadn't pilloried him? But then, would he have told her about it anyway? And would he have admitted the pleasure he had found that night, a new depth to his life, a desire he would never before have contemplated or imagined?

Thank you, dear Joan, for your understanding. Bitch.

Carl Stolford listened again to the voice. The quality of the speaker in the second-hand cassette player was less than good but the words, although metallic and distorted, were discernible.

> *Mr Stolford, you don't know me and you will never know who I am. Later you will realise that my identity is of no importance to you. All that should concern you is my offer to make you wealthier than you could ever imagine.*
>
> *All I ask of you is your skill and initiative as a leader of men, a relatively small group of men, on what will be an essentially military operation.*
>
> *The money you found with this tape-recording is to cover your initial expenses. In three months' time you will have the balance of twenty thousand dollars. And within a year you will receive one and a half million dollars, deposited in a Swiss bank.*

The operation will be illegal, yes. But, one might argue, what business transaction is truly legal? However, you will not be required to kill or maim unless as a last resort, and that decision will rest largely with you and how best you use your expertise.

During the three months you will be paid a weekly sum sufficient to keep you in modest comfort in the country of operation. This will be in addition to the twenty thousand dollars.

My anonymity is my security, Mr Stolford. You have a clear choice. To accept my offer or reject it. Either way, there is no possibility of tracing the money you have already received or this recording. Whether you keep the tape or destroy it is of no consequence. In itself, it is meaningless.

At four o'clock this afternoon, please telephone the TWA passenger terminal at John F. Kennedy Airport and page Mr William Hoover. Again, this name or the man using it will be of no use to you should you decide to report the whole matter to the police. He will merely be a go-between who doesn't know you or me. He is being paid simply to answer a telephone and accept a simple message from an unidentified male. The message from you will be one of two words, 'yes' or 'no'.

If you say no, Mr Stolford, you will hear nothing more from me. If you say yes, I will contact you again with fresh instructions.

I hope you accept. I know you have nothing to lose.

Shortly before four o'clock in the eyrie-like TWA terminal, a small and well dressed man with a goatee beard answered a paging call. Moments later he was walking to his chauffeur-driven Mercedes. The driver held open the rear door.

'Back to the office, sir?'

Lutz Feldmann nodded.

Only the graffiti on the walls of the elevator had changed. New names, old jokes, short on wit. And who the hell cared about 'Mary'? Her boyfriend? Her girlfriend? Mary?

The lift whined to a halt on the third floor and the aluminium doors rattled open. Peter Phelan hesitated before he stepped

27

out into the corridor. He should have had a drink. But she would have noticed it. His hands were sweating as he fumbled with the key ring. Another hesitation, then he quietly slipped the key into the lock.

A portable radio was pumping out commercials in the kitchen, but the room was empty. The bedroom door was closed. He eased it open. The room was tidy and unoccupied. Probably gone to buy some groceries. In the hall he paused to study his reflection in the ornate circular mirror. Too pale, too thin. His fingers found a short stretch of stubble under his chin. Funny how the shaving misses go unnoticed until long afterwards.

He turned and pushed open the sitting room door. His breakfast rushed towards his throat but stopped midway. Betty's mouth dropped onto the man's shoulder but it partly closed again with the next thrust. She gripped her lover's hair and brought her knee down in a ridiculously futile attempt to stop his onslaught. He, face down on her bare breasts, took this to be heightening passion and increased the tempo, buttocks clenching and unclenching with greater urgency.

'Stop, John. Stop,' she pleaded desperately, her voice vibrato from his pounding.

'Jesus, not now,' he wheezed. 'I'm too close.'

Phelan felt dizzy and sick. Air, quickly. He stumbled backwards from the room and slammed the door shut.

The lover's heart almost stopped with the sudden noise which jerked him upwards and sideways. He toppled across Betty's leg and onto the small round coffee table alongside the settee. The table overturned and he fell onto his back, ejaculating onto his legs and into the spilt cigarette ash on the carpet.

'What in the name of Jesus was that?' he croaked, cupped hand trying to stem the already dwindling white fountain.

Betty's eyes hadn't left the floor. 'Oh, sweet Mary, no, no,' she whispered.

'What was it?' the man demanded, his voice angry yet apprehensive.

'Your brother,' she answered numbly.

Lutz Feldmann sat behind the pine desk in his panelled office in

Manhattan and pondered the situation.

So far he had lost nothing but from now on it would be a gamble. The whole thing relied on too many people, all remote, uncontrolled, unknown. True, the reward could be great, but it would be the first time in his long and profitable career that he had personally helped in the execution of an operation. The role excited him in a way that he had long forgottten, but he wasn't sure yet that he was enjoying the sensation.

He swivelled his leather chair towards the picture window and studied the view of the east river. It had taken him a long time to buy that view and he intended to retain it. His rare profession depended on his continuing reliability. One miss and he could be finished, certainly a miss of this enormity. But he would make it perfectly clear that there could be no promises of success. Payment on delivery.

Feldmann was a procurer. In lesser leagues his role would be called a 'fence'. But the usual fences relied on business coming their way and then finding a buyer for the merchandise. Feldmann, after a lifetime clawing his way to the top, always had a buyer before the property was procured. The system worked for the benefit of all parties. The purchaser could depend on anonymity, often working through third parties such as lawyers or smaller agents. The amount of money required to interest Feldmann ensured that only the best would be employed in procuring the particular item required. The rewards were high for all and the results almost guaranteed at the outset. The network of contacts was worldwide: buyers, takers, traffickers, protectors. His organisation had found new homes for more than half the missing four thousand Old Master paintings on the Interpol list. The big-time activities of Feldmann had begun in post-war East Germany, his native country. In 1946 he had bribed his way across the border to visit his home village of Wechmar and his remaining relatives, the few to escape the Nazis. Feldmann had left the country in 1937, his instincts predicting the holocaust for Jews in Hitler's Germany.

Through Italy, Portugal and Ireland and with false papers he had made his way to the United States where his two years' art school training secured him a job in a small but thriving art gallery in San Francisco. It was during this period that he determined to fill the commercial void in the art world: the stealing and selling of treasures. These, once purchased, would never be seen again. Hung in the private galleries of rich American homes, they would satisfy only the peculiar lust of the individual.

The East Germans and Russians refused all applications to take money and possessions to the West in their 'co-operative' post-war rebuilding programme. But Lutz Feldmann had left with Albrecht Dürer's portrait of *Duke John the Good*, stolen from a museum in Gotha near Wechmar. His accomplices would, in later years, form part of his international network. The painting had since graced the basement wall of a television station giant at Tucson, glad to part with the asking price of a quarter of a million dollars to gloat over his unique piece of art.

Since then, the list of missing treasures increased worldwide while Lutz Feldmann's fortune multiplied. He had personally negotiated and organised more than half the world's ten most valuable art thefts including Corot's *Girl Musing by a Fountain* and Millet's *Portrait of Mme Millet*, both stolen in Montreal; Renoir's *Young Girl in a Garden* and Rubens' *Christ on the Cross* taken from Rome; and Titian's *Madonna and Child between Two Saints* stolen from a church in Pieve di Cadore in Northern Italy.

Feldmann's activities had expanded to every area of art, catering for all tastes but only the wealthiest buyers. Organisations such as the Fine Art Squad at Scotland Yard had had only limited success—about twelve million pounds' worth in their first six years of operation—in tracing stolen art treasures. His security was so complex that none of the finds had led the police to Feldmann himself. Only to lesser middlemen and occasionally to the thieves themselves.

Officially, he was owner and part-owner of cinemas and restaurants in five American cities including New York, where he had based himself for the past eighteen years. This gave adequate cover for his clandestine business and provided ideal meeting places for negotiating with clients. No negotiations were ever conducted in his Manhattan office. Lutz Feldmann had come a long way from the decaying buildings and dusty streets of Wechmar.

He lifted the receiver of his direct-line telephone and dialled the number of a stockbroking firm.

'Mr Melchoir, please...Lutz Feldmann.' His voice was accented despite the years in America.

He swung his legs under the desk again and hunched over the expanse of polished wood.

'Hello, Robert. So, how are things with you, Huh? Yeah, fine. And the kids? Good, good. Tell you what, Robert, I'm good for a bit of recreation and I was thinking maybe you and me should get up to Maine next weekend. Get us some fishing.'

Feldmann chuckled at the predictable response.

'Matter of fact,' he went on, 'I thought some of your pals might like to join us. Make it a real party, yeah?'

He ran his forefinger across the desktop, then wiped the invisible track with his knuckles.

'I thought maybe Boothbay Harbor. Party of, say, ten or twelve...Right, call me tomorrow to confirm. 'Bye, Robert.'

He replaced the telephone and sat for long moments, flicking imaginary spots of dust from the surface of the desk and smiling pleasurably.

Peter Phelan was an island in a sea of loud voices and clinking glasses. He had left his prison breakfast on the floor of the elevator at the apartment block and caught a cruising taxi to the dockside area of the city. There, in a bar on the south of the River Liffey, he coughed as the neat whiskey coursed down his throat into his empty stomach. Two more before he allowed himself a Guinness 'chaser'.

The dockers noted the stranger and his red-rimmed eyes. Embarrased, they studiously ignored him. Here were some of the city's toughest men who could cope with any physical challenge except another man's tears.

'Are you Peter Phelan?' the barman asked again. The crumpled man jerked from his morose thoughts. Phelan lifted his face to search the other man's expression, at first curious then quickly defensive.

'Why?' he asked quietly.

'Cause there's a call for ya, if y'are,' the barman replied, slightly ruffled.

Phelan rose unsteadily but shrugged off the helping hand from the barman, who nodded towards the public telephone on the wall beside the entrance door. Betty, who had somehow found him, would be whining her apologies and explanations. Jesus, was he going to tell her exactly what she was.

'What?' he snapped irritably at the barman.

'I said you'll have to shout. It's a lousy line or somethin' said the barman patiently, nodding again at the telephone.

'Yeah?' Phelan snarled into the mouthpiece. Conversation in the room subsided.

'Mr Peter Phelan?' the man's voice was distorted.

'Eh, yeah. Wha' d'ya want?'

'Right now, only a few seconds of your time. Outside the pub you'll see two dustbins. Under one of them you'll find a cassette tape wrapped in brown paper. Take the tape away and buy yourself a cassete player.

'What the fuck *is* this, anyway?' Phelan roared. Conversation in the pub stopped altogether.

'Steady, Mr Phelan. This is no joke.' The man's voice was now more hurried. 'Listen to the tape, Mr Phelan. It'll be the best offer you'll ever have to start a new life. It'll probably be the *only* offer.'

The line clicked dead. Phelan kept the receiver to his ear for some seconds before replacing it on the cradle.

'Stupid bollocks,' he muttered at the telephone and turned back to his table. As he moved, the babble of conversation resumed and faces that had been staring looked away quickly. He was an island once more.

He finished his drink without sitting down and left quickly. Outside, he looked around but he was the only observer, in the busy street. At the side of the building he saw the dustbins. He weaved towards them, one hand on the wall to steady his gait. He bent to lift the first bin, anticipating a weight. The bin was empty and it rose effortlessly, throwing him off balance, but in his drunken haze he misjudged the necessary movement and fell, face down, across the bin. A woman walking towards him holding a child by the hand stopped and shook her head sadly before stepping into the roadway to avoid the shambles.

Pulling himself up into a sitting position, he saw the small parcel beside his foot. He stuffed it into his jacket pocket and hauled himself to his feet. The woman looked back as the young man stumbled away towards the city centre.

'Drink,' she said disapprovingly to the smiling child. 'An' his poor wife probably waitin' at home for the week's wages. What some women have to put up with!'

The child, still smiling, wasn't listening.

Carl Stolford unzipped his trousers. Lager, filtered down to its basic ingredient, flowed along the steaming channel of cigarette butts and masticated chewing gum.

The noise from the group in the lounge of the 48th Street club surged briefly as the lavatory door opened. Two men walked in, one middle-aged and dressed in a creased lightweight brown suit, the younger man in a sheepskin jacket and flared trousers. Both were laughing and talking about the previous night's visit to another club and its overweight Malayan stripper.

They ignored the earlier arrival and continued their bantering. The younger of the two stood beside Stolford and shouted comments across to his companion at the wash-basin. The ex-marine looked back to the business in hand and tried to ignore the irritating decibels. He was not in good humour. Two hours of lunchtime waiting for his contact in the noisy lounge, with no indication that the barman had sent word to the 'Mr Mangen' to join him. The second tape had arrived that morning with instructions to find 'Mangen' at this club to get a passport. Another hour and he would call it a day and try again tomorrow.

The stream fell to a trickle and then stopped. He shook off the remaining drops and then froze with pain. His scream was stifled by a hand which reached across his shoulder from behind and muzzled him. A hard point was jabbed savagely into the thin flesh behind his ear and the voice of the middle-aged man said sharply, 'One sound, one sudden move...Understood?' Stolford twitched his head.

A hand frisked him quickly but thoroughly. His wallet was taken. Stolford twitched his head and the voice said, 'Right, now just step back real slow like.' The trio edged gently across the room, still locked together, until Stolford could feel his right shoulder against the door frame of one of the cubicles.

Again the voice. 'Now I'm gonna take this gun away from your head and my hand off your mouth, but Billy here has a

33

knife. Stupid heroics and your fatherin' days are all through. OK?' Stolford twitched again. The middle-aged man stepped from behind the ex-marine and put the gun under his nose.

'Now, move right back,' said the man, extending his gun arm which the younger man ducked under to retain his grip. Stolford stopped when the back of his legs touched the lavatory seat. The outer door opened and he could hear footsteps, but the captors ignored them. The footsteps stopped.

'Right, now,' said the middle-aged man, 'with your left hand, just reach across real easy and drop those trousers. And your underpants.'

'What the hell are you two...?' Stolford's question winced into silence as the younger man's grip increased.

'Not what you think,' said the middle-aged man. 'Point is, who are you?'

'I'm Carl Sto...' Again a tightening. The middle-aged man placed the pistol barrel against his own lips and tapped them twice. 'First things first. Trousers and underpants.' He motioned with the gun.

Stolford reached across his hand and fumbled with the buckle of his belt. It fell open and he inched the trousers and underpants down to mid-thigh. The anger had gone and now he felt fear.

'You're a very wise fella,' said the man. 'Now just squat down there and place both your hands over your pecker. And sit real still.'

As he sat down, Stolford felt the grip released. The younger man stepped back quickly and silently. His companion nodded to someone out of Stolford's vision and then he too stepped back. Stolford heard a sound of tinkling metal, and shuffling footsteps approaching the cubicle. A young blond-haired boy whom Stolford recognised as the vocalist from the pop group came into view. His trousers were around his ankles and he was naked downwards from the end of his short t-shirt.

Stolford started to rise from the lavatory seat but he was blinded by the glare of the electronic flash. When his eyes cleared the boy had already pulled up his trousers and was stepping out of sight with the photographer.

'Should be nice in colour.' said the middle-aged man, unsmiling, as be reappeared in front of Stolford. 'Should do

34

wonders for your reputation.'

'What's goin' on?' Stolford demanded, resuming his seat as the man motioned with the gun. The younger man appeared again, holding a long-bladed knife.

'Just insurance,' said the man. 'I'm Mangen.' He flicked open Stolford's wallet. 'According to this you're Carl Stolford. But in case you ain't, I've gotten me a little insurance,' he said, nodding towards the retreating footsteps.

'Look, I'm not the fuzz,' Stolford protested. 'I'm an ex-marine who's been offered some work abroad. But to get it I need a false passport and driving licence and I was told...'

'Who told you?' Mangen interrupted.

'Just a guy in a bar,' Stolford said lying.

'Who?'

'Just a guy. I don't know who he is. But I got to talkin' to him and he seemed to know about all kinds of things like he was in the rackets. Said to get a passport and driving licence I ought to come here and ask for you.'

'What nationality do you want?' asked Mangen quietly.

'Irish. A priest.'

Mangen stiffened.

'You mixed up in politics, fella?'

'No, of course not,' Stolford answered.

''Cause if you are, fella, you better go to someone else,' said Mangen. 'Those guys have their own contacts. Me. I stay well away from that.'

'It's a straightforward heist,' said Stolford, gesturing with a wave of his hand. 'But I need the passport.'

Mangen tapped the gun barrel on his lips as he eyed Stolford. He looked at Bill, who just shrugged. His eyes found Stolford's again. The automatic urinal flush behind him started up.

'When do ya need this?' he asked eventually.

'As soon as possible,' said Stolford. 'I may get a call any day.'

'OK,' said Mangen. 'You come back here in say, four days. Bring eight hundred bucks.'

Stolford's eyes shot up 'That's a lot of dough.'

'You want a good passport, you pay the price,' Mangen shrugged. 'Take it or leave it.'

'Alright,' said Stolford hastily. 'I'll be here. But what about that photograph? When does that get destroyed?'

'It don't,' snapped Mangen. 'If you turn out to be part of a set-up then that boy is gonna swear blind that you threatened to hurt him real bad unless he gave you joy.'

Billy slipped the knife into the belt at the back of his trousers and moved back. He clicked his index finger against his thumb and pointed to Stolford's trousers, still just above his knees. Stolford looked to Mangen for guidance. He nodded. Billy took the trousers and underpants from Stolford and rolled them into a tight bundle. Mangen threw the wallet to Stolford.

'Now, you just lock yourself in there and we'll take these outside. In about two hours, someone'll toss 'em over the top t'ya.'

Stolford stood and closed the door in their faces.

'Good,' Mangen said. 'Tomorrow you bring some pictures of yourself from one of them do-it-yourself machines. About four days later you get your passport.'

Later that day, when Stolford returned home, he found his apartment had been searched thoroughly. Mangen's men posed as detectives to question, and then get past, Mrs Schliemann.

Charles Casswell's smile froze as the group of newspaper photographers walked past with no sign of recognition. He snorted, twisting the ring on his little finger agitatedly.

'Remember, Charles,' said Simon Coates, his young companion, 'you haven't been on television for the past two years. I mean, they're not likely to spot you here in this crowd.'

Casswell exhaled gently. 'Yes, you're right, of course, dear boy. Come, let us find a taxi.'

They lifted the suitcases and walked out through the sliding glass doors of the airport. As they reached the waiting line of cabs, the ageing actor turned to Coates.

'You know, dear boy,' he said reflectively, 'the last time I was here in Dublin they had to have police outside those doors to hold back the fans.'

The young man nodded. But he did not believe it.

Only a quartet of hopeful seagulls, circling and hovering,

watched with more than scant interest the arrival of the white open-decked boat at the fishing ground, a mile and a half off Boothbay Harbor in Maine.

The conversation on the journey had been the inevitable mixture of business anecdotes, crude jokes and boasts of sexual liaisons. Now the eleven men were silent, sitting with their backs to the gunwales, the trailing fishing lines forgotten, giving undivided attention to the small man standing against the steps to the flying bridge.

Lutz Feldmann, the procurer, savoured the moment. Ten of these men were among the wealthiest in the United States and, although they specialised in, or had been born to, diverse arterial business empires and fortunes, they shared a common and consuming passion apart from money, a passion which was dependent on money: the ownership, legally or illegally, of the world's finest art treasurers. For a man of wealth, whose purchase of all other material possessions could be matched by another such man, the ownership of works of the finest art was the only remaining claim to individuality and uniqueness. Such a stake to such a man went beyond lust and avarice: it was as necessary as drugs to an addict. These ten men were addicts whose basement galleries, unseen except by their owners, housed many of the world's treasures officially listed as missing. It was to Lutz Feldmann that these men looked to cope with their addiction. For Feldmann was the supplier and Robert Melchoir, stockbroker and thirteenth man on board, was the pusher.

Melchoir moved now among the men, distributing copies of a glossy catalogue entitled. *Treasures of Early Irish Art, 1500 BC to AD 1500*. Feldmann watched for some moments as they scanned the coloured photographs, the masks of hardened businessmen stripped away suddenly to reveal unabashed, childlike expressions of pleasure. Some ran fingertips across the shiny pages as if to imagine the texture of the treasures illustrated.

'Gentlemen,' the procurer broke the silence, 'I expect to have these items available to you within the near future.'

'All of them?' asked one of his audience incredulously, his throat dry.

'Certainly all the principal items,' Feldmann answered. 'For instance, the Ardagh Chalice, the Cross of Cong, the Tara Brooch, St Patrick's Bell, The Crozier of Clonmacnoise and so on.'

'This is unbelievable,' another man whispered.

'Far from it, I can assure you, gentlemen,' said Feldmann, smiling confidently. 'The operation necessary to procure these treasures is already under way.'

Melchoir joined Feldmann at the steps. 'It will be the largest single haul of art treasures in history,' he beamed expansively. 'And you, my friends, are being given the opportunity to share these irreplaceable objects, the envy of museums and collectors the world over.'

Feldmann opened a small black pocket book and scribbled a line on the top of a clean sheet. 'The usual code names, gentlemen, for my records?'

The men grunted or nodded assent.

'Very well,' Feldmann said. 'Can we now start the bidding? Might I suggest we start with one of the smaller items, the Tara Brooch...'

One of the men raised a hand, almost imperceptibly. 'Half a million,' he said quietly.

The procurer smiled. 'Black Knight bids half a million dollars. I think we'll have to do better than that, gentlemen.'

The collectors laughed. 'A million,' one of them interrupted.

'Now we're getting places, gentlemen. White Bishop bids a million for the Tara Brooch...'

Two and a quarter hours later the last item had been 'auctioned' and the fishing boat turned for home – three mackerel and a small cod, which had been dead for some time, now on board.

'What was the final tally for the treasures?' Robert Melchoir asked Feldmann.

'Two hundred and forty-eight million dollars.'

'Jee-sus.'

Chapter Three

The tall 'priest' walked briskly down the stoop of the Brooklyn Heights walk-up and turned up the sloping road and past Prospect Park.

The horn-rimmed glasses beneath the black felt hat were already irritating the bridge of his nose, and the stiff dog collar chafed his neck. He felt conspicuous but drew only casual glances from the few passers-by on the sidewalk. The rapists and shoot-up artists were still in their holes waiting for the later hours of the evening. Only a group of three young Puerto Ricans on the corner watched his progress with vague interest.

He walked three blocks to the subway and took an E train under the river to 57th and 7th station. There he transferred to the downtown local, sitting with the battered suitcase on his knees, again comforted by the other passengers' lack of interest in him. At 42nd Street he made his way through the maze of the station to emerge at 6th Avenue and Bryant Park and walk east to the bus station on 41st Street.

The 'priest' smiled when he stood back to allow a young woman through the swing doors before him. 'Thank you, Father,' she beamed. He rode the escalator and then walked through the central area and out of another swing door to catch a Carey bus to John F. Kennedy Airport.

Two nuns, in light blue habits and large white bonnets, smiled across from the other side of the bus. He returned their smile but looked quickly out of the window to discourage any thoughts of joining their fellow cleric. The bus swung around and pulled down into the midtown tunnel, eventually threaded into the Van Wyck Expressway and then turned into the vast

JFK complex. He kept his eyes averted from the nuns during the journey, interrupted briefly at the various terminals: Eastern, American, United, Pan Am, Air France, Lufthansa and finally Aer Lingus.

'Have a nice flight, Father O'Mahony,' said the uniformed desk man, returning the green-covered passport to the perspiring 'priest'.

'Thank you,' said Stolford and turned away.

Peter Phelan stepped out of the Companies Registration Office in Dublin Castle and stood for a moment flicking through the sheaf of white and buff forms and information leaflets.

The last time he had registered a company it had been in his name and under the general heading of electronics. This time it would be incorporated as 'Matthews Pressure Cleaners Limited' and with a different managing director. His instructions had come in a second tape, as promised in the original found outside the dockside public house. The second message was left on top of a cistern in a south-city restaurant lavatory, after he had confirmed in a telephone call he had received during lunch that he would be willing to join 'the group'.

What was the group and who was in it? The caller, not surprisingly, had refused to answer those questions. But he had again reassured Phelan that the young engineer would be wealthy enough to leave Ireland and start afresh with a sizeable stake in another country, under an assumed name. The plan was foolproof and would guarantee everyone involved perfect cover before, during and after the operation.

Initially, his acceptance of the offer had been angry reaction to what he had discovered about his wife and brother on the day of his release from prison. Anger, disappointment and gut-tearing desolation, a betrayal which inflicted mental and physical pain beyond anything he believed possible. Would he have accepted the plan anyway? No, he was sure of that. And so, obviously, was The Voice, who knew he would be vulnerable, weakened beyond caring or sufficiently angry to go for broke.

The Voice had told him he would find a one-room furnished apartment booked in the name of Peter Phelan at Monkstown on the south side of Dublin. The owner of the apartment had been told that Phelan had been in England for years and was returning to live again in his native city. The Voice knew him well and had anticipated every action and thought.

...and there will be a reason for everything you will be asked to do, Mr Phelan. The reason will, in many instances, be obscure until the operation is at its more advanced stages. You will try, I'm sure, to jump ahead and guess at the reason. That is only to be expected. The danger, however, will be in reaching the wrong conclusions and trying to short-cut the moves. Don't, Mr Phelan...

Well, so far he had done what he had been told. This morning he had signed the unemployment register at the Labour Exchange, giving his correct name, his new address and his former residence: Mountjoy Prison. The official had seemed unperturbed. What kind of work was Mr Phelan looking for? Electronic engineering. Would he consider anything else if there was an opening? Not really qualified to do anything else. Right, Mr Phelan, keep in touch with us.

Having got the necessary company registration forms from Dublin Castle, he had one more task to perform. But that could wait until later in the day. He walked down along the River Liffey to the city centre and caught a bus to Ballymun.

The third-floor apartment was empty and silent. Tidy except for a cup on the draining board in the kitchen and a half-eaten slice of toast. The bed had been made, the dark blue quilt smooth. In the sitting room cabinet he found whiskey and a glass. He poured himself a generous three fingers and swigged at the neat spirit. He took the bottle and walked back into the bedroom and sat on the edge of the bed. He emptied the glass and poured himself another whiskey. He loosened his tie and walked over to the cabinet against the back wall of the room. In the top drawer were jumpers and blouses, but in the next one he found what he pretended he hadn't been looking for. He picked up a pair and stretched the elastic. He went back to the bed and lay back, kicking off his shoes onto the white carpet. With one hand he pulled off his spectacles and with the other caressed his face with the smooth nylon, rubbing it across his forehead, then down one cheek and finally masking his nose and mouth.

41

With one slow, painful sob, his body began shaking convulsively and the tears flowed and darkened the soft material still covering his face. In a while, he slept and dreamed.

His dream took him to warmth and sea air: golden grains filtering through his fingers onto oiled flesh, rising and falling with her breathing. Her bikini top lay loose, unfastened, across her breasts, wary of possible intruders into their sheltered mini-cove on the beach. He lifted it clear. She didn't move. The nipples, at first soft and partly hidden in the mounds, responded to his lips and rose, stiffened and red, from their white nests. Her hand reached out to him and found his body had also responded, taut and pulsing against the tightness of the swimming shorts. She straightened her hand and stroked the hardness with her palm.

Without opening her eyes she turned onto her side and pushed him gently onto his back, her bikini top falling between them on the sand. She kissed his nipples in turn and pinched them between her teeth, finally running her tongue in rapid circumnavigation before trailing it agonisingly slowly down his chest and stomach to the top of the shorts. Her hand slid up along the inside of his thigh and cupped his balls briefly before moving up to ease him from the top of the shorts. She giggled delightedly as it slapped onto her cheek, and he laughed with her.

Her fingers circled and pressed him for just a second before she parted her lips. In that brief moment he felt her warm breath on the tip before moisture enveloped it and the tongue stabbed and flicked. He reached behind her and she, without releasing him, moved her hips to shorten his stretch. The string covering moved easily off her buttocks and he slipped his fingers between, pausing only to tickle gently before moving them forward into the wetness to be gripped in unison with his own throbbing. It didn't last long but neither of them wanted to linger. His breathing came in gulps and his hips began to rise and fall as she pushed urgently down onto his probing fingers. She gagged once but regained her breath and kept him captive until he had subsided.

Phelan woke suddenly from his dream to find Betty studying his face with obvious affection. Her cheeks were flushed. 'Welcome home, Peter,' she said softly and moved up along the bed for his kiss.

The palm of his hand covered her face and pushed her across the bed away from him as he swung his legs over the edge to find his shoes. As he closed his trousers, he spat over his shoulder, 'You fuckin' slut!'

Carl Stolford left the terminal building at Dublin Airport at nine o'clock that morning after the twelve-hour trip from New York.

During the hour's stop at Shannon he had shaved and brushed down his black clerical suit. The flight had been uneventful and the only attempt to draw him into conversation had been abruptly aborted when he tipped back his seat and feigned sleep. His neighbouring passengers had left him alone after that.

An hour after he checked in to the cheap hotel on the north side of the city, the desk clerk tapped on his door. With a damp towel around his waist, Stolford padded from the shower stall. The clerk handed him a padded parcel with 'Father O'Mahony' in block letters on it. When the clerk had gone, Stolford tore open the parcel and found a cassette machine and tape. Wedged inside the leather case he found two hundred pounds in Irish bank notes.

The voice on the tape was the same as the one he had listened to in his New York apartment, metallic and toneless.

Two miles away, Charles Casswell and his young companion stepped onto the balcony of their executive apartment overlooking the south side of Dublin Bay.

'You still haven't told me what work you've to do here,' said Simon Coates, cautiously aggressive.

'Dear boy,' said Casswell, resting his hand on Coates' shoulder, 'I haven't the faintest idea myself. All I know is what I was told in that last telephone call: Come to Dublin immediately; accommodation has been arranged; go through the motions of finding acting work with one of the theatres but don't actually take the job.'

'Sounds ridiculous, if you ask me,' said Coates huffily.

'I didn't,' said the actor abruptly. Then more gently, 'Relax. It'll be just fine, I'm sure.'

When the telephone rang forty minutes later, both men had showered and changed.

The toneless voice told Casswell to expect visitors at nine o'clock that night.

At twenty minutes past the appointed time Carl Stolford decided to go into the red-brick apartment block, Raglan House.

He had stood watching the only arrival, a thin young man wearing gold-rimmed spectacles and dressed in faded denims and a dark blue anorak, hunched against the biting wind whipping around the towered buildings. The area was quiet. Only a dozen cars parked in bays fronting the separate apartment blocks in the complex. A city-bound train rattled past on the nearby line.

He stepped out of the shadows and walked to the glass double doors of the block. He pressed the button marked 'Byrne' and waited. A voice crackled in the tiny speaker set in the aluminium board: 'Yes?'

'You're expecting me,' said Stolford quietly, leaning towards the speaker.

'Am I?' the accent was English, theatrically refined.

'I'm a bit late. Got lost.'

'What time should you have been here?'

'Nine.'

The speaker clicked to silence and a soft clunk indicated the activation of the electronically controlled door lock. Stolford transferred the paper-wrapped cassette machine to his left hand and pushed open the door. Inside, the elevator doors slid open. He travelled to the second floor. He padded quietly along the carpeted corridor and stood outside the apartment door, head inclined, listening. He heard the muffled tones of the Englishman inside.

The door opened immediately to his single short jab on the buzzer. A silver-haired man stared at him briefly and then smiled broadly, capped teeth whitely contrasting with the slight tan.

'Come in, old chap,' he said warmly, stepping back to pull the door wider.

In an armchair near the curtained windows sat the young

44

man Stolford had seen arriving earlier. He still wore his anorak despite the oppressive heat of the room. A second young man turned from a drinks trolley and eyed the newcomer keenly. His stare moved from the grey eyes in the strong face, past the priest's collar and down the well built body in the black suit. The young man made no attempt to veil his admiration.

'Well,' said the silver-haired man warmly, 'should I call you 'Father' or what?' He extended his right hand. Stolford ignored the proffered hand and glanced around the room. The man in the anorak met his glance and looked away.

Stolford said sharply to the older man, 'Carl Stolford. And who are you?'

Casswell's smile faded and he withdrew his hand. 'Charles Casswell,' he said stiffly. 'Care for a drink?'

Stolford nodded briefly and advanced into the room. 'Whiskey.' He stood in front of the man in the armchair who matched his stare for a few short moments but then softly muttered, 'Peter Phelan'.

'And I'm Simon Coates,' said the other man brightly behind Stolford.

'Yeah,' said the big man, accepting the glass of Bushmills whiskey and Club mixer, and moved over to the second armchair. The others watched unspeaking. The pecking order had already been established, a leader undisputed.

The big man sat deep in the chair, elbows on its arms, glass rolling gently between his fingers before his mouth, the parcel on his lap. He glanced at each in turn and sipped slowly. The others, uncomfortable, waited. The music from the small corner speakers ended and the mechanism clicked twice, dropping another disc onto the turntable.

'Kill it,' said Stolford quietly to Coates, jerking his thumb towards the unit. The man reacted instantly. The orchestra slowed and faded into silence. Coates stayed beside the unit. Casswell cleared his throat and moved to the centre of the room.

Stolford had assessed them as he had done with countless fresh troops throughout his military career. The strong, the weak. The strong who could weaken and the weak who could, by word or circumstance, be raised to a strength undreamt of. Casswell, immaculate in attire, a vanity rooted in insecurity.

His companion, effeminate but for that more difficult and therefore dangerous. Coates was a follower but only to a point. He would be led until angered by indifference or scorn. His courage would come from temper, a natural coward. The third man, Phelan, was also a follower but his subordination would be reasoned, calculated. A more reliable loyalty in some ways, but he would have to be given a looser rein than the others.

The ex-marine had been wrong in the past but not often. Time would tell, perhaps force him to modify his assessment and his approach to the individual. But for now, each would be pigeon-holed according to the tried method. He had nothing else.

Casswell tried to regain lost equality, as Stolford guessed he would. The actor cleared his throat again and straightened his shoulders. The nervous thumbing of the ring on his little finger belied the brave stance and the words. 'Well, dear chap,' he projected. 'Do I gather that you are the, eh, gentleman who has brought us here?'

Stolford sipped again before speaking. 'Is that with *you*?' he said disdainfully, nodding in the direction of Coates whose face dropped. Casswell stiffened. Peter Phelan glanced at them in turn and smirked. Nice one.

'Simon is my friend, yes,' Casswell blurted defensively.

The big man matched his glare. 'Who told you to bring him with you?'

Angry, Casswell retorted, 'No one told me *not* to, to come alone.'

Stolford had scored enough for now. He put his glass on the arm of the chair and stripped the brown paper off the cassette machine in his lap. He placed it on the other arm and pressed the start button. The tiny speaker hissed for a few moments before the now-familiar voice rasped:

Welcome to Ireland, Mr Stolford. At nine o'clock tonight go to number 2, Raglan House, Serpentine Avenue, Dublin 4, where you will find Charles Casswell and Peter Phelan who will assist you in your work here. They will work directly under you until such time as the work has been completed. Their roles will be made known as each stage of the operation approaches. If any one man fails to carry out his instructions to the letter he will jeopardise the entire scheme, so it is in everyone's interest to see that my orders, through you, are carried out specifically and unquestioningly. Stop the tape, Mr Stolford.

Stolford stopped the machine and waited for comments. There was none. He restarted the tape:

There is a lot at stake. Too much for defection once we have embarked. For that reason each of you must now finally decide whether you wish to proceed. If you do decide to continue you will be rewarded with wealth. But if you change your mind and try to pull out after tonight you will have learnt too much, you will present a threat to those who want to carry on. I am sure I make myself perfectly clear. You must do the same. Stop the tape, Mr Stolford.

Casswell sat heavily onto the settee and stared at the machine. Coates licked his lips and looked at the actor for guidance. Phelan opened a packet of cigarettes and lit one, fighting to appear unconcerned. He was also fighting for time. Stolford emptied his glass and held it towards Coates. The young man gratefully turned his back to slop whiskey from the trolley.

'Well,' Casswell began uneasily, 'I'm sure I don't know quite what to make of it all. I mean, I take it you are not the man beind the voice, Mr Stolford?' Stolford shook his head slightly and reached out to take the glass from Coates. The young man looked miserable.

'Then, who *is* he?'

'Someone who knows some, or all, of us,' said Stolford, casually. He looked at each of the faces and added, 'Or enough about each of us to know we meet his needs and that we're likely to accept. We've already proved that by coming here.'

'Yes,' said Casswell, 'but who could know us all or know that much about us?'

'Someone in organised crime, maybe,' Stolford shrugged. 'Could even be a government official with access to security files at an international level. Maybe even a cop.'

'A member of a prison visiting committee,' suggested Phelan

quietly. His sudden interjection jolted Coates. The others turned and waited for elaboration.

'I've just come out,' said Phelan, studying the glowing tip of his cigarette. 'These people get to know a lot about you...and your family,' his voice tailed off. The others still stared. 'We're losers and this guy knows it.'

'Yes, yes, quite,' said Casswell. 'But I've never been in prison, so how...'

'But you've been in the papers,' Phelan interrupted. 'Even the Irish read the newspapers, Mr Casswell.' He smiled ruefully at the pained expression on the actor's face.

Phelan turned to Stolford. 'I couldn't place *your* name at first. But the accent put me on the right side of the world. Vietnam, right?'

Stolford nodded almost imperceptibly.

'Something I read about you in an old magazine,' Phelan went on. Stolford studied his drink.

'Not very nice that, was it?' the engineer persisted.

The big man kept his eyes on the glass as he spoke, softly. 'Word of advice, fella. Next time y'throw that one up make sure y'got both hands real tight 'round y'twins.' He looked into Phelan' eyes. 'Read?'

Phelan looked away.

Casswell eased the tension. 'Well now, gentlemen,' he said soothingly. 'Let's not draw swords among ourselves. I mean to say, we all seem to have some kind of eh, should we say, *background*, what? Point is, what do we do now?'

'We make up our goddam minds, that's what,' said Stolford, still rattled.

'Yes, quite so,' said Casswell hurriedly. He stood up and walked over to the drinks trolley. He poured himself a vodka laced with white lemonade, then added more vodka. Coates stood rooted, eyes darting from Stolford to Phelan who were studiously ignoring each other. Casswell placed a reassuring hand on his companion's shoulder. Coates tried to acknowledge the gesture with a smile and failed.

Stolford glanced at his wrist-watch. 'We've got twelve minutes, accordin' to The Voice.' He pressed the button on the cassette machine:

*If you unanimously agree to go ahead, open and close the
curtains of the apartment where you're meeting. I'll be
watching for the signal. If you are not unanimous, open
them twice. In that case, I will contact each of you indivi-
dually tomorrow to find out who goes on and who drops
out. I say again: if you're in, stay in. Be sure. Make the
signal before ten o'clock.*

Peter Phelan drained his glass and said simply, 'I'm in.'

'So am I,' said Stolford looking at Casswell.

The actor shrugged and smiled. 'Well,' he chuckled, 'Why
not? Me too, I suppose.'

'Suppose' ain't good enough, Casswell,' said Stolford
sharply. Casswell's smile faded instantly.

'You fuck up later and maybe you get us all gutted.' Stolford
went on. 'Y'better be real sure an'...'

'Alright, alright,' Casswell interrupted, face flushed with
annoyance. 'I'm definitely in. Does *that* make you happy?'

'No,' said Stolford. Even Phelan was surprised.

'What *more* do you want me to say?' asked Casswell,
exasperated.

'I want you to say what's goin' to happen to your asshole,'
he said, thumbing in the direction of Simon Coates. The young
man jerked erect and, with courage born of hurt, launched
himself at the ex-marine arms raised, a roar rising in his throat.

The speed of the big man surprised everyone. He rose and
stepped slightly to his right, at the same time jabbing stiff
fingers into the belly of the attacker. Coates dropped instantly
to his knees, his face burying itself in the cushion of the
armchair where Stolford had sat. Both hands gripped his
injured pelvis as he struggled to breathe. Stolford gripped the
young man's hair and pulled his face back off the cushion.

'Now what do *you* say, pretty boy?' said Stolford quietly.
'In or out?'

Casswell moved to the side of the chair and looked into the
agonised face. He moved his hand towards Stolford and then
changed his mind. Coates swivelled his eyes to meet his. The
actor's face showed an admiration he had never seen before.
Admiration and amazement.

'In,' wheezed Coates. Stolford released his grip and the

49

young man's body slumped sideways onto the carpet. Phelan looked from Coates to Stolford but couldn't decide who he disliked more.

Stolford glanced again at his watch and stepped back. He turned and poured himself another whiskey. He felt slightly ashamed and knew he showed it. He moved back to the fallen Coates and lifted the unprotesting body onto the chair. Coates covered his eyes with one hand and nursed his stomach with the other.

'It's your apartment,' said Stolford, sweeping his hand towards the curtains.

'Is it time?' Casswell asked unnecessarily, looking at his watch. He moved to the side of the drapes and rummaged for the drawstrings. The curtains moved slowly apart revealing the blackness of the night and the water on the glass. It had started to rain. Casswell felt strangely vulnerable and naked, staring into the void. He closed the curtains quickly and turned to Stolford.

'Now what?'

'Now we listen again.' Stolford lifted the machine from the arm of the chair and restarted it.

By now you have signalled your intentions. Those of you who have decided to stay will receive a sum of money equivalent to twenty thousand dollars as a sign of my good-will. It will be paid into individual Swiss bank accounts within two days. You will be notified of the numbers when that has been done. In addition, you will receive weekly amounts of cash to cover your living costs. Finance for other necessities will be delivered to you at times and places I will signify in later messages. If you, Mr Stolford, have agreed to go on you will be the leader of the group, and all instructions will be delivered to you. Instructions will be issued in stages. In that way, you won't know until the last possible moment exactly what the aim of the operation is. You will make guesses, of course, but I expect most of them will be very wide of the mark. I would, however, advise you not to anticipate my intentions. Do only what I tell you. But do it exactly as I instruct you and we will be rich men. Mr Phelan has already, I trust, carried out one chore for me. Its significance will become obvious in time. I will contact you again tomorrow, Mr Stolford. In the interests of security for all concerned, my messages, in future, will be to you alone; how much you disclose to the others involved will be for you to decide as the plan and operation progress.

The quartet listened for some moments to the now voiceless tape as it hissed in the little speaker. Casswell was the first to speak when the American pressed the stop button.

'Hm,' he pondered heavily. The thinker was grossly over-acted. 'Seems fair enough, I suppose. Except for one thing.'

'Yeah?' Stolford was unimpressed.

'Well, I mean, it's obvious, isn't it?'

'What is?'

'The money, of course,' said Casswell patronisingly. 'I mean, this chap, this *voice* knows the numbers of the Swiss bank accounts so he waits until we've done all we're required to and then he withdraws the money. Or he could even do it right away. We end up with nothing.'

Stolford sighed. 'As soon as we know the numbers, we contact the bank and transfer the money to fresh accounts. Then only *we* know the numbers. He knows damn well we'll do just that.'

'Ah, yes. Quite so,' said Casswell hurriedly. 'I was going to suggest that.'

Stolford turned to Peter Phelan. 'What did The Voice ask you to do already?'

Phelan reached into the side pocket of his anorak and pulled out the papers he had brought from the Companies Registration Office. He handed them to the big man, who unfolded them and scanned the pages.

'I was told to get forms to register a company,' said Phelan, 'called "Matthews Pressure Cleaners Limited".'

'Mean anything to you?'

The engineer took off his glasses and rubbed his eyes. 'No. Not a thing.'

'And that's all the message told you?'

'Yes.'

'What are "pressure cleaners"?'

Phelan put on his glasses and turned to the ex-marine. 'Well, they clean out boilers and pipes and things with pressure hoses.

51

You know, in factories and hospitals. Clean out all the gunge that gathers over a period of time.'

'Does that give us any clues?' asked Casswell.

'Doesn't tell me anything,' said Stolford. 'But The Voice was right. It's sure got me guessin'.'

He turned to Phelan. 'Any ideas?'

Phelan shook his head. 'Nor does the business address. It's a big lockup garage in Rathmines, on this side of the city. I went up there. Empty.'

Stolford turned to the drinks trolley and cleared a space for the cassette machine. He removed the cassette and walked into the kitchen. He took a knife from the drawer and levered open the plastic cassette.

Casswell had followed him and stood watching from the doorway as Stolford pulled the tape from the tiny reels and placed it in the sink. The big man opened the window and then set fire to the heap. It burned badly but it melted and contracted into a black mess. He prodded it a couple of times to be sure and then dumped it into a waste disposal bucket in the corner.

He turned to Casswell and asked, 'You been asked to do anything, by The Voice?'

'Only to go through the motions of trying to find an acting job. But really stay free.'

'Right. Then you do that. I'll be in touch.'

'When?'

'Soon as I hear from him.'

Stolford walked through the lounge without even glancing at the others, and out of the apartment.

'That bloke's full of shit,' said Coates painfully but not too loudly.

Phelan was tempted to agree but saw how things were. He put the papers back in his pocket and followed the American.

'Thank you for a most delightful trip,' said the flamboyantly dressed man to the hostess standing in the open doorway of the Boeing 747 at Dublin Airport.

She smiled at his old-world manner and soft American accent. He had provided refreshing company on the flight from San Francisco with his politeness and good humour. She

52

guessed his age to be mid-fifties though his charm and good looks made the differential the least of her considerations. She found herself blushing and wondering. He smiled again and the grey eyes twinkled before turning away. The girl sighed inwardly, a little sadly. 'Goodbye, Mr Stanley,' she murmured to his back.

Sebastian Stanley took a taxi to New Jury's Hotel and registered for a five-day stay. He was going to postpone his business until the following morning but changed his mind and, after freshening up, went out again into the sunshine. The overnight rain had cleaned the street and washed the leaves on the kerbside trees of Pembroke Road. He smiled gratitude to the uniformed commissionaire at the front door. No, he would walk, refresh his memory of his favourite city.

Five years since his last visit. The Georgian architecture had taken a pounding in that time. Fewer uniform terraces, more decay, dirtier. The grey and brown slabs with reflective glass now encroached, dominated. Brave pockets still remained, contemptuous of the towering youngsters and trendy town-house sisters. But they were in a state of siege with no hope of victory. Was it only foreigners like Stanley who appreciated the age of others' cities?

The official at the Arts Council headquarters beamed his recognition and extended his hand. 'It's nice to see you again, Mr Stanley.'

'And you, Mr Walshe. It's good to be back.' He shook the hand warmly and sat before the desk.

'As I said in my letter,' said Walshe, 'we're delighted with the idea of an Irish-only gallery in San Francisco.'

'And so am I,' Stanley smiled. 'It's long overdue.'

'You said in your initial approach that the gallery would provide a broad platform for Irish art,' said Walshe.

'Quite. Everything from paintings to sculpture.'

'And not just established artists?'

'Oh, no. We particularly want to encourage the newcomers, the unknowns' said Stanley assuringly. 'A blend is what we need. A blend of old and new.'

Walshe's smile broadened. 'That's marvellous. To have someone of your calibre pushing out the boat for a newcomer will mean a great deal internationally for him.'

'I hope so,' said Stanley modestly. 'Of course, the Irish art treasures' American tour has provided a terrific springboard for a gallery such as this.'

Oh, yes. I expect so. We've been delighted with the response to the exhibition. I've lost count of the number of times we've had to postpone returning them to Dublin.'

'It's understandable, or course.' said Stanley. 'Word of mouth is the best recommendation in art appreciation, I've found. And, well, with literally millions of people having already seen them throughout the States, millions more will want to see them.'

Walshe nodded. 'Perhaps amongst all our young artists you'll find someone to create a similar stir in public interest.'

Stanley laughed gently, his long grey hair shaking in rhythm. 'Perhaps. At least it's a real beginning.'

'We're very grateful to you, needless to say,' said Walshe sincerely.

Stanley held up a protesting hand. 'Don't thank me. Thank my principals who are financing the project. I am merely their agent, their field representative.'

'But without your support and enthusiasm it might never have got off the ground,' said Walshe truthfully. 'You say the gallery owners are collectors themselves?'

'Yes, that's right. Never been connected in what you might call the professional side of art exhibitions. That's where I come in.'

'A great asset to any new art gallery,' smiled Walshe. Stanley enjoyed the flattery.

Walshe opened a drawer in the desk and brought out a single sheet of paper.

'We've prepared a list of artists who might interest you,' he said, handing the sheet to Stanley. 'We think they're all very good. Painters, sculpters, potters, weavers.'

Stanley scanned the names and addresses listed according to category.

'I hope that's sufficient for you,' said Walshe.

'Exactly what I wanted,' said the art critic without looking up from the page. 'And the export of the items when the time comes?'

'Oh, we'll take care of everything,' said the official hastily.

'Export licences, customs clearances, all the paper work. No problem whatsoever.'

'Well that will certainly make my task so much easier,' said Stanley warmly. 'I'll take care of the transport and costs, of course. But to know you'll shortcut the bureaucracy will certainly encourage my principals.'

'Only too pleased to help,' said Walshe.

Stanley rose and shook hands with the happy official. He promised to call again after his visits to the various addresses on the list.

Outside in the street, Stanley folded the paper carefully and put into his inside pocket. He smiled at a passing girl and at the world in general.

That same morning, Carl Stolford received, as promised, another message from The Voice.

He had been tempted to satisfy his curiosity about the identity of the man by leaving the hotel early in the morning and watching from a discreet distance for arrivals. But, he realised, if The Voice personally delivered a tape he would be watchful for Stolford and would avoid the hotel. After breakfast Stolford returned to his room and waited.

The telephone buzzed at half-past ten. 'Call for you, Father O'Mahony,' said the desk clerk. Then the voice he had heard on cassette the previous day.

'Good morning, Father.' The man's voice was jovial.

'Good morning.'

'Why don't you come along now and say hello?'

'Sure. Where?'

'The Burlington Hotel in Leeson Street. Bring your tape machine and wait for me in the foyer.'

Stolford left the hotel and walked down the wide expanse of O'Connell Street. Opposite the General Post Office he caught a taxi and feigned interest in the driver's family's service to the Church. A brother a Benedictine monk at Buckfast Abbey in Devon and a sister in a nursing order in South Africa.

In the carpeted foyer Stolford saw only two waiting people, both women. He bought a newspaper from the shop and sat opposite the front doors. A slow twenty minutes passed but no one approached him. Then a uniformed desk clerk summoned him to an external telephone. The voice was the same one as earlier.

'Sorry to put you through this,' the man said apologetically. 'But I couldn't run the risk of the desk clerk at your hotel listening in on our call. Small hotel, little for him to do except maybe be curious about the guests.'

'Yeah, sure,' said Stolford.

'I want you to be ready for a sudden visit to France. To collect something of great importance.' The man went on, 'You keep on your dog collar for the trip.'

'Where am I goin'?' Stolford asked.

'It'll all be on another tape which you'll find waiting for you now at Casswell's apartment. Keep in touch with him by telephone afterwards. Everything will be on the tape except the departure date. I'll leave a message with him when that's known.'

'Will I have any trouble importing this thing, whatever it is?' asked Stolford suspiciously.

'No problem,' said the man firmly. Then with a note of caution, 'Provided you do exactly as you're instructed.'

Stolford made no reply, which prompted the man to add encouragingly, 'It's all right. It's not a gun or anything like that. OK?'

'OK,' Stolford answered, unconvinced. 'But it's that important to us?'

'That important.'

Neither spoke for a few moments. Finally Stolford moved to another tack. 'You know that Casswell brought his boyfriend?'

'Can you handle him? It's up to you. You're the group leader.'

'I already have,' said Stolford with a coolness which apparently alarmed the man.

'Nothing too rash, I hope?'

Stolford chuckled. 'No. He's joined us.'

The line went dead and Stolford left the hotel. A ten-minute taxi ride brought him to the apartment complex in Serpentine Avenue. In Casswell's apartment, Coates handed him a cassette tape tightly wrapped in paper and tape. The young man had been tempted to open it before Stolford arrived, if

56

only to show contempt or defiance. But the thought passed quickly with the memory of his previous encounter with the big American.

They all sat and listened to the tape. Stolford rewound it and listened again. Each of them was given instructions for the next ten days, most of them for Stolford and Phelan.

'I'm goin' t'see Phelan now,' said Stolford, removing the tape from the machine. He moved to the door. 'You been in touch with the theatres yet?' he asked Casswell.

'No. I was waiting to hear from you first,' said Casswell, spreading his hands.

Stolford smiled reassuringly. 'Yeah. Well, make a few enquiries today. But, like the man said, stay loose. Huh?'

Casswell returned the smile. 'Yes, of course.'

The ex-marine in priest's clothing walked out of the apartment complex and asked a passerby directions to Monkstown. He caught a bus at the top of the road and eighteen minutes later, was admitted by a bleary-eyed Peter Phelan to the one-room apartment, four miles south of Serpentine Avenue. The engineer was wearing only underpants. His thin body contrasted with the bulk of the American.

In comparison with Casswell's luxury apartment, the furnishings were simple and worn. A single bed, unmade, in the corner with a straight-backed chair alongside. An over-full ashtray on the edge of the chair had spilled some of its contents onto the faded brown carpet which covered most of the floor. Two armchairs of considerable vintage faced each other from opposite sides of the room, and a small Formica-topped table hugged one wall. On it were the remains of a bag of potato chips and a cup of coffee. Only the latter showed any signs of recent life. A small sink and draining board stood beneath the narrow window overlooking an overgrown garden.

'It should be nice when it's finished,' said Phelan ruefully, watching Stolford's glance around the temporary 'home'.

Stolford smiled sympathetically. 'You wanna bet?' he asked derisively. He sat gently on one of the armchairs. It creaked under his weight.

'You hear from The Voice?' Phelan asked, reaching for a cigarette packet on the bed cover. It was empty.

'Yeah, another tape.'

Phelan crushed the packet and threw it into the corner. 'You got any cigarettes?'

'Don't smoke.'

'Shit,' said Phelan, 'I knew I'd forget to get some last night.'

'Looks like you weren't in much condition t'remember anythin',' said Stolford wryly.

Phelan sat on the edge of the bed. 'I've been making up for lost time.'

A warning bell sounded for Stolford. 'You ain't been talkin'?'

Phelan stared unblinking through the lenses of his spectacles. He was in no mood to be patronised or rebuked. 'One thing I learned inside was to keep my legs and my mouth shut tight.'

Stolford dropped his eyes and busied himself with the cassette machine. He pressed the button and sat back. Phelan rummaged in the bedside ashtray and retrieved a crushed butt. He lit it with difficulty and sat cross-legged on the bed, pulling the clothes around his shoulders. Neither man spoke until the tape had finished.

'Still tells me fuck-all, doesn't it?' Phelan asked.

'Only that The Voice is obviously connected internationally,' Stolford answered. 'So, he can't be all shit.'

Phelan sucked the last smoke from the butt. It tasted of filter. He jabbed it into the ashtray. 'What about the two fairies? What do they do? Apart from setting themselves up as the directors of "Matthews Pressure Cleaners"?'

The American shrugged. 'No idea. Except that Casswell must be needed real bad.'

He got up from the armchair. 'You clear on what you've t'do?'

Phelan nodded but looked troubled.

'Somethin' botherin' you?' Stolford asked.

'Just that we don't know what we're getting into,' said Phelan. 'And no way of knowing that we're going to get any more than we already have for what we do.'

Stolford measured his tone, careful to avoid causing offence. 'Have we anythin' else on offer right now?'

The young man sighed and pulled the clothes tighter around his shoulders.

'Besides,' Stolford went on, tone hardening. He stopped himself suddenly.

'Yes?' Phelan prompted.

'Nothin',' Stolford smiled. 'Forget it.'

He moved to the door.

'I'll be in touch.'

Phelan stared for seconds at the door but constructive thought failed to penetrate the alcohol fog. He pushed his legs out over the side of the bed and scanned the room. Reluctantly, he stepped onto the cold floor and reached beneath the bed until his fingers found and grasped the whiskey bottle. He smiled relief and withdrew his hand.

The bottle was empty.

Chapter Four

Since the collapse of the French underworld empire of Barthélémy Guerini, life had been hard for Adrien D'Albe and his beautiful wife, Fabienne.

The house had been sold with the last of the sleek cars some years ago to cover gambling debts and buy the small café on the outskirts of Toulon. Reluctantly, he had agreed when Fabienne suggested selling her furs and the bulk of her jewellery to keep them solvent in the first few difficult years.

As assistant to one of Guerini's liutenants, ex-safebreaker and lockpick D'Albe had commended himself to the Organisation by consistant reliability and unquestioning obedience. Whatever was required would be supplied: men, equipment or simply information. Gradually his work made him indispensable to the machinery of the vast empire. A latecomer to the banner of the first of his bosses and with no knowledge of the politics of the underworld structure, time proved his choice of master to have been the correct one. The reward was increasing trust, power and wealth, and an introduction to the beautiful Fabienne, daughter of one of Marseilles' oldest and richest families.

Pampered, spoilt and bored, Fabienne had seen in Adrien D'Albe only a source of amusement at first; she would challenge his apparent inverted snobbishness and his seeming contempt for her class. In the process, she fell in love, to the surprise and enmity of her family, an enmity which merely strengthened her resolve to marry Adrien D'Albe.

He was a careful man with a shrewdness rooted in the poverty of his background. Son of a tailor who died when

Adrien was just nine years old, he lived in a two-roomed home with his mother and three elder sisters. He left school at the age of fifteen to find work to supplement his mother's seamstress income. By then, one of his sisters had married. The second girl died of an accidental drug overdose at a party in Paris. The mother never recovered from the blow and died, broken, less than a year afterwards. The third girl, Léa, left the apartment one day with a boyfriend to find work in Toulon. She promised to send for her young brother when she had found a place to live.

Apart from one postcard, she never contacted him.

He drifted into petty crime and graduated in safe-blowing and lockpicking under a 'master' in Marseilles. It was never rewarding to a man with D'Albe's ambitions, but it did give him an introduction to the Organisation in Marseilles. At first the pickings were small, to suit the chores he was asked to undertake. But his loyalty and efficiency were quickly recognised and his stature increased, at first locally and then nationally. His only serious questioning of the morality of his activities and those of his employers came on a trip to Toulon.

He had been sent to investigate complaints by local prostitutes who had refused to work with a particular pimp. They claimed he was not only ripping off the girls but also the Organisation. Under an assumed name he set up a temporary 'office' in a small local hotel and sent for the girls for individual interview. Each had been beaten and threatened by the pimp. Such treatment was not uncommon in that occupation, but this had been so savage that it had kept several of them off the streets. The last girl interviewed by D'Albe had a heavily bandaged nose which had obviously been broken. Her eyes were almost completely closed by spreading bruising. She took one look at D'Albe and tried to leave the room again, but he caught her arm and brought her back and wrapped his arms around the aged and pitifully thin woman. It was Léa.

That night the pimp was picked up in the street by three men in a Peugeot 504. Found gagged and bound on a roadside six miles outside Toulon, a post mortem on his mutilated body revealed that the primary purpose of the heavy tape gag was to force the pimp to swallow what his killers stuffed into his mouth before death.

Léa returned to Marseilles with her brother and was given work in a nightclub. Adrien involved himself no more with the call-girl business of the Organisation and they never called upon him again to do anything connected with it.

With the collapse of the Guerini empire he had slipped into relative obscurity, although his café was occasionally visited by underworld characters who sought information or assistance. But it was small low-key stuff, a mere reminder of his successful days. Until now he had been unaware that he was anything more than a vague memory in the top tiers, the *capi*, of the international Mafia. True he had again figured briefly in newspaper reports when he was brought in for police questioning after the escape from custody of Albert Spaggiari in 1977. Spaggiari was the leader of the gang which robbed the Société Générale bank in Nice of an estimated thirty million francs in cash, gold and jewels.

D'Albe was, in fact, one of the few of the many hundred questioned who had helped Spaggiari out of the country. As always, he had covered his tracks well and easily withstood the police questioning about his possible, and to them probable, involvement in the daring escape.

But D'Albe was now flattered that the famed Lutz Feldmann had made contact with him for help with a very important assignment. It would involve two trips but, before that, the purchase through his own channels of a very special item. If he was found with it, or if it was traced back to him, he would spend many years behind bars. He had not asked why it was wanted. He would know soon enough. On the second trip.

The purchase took longer than expected. Guns, explosives and manpower could be bought with one discreet telephone call. But this was different. He was the first, he was told, to make such a purchase and he had no reason to disbelieve his contacts. It arrived five days after his initial enquiry. The bottle was packed in a wooden box lined with polystyrene. The box was wrapped in polythene heavily sealed with yellow masking tape. It scared the hell out of him despite the assurances that the bottle inside was airtight and completely safe to handle.

He telephoned a friend in Paris with a pre-arranged message which would seem innocuous to an eavesdropping operator or someone who by chance had cut in because of a crossed line.

63

The friend then called another man in Paris who placed a call to New York. It was four in the afternoon local time and Robert Melchoir was fighting an attack of indigestion brought on, as always, by pancakes.

'Monsieur Melchoir?' The English was heavily accented.

'Yes.'

'This is Flaubert.'

Melchoir straightened in his chair. 'Oh, yes. Of course Mr Flaubert.'

'I wish to sell those shares.'

'When?'

'Friday, noon onwards, French time.'

'We'll be glad to find you a buyer, Monsieur Flaubert,' said Melchoir smiling. 'Thank you for calling.'

The line went dead. Melchoir immediately telephoned Lutz Feldmann and arranged a meeting for ten minutes' time in a restaurant.

Melchoir was already seated when the procurer arrived. Feldmann slid into the booth alongside the stockbroker. 'That French item is almost ready for collection,' said Melchoir quietly.

Feldmann smiled. 'Good, excellent. When?'

'Friday, any time after noon, their time.'

Feldmann glanced at his watch unnecessarily. 'Doesn't give us much time. Why after noon?'

'Must be a good reason for it. Probably to prevent the pickup clashing with the time of church services.'

'Oh, yes,' said Feldmann, nodding. 'That must be it. The French wouldn't be keen to hang on to that stuff for longer than they would have to. I'll get on to The Voice in Dublin.' He got up and shook his head at the approaching waiter. 'Did you transfer that money to the numbered Swiss accounts for the boys, Robert?'

Melchoir nodded and smiled. 'They don't trust us much. They moved it to other accounts the following day.'

Carl Stolford travelled south from Dublin on Wednesday afternoon to take the five o'clock sailing of the Irish Continental Line passenger and car ferry from Rosslare in County Wexford to Le Havre. He travelled tourist class and avoided conversation with his fellow passengers in the four-bunk cabin. He brought with him a suitcase of clothing and a briefcase containing a bible, a missal, and several religious magazines. The ship docked in France the following afternoon at three o'clock and Stolford went straight to the Hertz offices in the Place de la Gare where he produced his false driving licence to rent a Renault 5 for 'at least a fortnight'. Having eaten lunch on the ferry he set off eastwards to Beauvais. He drove slowly to arrive late in the evening. At Rouen he halted for an evening meal in a restaurant and moved on after a two-hour rest. He reached Beauvais at eleven o'clock and booked into the Hôtel du Palais. After a whiskey nightcap he showered and went to bed.

Stolford ate a continental breakfast in his room at eight-thirty the next morning and packed his suitcase. The hotel manager was standing at the reception desk when the American priest walked across from the elevator.

The manager spoke in English. 'I hope you enjoyed your stay with us, Padre.'

Stolford said warmly, 'Yes, indeed. Very comfortable.'

'You're here in your professional capacity, no?'

'No', said Stolford casually. 'Vacation. Promised myself this trip a long time ago.'

'You're heading south?'

'Yes. Paris and on down.'

'I hope you enjoy our country.' The manager took Stolford's cash and handed it to the waiting cashier.

'Thank you for your hospitality,' said Stolford, extending his hand. The manager shook his hand warmly.

'Goodbye, Father O'Mahony.'

Stolford left the hotel and went to the car park. He put his suitcase in the boot and took out a rigid black briefcase. He locked the *trunk* and walked northwards into the Rue St Pierre. Facing him was the huge grey sprawl of the magnificent cathedral, towering above its younger neighbours. He turned away. The pickup was not to be made until after midday. He strolled around the town, enjoying the brief role of sightseer, admiring the famous astronomical clock, the fortified gate erected in the fourteenth century, and the Norman-Gothic Church of St Etienne, described in detail in

65

the guidebook he purchased at a local tourist office.

He returned to the Cathédral Pierre shortly before one o'clock, climbing the fourteen stone steps from the cobbled forecourt and entering the building by the main south doors. Above and around the doors was the flamboyant, almost crazed, Gothic stonework of the thirteenth century, with its numerous carved tabernacles and huge rose window.

A cold draught hit him as he walked inside, a welcome relief from the sticky heat of the street. He moved across the aisle and then stopped beside one of the huge compound roof piers, stunned by the enormity of the construction. The vaulting, the highest in Europe, soared one hundred and fifty-seven feet from tiled floor to ceiling. The guidebook told him that in 1284 the townsfolk had paid heavily for the extravagance of the builders when the vaulting caved in. The cathedral, begun in 1225, was not completed. After the choir and transept had been finished, interest and finance had gone and work on the nave never begun.

Stolford sat in one of the rows of upright wooden chairs, placing the briefcase between his feet and watching the movements of the few other people in the building. A couple of elderly tourists appeared from the cloisters, talking in whispers and stopping frequently to admire the statues and tapestries. Three teenage girls with haversacks overtook the couple to reach the doors. One of them glanced at the big American, smiled self-consciously and looked away quickly. Near the high alter a soberly dressed woman stood before one of the ornate 'stations', hands joined. After a few moments she turned towards the altar, genuflecting and making the sign of the cross. The slight bending of the right knee was more habit than conscious reverence. She moved slowly towards the doors, half-walk, half-tiptoe. Early thirties, Stolford guessed. She looked worried. Was she the one? She caught his glance and for a moment it seemed she would walk across to him, but she moved to the back row of chairs and sat staring at the tracery in the windows above the high altar.

Stolford lifted the briefcase and stood up slowly. The elderly tourists looked across and smiled. He nodded and moved quickly but gently to the right aisle behind the choir. The confession box was partly recessed in the wall, its dark wood

66

contrasting with the grey of the stone. He heard one of the main doors opening and footsteps which stopped. The temptation was great to look behind him but he realised the move, however casual, might seem furtive. He opened the central door of the box and stepped quickly inside. His knees touched the seat. He turned around and sat on it, placing the briefcase flat on his knees. Only small chinks of daylight from around the door broke the darkness of the confined area. He waited, listening to the silence, then reached down with his right hand and felt around beneath the seat. Nothing. His heart sank. Christ, all this way and nothing. He changed hands and tried the other side, movements becoming more agitated. It was there, near the wall. His fingers felt the stickiness of the holding tape and began working it free, slowly and gingerly. It came loose and he brought it out. The dark blue bottle resembled those used by the manufacturer of a popular patent medicine. No way, Stolford thought, and put it into his briefcase, easing the catch closed.

Approaching footsteps froze him. They slowed and stopped. He held his breath straining to hear any movement. Whoever was outside was also listening. After some moments the footsteps resumed and Stolford gratefully emptied his bursting lungs with a long hiss through his teeth. But the footsteps stopped again. The woodwork vibrated as one of the penitants' doors opened and closed. He pressed his ear against the wooden partition. He could hear soft breathing.

The sharp raps on the other side of the partition lifted him into a standing position. The temptation was to throw open the door in front of him and run from the cathedral, but he held himself in check. Who the hell was knocking? Another priest, a real one? Or the sacristan? Why didn't they come to his door instead of the penitants'? Maybe they'll go away. Another heavier knock on the woodwork destroyed that ridiculous optimism. How the hell would he talk his way out of this one? Keen collector of confession boxes? Feign deafness? Stupidity?

He reached to his right and slid open the small panel separating him from the person next door. Through the wire mesh he could see the troubled face of the woman he had seen leaving the cathedral. He rested his elbow on the narrow ledge beneath the hatch, covering as much of his face as possible with his hand. 'Bénissez moi, mon Père,' the woman whispered, but with a firmness of resolve. 'J'ai péché contre mon Dieu. Il fait six semaines depuis la dernière fois que je me suis confessée.'

Stolford's grasp of French was never firm, even when the verbs and nouns were pumped into his uninterested schoolboy head. Now, apart from a vague memory of one or two words and phrases, he was in a fog of ignorance. Besides, this woman was pouring it out in an accent and at a speed he had never had to cope with. His schoolteacher had had a soft North Carolina drawl which was never disguised. This was something else. Senior league, natural, incomprehensible.

The woman raced on, Stolford struggling still with what she had already said. Only one word, 'confessée', seemed recognisable. Christ, he thought, the woman is telling me her sins. She's confessing. He peered with one wide eye through his fingers. She held her hands beneath her chin, fingers entwined, and never lifted her eyes to him.

'...et j'ai couché avec un homme.' Man? What about the man, Stolford wondered. 'Et sans le vouloir je me suis trouvée dans les bras d'un autre homme,' the woman went on. Stolford sunk low into his seat.

The woman looked up into the wide and unblinking eye between the fingers. 'Je demande pardon au seigneur,' she ended quietly. She waited patiently. So did Stolford. After some moments he realised the next move was his. Some non-verbal acknowledgement. The Sunday Baptist lessons and his years in the Marine Corps had never prepared him for this situation.

Television rescued him. At least his memory of the two recent papal elections shown on television newscasts rescued him. The successive pontiffs had motioned to the crowds in St Peter's Square and made signs of the cross. Keeping his right hand in the same position, Stolford stroked the air with his left. He paused for a moment, then added another flourish. Just in case.

Relief showed in the woman's face but she made no move to leave. He blessed her again. Stupid bitch. Still no move. His left hand was still hovering vaguely beside his face. He became aware of it and dropped it self-consciously onto his lap.

Eventually the woman spoke. 'Pénitence, Père?' she prompted gently.

'Ah...' Stolford began, but stopped himself translating the word into English. He lifted his left had again and waved it, spread, from side to side. The woman watched the movement. She seemed puzzled and he hardly blamed her. But she obviously made some kind of interpretation. She smiled, lifted herself from her knees and walked out of the confessional, shutting the door quietly beind her.

Stolford sighed gratefully and licked his upper lip. It was salty with perspiration. Why the hell couldn't The Voice have sent someone to France who could speak the bloody language? He waited for some minutes anxious to leave before someone else thought he was a priest, but wary of meeting the same woman face to face.

When he eventually left the confessional the woman was near the altar, lighting a candle in front of a statue. He slipped quietly from the cathedral and gulped the heavy air outside. He walked briskly back to his parked car and drove out of town southwards along the N321 until he reached Méru and then swung west onto the N323 to reach Chaumont. He registered in a guest house on the outskirts and lunched before driving away for some sightseeing in the surrounding countryside.

Between the villages of Hardivillers and Jouy, north-west of Chaumont, he pulled off the road into a lane bordered by hedges and some trees. He took the briefcase to the boot of the car and transferred the blue bottle to the toilet bag resting on top of his clothes in the suitcase. Curious, he took the bottle out again and held it up against the weak sunshine. It held a thick white liquid. The screw top was sealed with tape which he would remove before he boarded the ferry at Le Havre. What the hell was in the bottle? What made it so important and so lethal?

'...and under no circumstances open the bottle. To do so would undoubtedly cause you to die. You must believe this...' – the words of The Voice on the last tape came back to him. Just holding the bottle made his neck creep. What game had he got into? And was he ever going to get the promised reward?

...and the reward for you all will be great. Greater even than anticipated when the operation was planned. Each of you will receive exactly one million dollars in addition to

what has already been paid into the Swiss numbered accounts...

Promises, but what guarantees? None. And what would prevent The Voice disposing of him and the others as soon as the operation had been carried out? Stolford had asked himself this pointless question repeatedly since the whole thing began. The organisation was obviously international, possibly Mafia, and therefore inescapable. They would find him wherever he tried to hide, whether or not he went on with it. No choice. He returned the bottle to the bag and closed the suitcase.

In Le Havre the following day he returned the Renault to the Hertz office and explained his curtailed visit by looking suitably worried and saying a message had awaited him in Beauvais about his elderly mother in Dublin. Stroke, serious, hoped he would make it back in time. Terribly sad, the Hertz girl agreed.

At customs in Rosslare, early on Sunday morning, Stolford made for the first officer in the line behind the tables and threw open both cases, the toilet bag open and lying on top of the clothing. The young officer glanced at the contents and reached for the bag. He was not in a good mood. Another row last night. The wife and her whining mother and the whole lousy family could go to hell as far as he was concerned. Passengers were in for a tough time today.

He pulled the clothing aside to look at the bottom of the suitcase. The open toilet bag fell to one side, tumbling the bottle towards the lid of the case. Stolford dived and stopped it falling onto the floor. It took real effort to unclench his teeth and force a smile. A man in plain clothes who was standing behind the officer looked curiously at the sudden movement. Police Special Branch dectective. 'Couldn't do without that,' said Stolford jocularly. 'Stomach needs all the help it can get.'

The customs officer looked up through his eyebrows at the priest. Trust a sky pilot to be happy at this hour of the bloody morning, he thought. He took the bottle from Stolford's hand and straightened. 'Have you anything to declare, Father?' he asked coolly. He held the bottle by its neck and tapped the bottom edge of it against the palm of his other hand.

Stolford wanted to snatch the bottle from the officer and

clutch it protectively in his arms. He also wanted to smash his fist into the guy's mouth. Instead, he smiled again, but this time almost apologetically. 'No, I'm afraid not. Hadn't time to buy anythin'. You see, I got this message...'

'Right,' the officer interrupted. 'Thank you.' He threw the bottle back into the clothing in the case and slammed down the lid. Stolford swallowed hard and moved the case a little way along the counter to make way for the next passenger. He settled the bottle between layers of clothing, locked the suitcase and walked away. He had done it.

'Just a minute, Father.'

The harsh voice of the customs officer stopped him in his tracks. He turned slowly to face the officer; a pathetic attempt to show nonchalance was the best he could manage. The detective was now standing beside the officer. Stolford walked slowly back to the table. He might be able to make a break but the odds were bad. The detective was probably armed. Other passengers had now turned to watch developments. Stolford reached the table.

'Forget something, Father?' the detective asked.

'Forget?' Stolford asked in what he hoped was a tone at least approaching innocence. 'Sorry, I don't understand.'

'That,' said the detective.

Stolford looked down to follow the policeman's pointing finger. The briefcase was lying where he had left it. He looked back into the detective's face which was now creased in a broad grin.

'Oh, yes, of course.' said Stolford. He wanted to smile, chuckle, anything to show gratitude, friendship. But his jaw was locked tight with shock. 'Just not my day, I guess,' was the best he could manage.

He took the briefcase and walked away stiff-legged. He badly needed a drink.

Later that morning, he put the suitcase on one of the armchairs in Charles Casswell's apartment. Casswell and Coates gathered cautiously, almost reverently, around the case when Stolford opened the lid to show the blue bottle lying on the clothing. The three men stared for seconds at the bottle as if some inspiration might suddenly fill one, or all of them.

'What's in it?' asked Coates, breaking the silence.

'Don't know,' Stolford shrugged. Then grimly, 'And I don't intend t'find out.'

Casswell glanced at his watch. 'Plenty of time. Lunch first?'

Stolford nodded. 'Did you rent a car?'

'It's outside.'

Just under four hours later Casswell swung the rented Fiat 132 off the coast road running north of Dublin City and onto a long wooden causeway which linked the mainland at Clontarf to the North Bull Island, home of two golf courses and thousands of sea birds. The wide expanse of beach on the seaward side of the island consisted of hard-packed sand, rolled smooth by the wheels of weekend family saloons and the sports cars of necking couples. The beach was headed by low sand dunes which formed the boundary of the golf courses and provided privacy for those who did not own motor cars.

The Fiat pulled left onto the beach and drove north parallel to the sand dunes for exactly one mile.

'Here,' Stolford said, tapping Casswell's arm.

The actor swung the car towards the dunes and stopped. Then he reversed it towards the sea, stopping at what he judged to be halfway between the dunes and the sea. He switched off the engine.

The American, carrying the blue bottle, left the car and walked up into the dunes. In a small depression, sheltered from land and sea, he scooped a small hole and buried the bottle. To mark the spot he used his handkerchief weighted with sand.

Back at the car he scanned the dunes again. Nothing. He sat in the passenger's seat and shut the door.

On the main road towards the city, Charles Casswell said, 'I'd give a lot to know what was in that bottle.'

A golfer on the Royal Dublin course, playing alone, badly sliced a shot into the rough. He moved into the dunes as if to retrieve the ball but, in fact, to locate the expected handkerchief and the blue bottle beneath.

The engineer, Peter Phelan, had been busy in the last few days. The money, as promised on the last tape, had arrived at his apartment.

The four-ton open-backed Dodge truck he had bought was four years old but looked ten. The milometer reading was much too low for the condition of the vehicle, but this was part of the price of silence Phelan had to pay to the rough-tongued scrap-dealer in the midlands. The truck was driven to Rath-mines and locked in the garage provided by The Voice.

Other purchases were made in the Dublin area and now awaited collection at various locations around the city. More vital equipment would be driven across the border on un-approved roads from Northern Ireland. Some pieces could be bought openly for his registered business, Matthews Pressure Cleaners, while others had to be purchased separately and from different sources to avoid suspicion then or later.

Sebastian Stanley, the American art dealer and critic, had also made progress.

Since his meeting with the Arts Council official he had visited three galleries and the studios of fours artists in the south of Dublin County and in County Wicklow. He now had all he needed and had already made provisional arrangements for the artists' works to be moved to Dublin for shipment to the United States.

He was suitably vague to everyone about the exact date of collection and shipment.

The Arts Council, as promised, would look after the necessary documentation for customs clearance when neces-sary.

They were pleased, the artists were pleased and Stanley was pleased. Lutz Feldmann would also be pleased.

The Voice would be unsurprised.

Across the English Channel, in the port of Brest, the two old friends were pleased to see each other again. It had been four years only but seemed a lifetime.

Adrien D'Albe hugged Edouard Dufour on the quayside overlooking the diver's boat. He stood back to take stock of the former paratrooper turned underwater demolition expert. More pounds and less hair perhaps, but just as fit and strong as he remembered.

Dufour had seen action with the elite French Parachute Corps in the fifties, including the disastrous battle at Dien Bien Phu. After his release he had tried fishing, but the necessary routine was unacceptable and he turned towards diving, making use of the explosives experience of his army days. He was a willing student and learned surely the techniques and dangers of underwater work.

During a refit of the Cunard liner *Queen Mary* he bought one of her huge steel lifeboats which was being replaced. For eight months he toiled, sometimes with help but often alone, converting the boat to suit his new profession of diver. He built living accommodation and installed large stowage lockers for his equipment and accessories. The spacious cabin could sleep six, although bachelor Dufour seldom entertained more than one woman at a time. The bridge was equipped with the best radar, radio and depth-sounding equipment, and her size, design and build made her capable of sailing any waters.

The late fifties and early sixties were good years with sufficient work and challenge. Sunken ships and anti-landing obstacles still blocked some ports and channels despite the lapse of time since the Second World War, and his services were in constant demand. In winter he operated around the French coast and during summer moved along the English coastline and among the Channel Islands.

But need for his work decreased as the coastlines became free of obstacles – through his own efforts and those of the increasing band of divers on both sides of the Channel. In recent years he had moved far north to the oil-drilling platforms and their maintenance in the dark and chilling waters off Scotland's coast.

He hated it.

Every few months he broke loose and sailed back in his converted lifeboat to the French ports to hunt for freelance work. The opportunities seldom improved and, when his oilrig payrolls ran out, he had to head north again.

At a guess, thought Adrien D'Albe as he sat on the edge of one of the bunks in the comfortable but untidy cabin, Dufour must be forty-seven but looked ten years younger. The brown hair was receding a little from the weather-bronzed forehead and the side-boards showed flecks of grey, but his face was hardly lined. The diver's body was powerfully built, without the grossness of the muscle-builder but with the hardness of a man who had always known a strenuously physical life. His hands were big, perhaps disproportionate, thought D'Albe as he watched him pouring drinks, but otherwise perfectly scaled to his six-feet-two-inch frame.

'Well,' Dufour said, handing the brandy to D'Albe, 'what do you think of Marie?'

'Marie?' D'Albe queried, glancing quickly around the cabin.

'The boat,' Dufour chuckled, sweeping his hand around him. '*Marie.*'

'Ah, yes,' D'Albe recovered, 'the boat. Very nice.'

'I think, my friend,' said the diver teasingly, 'you would not know a racing yacht from a canal barge, no?'

His eyes twinkled amusement.

D'Albe smiled agreement. 'Cars, my dear Edouard, and women. But boats...' he shrugged, leaving the sentence unfinished.

The men drank again in silence.

'So,' Dufour said eventually. 'What's the reason for the visit?'

D'Albe outlined the offer he had been asked to make to his friend. The money, he knew, was good but the decisive factor for Dufour would be the prospect of adventure and excitement. The offer, therefore, was irresistible.

After a few short moments the diver looked up from his drink and grinned.

'Let us drink to challenge and wealth, my friend.'

In New York the following day, Robert Melchoir received another call from 'Monsieur Flaubert' in France. The coded conversation—talk of bonds and shares to an eavesdropper—pleased the stockbroker.

He met the procurer, Lutz Feldmann, in a restaurant nine minutes later.

'We've got the diver,' Melchoir said simply.

Feldmann smiled. 'And the Belgian equipment?'

'That too.'

'Good. Then we tell the man in Dublin to begin the operation.'

Part Two

THE PREPARATION

Chapter Five

The drunk wove his unsteady course through the dark alleyway to his home near Dublin's dockland, the rain drizzling onto his flat cloth cap and the shoulders of his jacket.

It had been a good night in the bar. Not a great night, but good. He hadn't beaten the big ape, Condon, in the darts match but, by Christ, he had given him a hell of a run for his money.

He took his hand from his trouser pocket and threw an imaginary dart, face smiling the memory. Next time, he vowed.

Then he was falling, hand extended in a useless attempt to ease the impact with the wet-blackened concrete. His cheek-bone grazed the wall but the pain would take some hours to penetrate the alcohol barrier. His downward collapse was checked, momentarily, by the plastic bags of garbage at the base of the wall, then he rolled sideways into the centre of the alleyway.

He laughed then, looking up into the falling rain. Shock had made the incident amusing.

'Christ, I'm pissed,' he told himself unnecessarily. But the laughter froze in his still open mouth when the other sound intruded.

The low growl was a challenge. Another, slightly higher than the first, formed a thin chorus. They were close. But where? The drunk was more sober now, adrenalin combating booze. He lifted himself carefully onto one elbow.

How many? Two? Three? The light at the end of the alleyway showed the animals in silhouette. Huge, they were, or so they seemed, shoulders hunched and ready. The third dog turned its attention back to ripping and tearing something against the far wall. But the other two held their position, ears back, neck hair upright.

'Nice bow-wows,' the drunk mumbled hopefully, placatingly. 'Good boys, good boys.'

One of the dogs closed its mouth and turned away quickly to salvage something of its supper. The other stood, growls less frequent but still watching the drunk. The man drew his knees up slowly and wormed his backside away from the dog. The animal growled once more and moved over to the others. The drunk lifted himself slowly and, on trembling legs, backed off for some distance before turning his back to the animals and continuing his staggering journey.

'I've a good mind to go back there and kick their teeth out,' he slurred angrily to the night.

Back in the alleyway, the dogs licked the final traces of the raw cow's meat from the ground, sniffed around for a few moments and then wandered away, two to find some kind of shelter from the drizzle, the third to his home a mile away.

The converted lifeboat slipped out of the busy port of Brest under cover of darkness and turned north-east to the English Channel.

Edouard Dufour had let it be known that he was returning to the North Sea oilfields. Financial necessity, he had told port officials and Hélène. Tolerant, passionate, Hélène. She would miss him, would always love him, would wait for him, faithfully. The hell she would, thought Dufour, chuckling to himself as he peered through the windscreen of the bridge.

The memory of their parting earlier that night brought a warmth, stirring him again. For ten years she had loved, humoured and comforted the diver whose cavalier personality hid a basic insecurity. Supremely confident in his professional ability but reluctant to give anything of himself emotionally, he showed his fondness for Hélène in unconscious gestures but never in words. They were good together, in and out of bed, but his only admission of this was his seeming reluctance to seek other company on his return to Brest after each job. He had not told her about the financial prospects for this job in

Ireland, but if all went well it might decide him to make their relationship permanent. It might, he thought. But, as always, first things first.

He brought the *Marie* to a heading which would take him to the west of the Channel Islands of Guernsey and Alderney and on to Cap de la Hague before moving into the shipping lanes of the Channel. He sat behind the small wheel and finished Hélène's second bottle of 1976 Chiroubles with a silent toast. The single heavy diesel engine throbbed rhythmically behind the wheelhouse, pushing the boat through the slight swell at six knots. He felt good. Better than he had for years. In four or five weeks' time he would be back in Brest with Hélène and with a staggering bank balance in Zurich.

Wealth, the dream of every diver. Well, most of them. Especially in the North Sea operations where the risks were high; not only fatalities but other injuries, unrecorded except in hospital reports and occasional newspaper articles. He had seen them all. The bends and the lesser cousins known as 'niggles', the bubble of helium gas forming in the body. Sometimes the bubble hit the spine causing paralysis, or the ear which often meant permanent damage to the diver's sense of balance. Two of his friends had died because the helium had reached their brains. Then there were the 'shadows', the dark areas which showed up on annual X-ray pictures, confirming that the diver had necrosis of the bones, the gradual rotting thought to be caused by compression.

Dufour had done it all, saturation and bounce diving, and escaped the shadows. Now just one more operation.

In Dublin, Carl Stolford had settled his account and moved out of the hotel. Too long in one spot could cause questions to be asked by inquisitive detectives doing their routine rounds of such establishments.

Moving south for a few days and then back to the States, he had told the desk clerk. In fact, he moved to Peter Phelan's one-room apartment in Monkstown. The engineer had moved in an old camp bed for the ex-marine which could be easily folded and hidden should the landlord arrive for a spot check.

Together, the two collected the pieces of technical equipment which had been purchased by Phelan for their 'pressure cleaners' business. Then in a city-centre store specialising in camping equipment and protective clothing, they bought four ex-British Army combat uniforms and four pairs of black boots. They cost a total of ninety-eight pounds. The purchase of the old uniforms would cause no suspicion despite the fact that the Irish Army wore the identical uniform. The NATO green jackets and trousers were popular with civilian outdoor workers because of their durability. The leather boots, rubber-soled, were often bought by hitch-hikers and campers. They needed four black berets to complete the basic uniform, and made the purchases in different shops to avoid arousing curiosity. Black berets were recognised headwear for Northern Ireland paramilitary groups. In a small shop near the Coombe they bought three pairs of green woollen gloves and one brown leather pair.

Insignia had then to be found and this proved more difficult. All the uniforms had to bear Southern Command flashes and all represent the same unit of that command. The command flashes were found in junk and militaria shops in Dublin and Cork, but the unit flashes were bought by Stolford in a series of meetings with a cheery quartermaster-sergeant in the town of Kildare alongside the Curragh, the country's largest army camp. Stolford, dressed in civilian clothes and carrying a camera, stayed in the town for four days, posing as a tourist with a great interest in armies and their insignia. Because of its location, the town was essentially 'military' and it was not difficult for the American to strike up conversations with soldiers in bars. Eventually he made contact with the one man who could get him the unit flashes and private first-class stars to add to Stolford's 'military collection Stateside'. And, as a bonus, a set of sergeant's stripes and a captain's epaulettes and pips. For two nights the quartermaster-sergeant drank his fill of Irish whiskey at Stolford's expense and then bid the tourist a fond goodbye and a safe return journey to America. The method of obtaining the insignia had contained an element of risk, but he had no choice and guessed rightly that the freeloading quartermaster-sergeant would never admit he had furnished the items to the so-called tourist.

Stolford returned to Peter Phelan's apartment to find the young engineer very drunk.

A crumpled evening newspaper lay on the floor of the smoke-filled room and a half-empty bottle of whiskey sat, with Phelan's spectacles, on the chair alongside the bed. He lay on his back, one arm across his eyes, the other hanging over the edge of the bed, an empty glass in his hand. He moved his arm reluctantly from his face to reveal bloodshot eyes. He could barely reply to Stolford's obvious question.

He repeated his question and this time Phelan motioned towards the newspaper. 'My brother,' he muttered.

Stolford lifted the paper and scanned the uppermost page. At the bottom of the page was a three-paragraph description of a car crash in the early hour of that morning. It told how John Phelan, a thirty-eight year-old unmarried accountant, had crashed into a wall on a lonely suburban road on the north side of the city.

For a long time Stolford sat on the edge of the bed without speaking. After a time, Phelan told him the story in detail.

A mile from the Belgian coast, Edouard Dufour took a final fix on his position and dropped his storm anchor over the side.

The sea was calm with only a whiff of fresh wind from the south-west. He had made good time despite the tides–too good. He would have to wait for five hours for the rendezvous. He catnapped in the chair behind the wheel of the converted lifeboat, waking regularly to check his position and restart the diesel to bring the vessel back onto station, due east of the small seaside town of Koksijde.

Just before three in the morning he woke to the distant sound of another engine. He reached for the night glasses and scanned the moonless darkness towards the shore. For a long time he could see nothing although the engine noise increased steadily. Then a stab of red light penetrated the blanket, twice and twice again.

He reached outside the wheelhouse and tilted the spotlamp on the roof bracket. He stabbed the console switch three times and repeated the sequence. The red light answered once. Through the glasses he could now see the high bows of the open clinker boat rising and falling in the slight swell as it approached. He stepped outside and up onto the flat wooden deck, steadying himself with the mast's forward guy rope. The open boat's engine cut back to neutral and the vessel edged gently bow-first into the side of the converted lifeboat. There were three men on board, the one in the bow holding a submachine gun at waist level and pointed at Dufour.

'What is your name monsieur?' the accent was French.

'Dufour,' the diver answered flatly.

The man put one foot on the bow of the open boat and sprung up onto the deck beside Dufour. He paused for just a second and then moved cautiously towards the wheelhouse. Dufour glanced back at the open boat and saw that a second man now had a submachine gun trained on him. He could hear the first man moving about in the cabin beneath his feet, opening doors and hatches. He reappeared and nodded to his companions. The engine clunked into gear and the boat brought her beam alongside the lifeboat. The man at the wheelhouse door caught a rope thrown by one of his companions and made it fast to Dufour's boat.

'We must do this quickly, monsieur,' said the first man, nodding again to his own boat where the other two men were removing a tarpaulin from cases and parcels.

Dufour bent down to help pull up the first of the wooden cases, long and narrow and with a rope handle at each end. It was unmarked. As the other cases and equipment were brought onto the deck, the first man walked forward to Dufour and extended a wide-blade sheath knife to him.

'Please check each item carefully,' he said quietly.

'Oh, I'm sure it's all in order,' said Dufour, anxious to get under way.

'Please check,' said the man. The tone left no room for argument.

Dufour took the knife and knelt beside the cases. He prized open the lid of the first one and peered inside. The red light of the torch which had been hanging at the belt of the stranger lit up the inside of the case. Dufour could see four rifles, heavily greased, sights uppermost.

'As requested, no?' asked the man. Unsure, Dufour took the easy way and nodded confirmation.

'FN. Semi-automatic,' said the man. 'And magazines,' he added, tapping a smaller case with the toe of his canvas shoe.

Dufour opened it and counted six magazines, unloaded.

Beneath them he could see rows of brass-nosed rounds of ammunition laid between layers of padding. He tapped the lids back into place and stood up.

'The other equipment?' he asked 'And the explosives?'

'Everything asked for,' the stranger assured him.

Dufour looked at the diving equipment being stacked on the deck. Now he was in familiar territory. He stepped across and examined each piece, testing valves and tanks before moving on to the masks and suits. It was all new and the best. He was about to stand up when he noticed two other bundles, one large and the other much smaller, both wrapped in polythene and tied with string.

'What're those?' he asked.

'Four flak jackets and webbing equipment in that one,' said the stranger, shining his torch onto the larger parcel. 'One 9mm Browning pistol, two suitable full magazines, and holster and belt in that,' he finished, flashing the beam onto the smaller bundle.

Dufour nodded briefly and then rose to look at the man. 'Have you been told what all this is for?' he asked gently.

'No,' said the stranger. 'And I have no wish to know, monsieur.'

He turned to his companions and then back to the diver. 'Can you manage to put this below without help?'

'Yes,' answered Dufour.

'Good. It is best that we do not stay here too long.'

All three jumped back down into the open boat and waited for Dufour to release the mooring line before starting the outboard engine.

'Good luck, monsieur,' said the stranger and waved.

Dufour returned the wave but his thanks were lost in the roar of the engine as the boat pulled away sharply. In moments it disappeared into the darkness and soon even the sound had gone. The diver ferried the equipment and arms below and placed them in storage lockers behind the wheelhouse and in the bow.

Twenty minutes later he started the diesel and swung the boat onto a southerly course. At the north-eastern side of Cherbourg he would take on board the man who had arranged the delivery of the cargo, Adrien D'Albe.

The following morning, while Peter Phelan went to the hospital and the undertakers to arrange the funeral of his brother, Carl Stolford picked up Simon Coates at Casswell's apartment. They went first to a car accessory shop, where they purchased a roof rack and had it fitted to the Fiat, and then out to the small harbour of Bullock. On the quayside they found the huge warehouse described in the telephone yellow pages, Western Marine. Inside, they moved slowly through the rows of boats and engines, stopping at the inflatables section. They told the saleswoman they were looking for a small fishing boat and thought an inflatable with outboard engine would be best. They were appropriately vague about the size needed. The woman was most helpful, translating the technical blurbs for the benefit of the two landlubbers. Eventually, they decided on an Avon S100 measuring ten feet six inches long with a beam of four feet ten inches. The medium-speed boat could carry up to four people and could take a fifteen-horsepower standard shaft outboard. They bought an electric-start Chrysler 10. For both they paid cash and asked, unnecessarily, for help from the warehouse workers to get the boat onto the roof rack of the car. The engine was put into the boot. As an apparent afterthought, Stolford also bought a set of paddles and a wrist compass. Beaming pleasure and muttering comments about their intended vacation on the River Shannon, the two thanked the saleswoman and pulled away from Bullock Harbour. They drove to the lockup garage in Rathmines and unloaded the boat and engine. The roof rack was removed and locked inside with the boat. Later that day they purchased anoraks, three fishing rods, multipliers and sea traces.

Everything was on schedule.

At eleven o'clock the next day, Peter Phelan stood before an open grave in Dean's Grange Cemetery, south of Dublin city, aware of, but not hearing, the intonation of the elderly priest in the wind-blown surplice.

Most of the small group were friends of his brother or distant relations. The boys' parents had died in a motorway accident while holidaying in England seven years earlier. Now John was with them in the vast granite and marble burial ground. On the heaped earth alongside the grave and on the wooden temporary covering were two wreaths and a dozen plastic flowers.

The anger had gone when he saw the body in the mortuary, but so too had other feeling he had known in the past. Now he stood with head bowed, more to shelter against the cutting wind which whipped through and around the celtic crosses and ornate headstones than as an outward sign of respect. Others in the group wiped tears from their eyes, but they were wind-made. Only Betty's were real.

She stood behind him, near the back of the group. He had looked at her several times during the Mass and afterwards in the yard as they brought the coffin from the church to the waiting hearse. But there was nothing in the eyes, no sign, no depth. Now she edged gently through the gathering to stand at Peter's side. He gave no indication of knowing she was there, but he knew.

When the last prayers had mumbled into silence and the priest turned to place his hand on Phelan's before moving away, Betty reached across and held her husband's arm. Others came and spoke softly to him but the words were just words, a sound and a tone deemed correct, acceptable and therefore accepted. None would be remembered.

For some time they stood, unaware of the waiting workmen with shovels. The last car door had long closed on the grateful departing group when Betty spoke.

'I'll have to go Peter,' she said, softly apologetic.

'Huh?' he asked vaguely.

'I said I'll have to go,' she said patiently. 'I've invited some of them back to the flat. For drinks or something.'

'Oh, yeah. Sure,' he said, moving away from the grave and towards the only remaining car.

'Who's that?' he asked.

'My friend Anne, from the office,' she said. 'Are you coming with us? Come back with us.' She increased her grip on his arm. 'Please Peter.'

He stopped and faced her. For the first time he looked and saw.

'Not now. I'll be in touch. You go ahead.'

Wrongly she sensed a lie. 'Well, at least let me explain

87

what...why it happened.'

'Not now, Betty,' he said, covering her hand on his arm. 'I've some things to sort out. Maybe then we can, you know...sort us out.'

He squeezed her hand. 'Not now,' he repeated, 'but I *will* come to see you. I promise.'

She wanted to throw her arms around him, hold him, love him, make him understand, make it right again. So much to say, yet so little. Instead, she just forced a smile.

'Well, then,' she said, motioning towards the waiting car. 'Can we give you a lift to somewhere?'

He shook his head and said, 'You go ahead. I'll be in touch.'

She lifted herself onto tiptoe and kissed him gently on the lips and then quickly turned away. He stood and watched the car drive away along the concrete road towards the gate.

Across several rows of graves a tall man in a black raincoat and hat watched as he knelt before a headstone. He waited until Phelan had walked slowly after the car and then he stood and moved towards the other gate, dumping the flowers he had bought outside the cemetery into a refuse can.

Chapter Six

He waited, in the darkness, with the patience of the natural assassin. How long he had lain there, unmoving, crouched, was of little importance in the scale of his plan, instinctively conceived.

He had once seen a killing, but it had been a spontaneous act, born of ill temper, coarse and unpremeditated. Brute force and not skill had won that day. He had stood at a distance, the only spectator, frightened by the increasing intensity of the fight until suddenly the victor stepped back from the bloody heap, stunned, and limped from the arena to nurse his wounds.

Now, suddenly, he sensed the approach of his target, knew it would be peering over the rough stone wall before easing itself onto the sloping roof of the shed just below the edge. A slight creak confirmed the progress and position. Six more seconds passed before the assassin heard a muted thud signifying arrival at ground level. It was almost time. For just a second the target paused for reassurance before setting out across the open ground towards the partly open ground-floor window and the room beyond. The assassin moved quickly, silence forsaken for speed.

The cat heard the approaching attacker and turned, too late. The mongrel sank his teeth into the middle of its back; the momentum of the charge pushed it down and onto its side, bringing the dog's head and neck above the squirming cat. The victim's back paws kicked out in unison, the bared claws raking the soft flesh of the dog's howls and forcing the terrier to release his hold and step back momentarily. The bared teeth lunged again at the cat, which was now on its feet. The right forepaw swept downwards and across, tearing tracks along the length of the wrinkled nose.

Now, for the first time, the dog felt fear and he backed off a pace to reassess the target. He stood, motionless, except for the vibration caused by the growling from deep within his chest. The cat's back was arched, hair upright, mouth partly open, its long growls rising and falling, part snarl, part whine.

A light came on in the upstairs window of the house, illuminating the back yard and the motionless animals. A woman's voice muttered and a man, closer, replied, 'I don't know, for Christ's sake. A cat fight or something!'

A shadow fell across the bloodied face of the terrier as the man reached the window and wrenched it upwards. The sudden sound from behind startled the cat, and the dog saw his only chance. The weight of his charging body pushed the hissing feline onto its back as it raised both front paws in defence. White foam streaked the cat's fur as the dog tried to find a grip for his teeth on the squirming opponent. All four paws now lashed out at the dog, scraping, cutting.

'It's our dog and cat, for Christ's sake,' said the man above. 'I'm goin' t'kick their arseholes off...' his voice trailing away as he moved from the window and made for the stairs.

The dog, flinching from the onslaught of the flailing barbs, was fighting almost totally blind, eyes drawn into protective slits. Now any spot on the cat's body would suffice to try to redress the balance of pain. He found the underside of the cat's right shoulder and bit hard into the sinew to lock his eye teeth behind the tearing fibres. The rising screech from the cat encouraged him, and he brought both back legs forward to balance his body and concentrate his weight behind his head now working from side to side to tear the flesh from the wound he had inflicted.

But in moving forward he had brought his testicles directly above the kicking back legs of the cat. Both sets of claws struck together, ripping the delicate membrane of the bag. The dog howled, releasing his hold, and arched his back in an attempt to rise above his own testicles and therefore the pain. The cat wriggled free and upright as the dog sank onto his haunches and buried his bleeding nose into the lacerated balls to lick furiously at first and then, wisely, more gently.

'What's goin' on, for Christ's sake?' said the man, throwing open the back door. It caught, as it always did, in mid-arc on the concrete threshold and he thumped into the edge of it as he stepped forward, catching the side of his forehead and bicep.

His wife, sitting upright in bed, had heard the howl of agony from the dog. Now her husband was bellowing obscenities and apparently kicking or punching at the back door. The whole neighbourhood would be awake soon.

'Will ye stop that cursin',' huffed the woman as she padded down the narrow staircase, her large breasts rising and falling beneath the pink nightdress. 'Whatever's the matter wit'ye, anyway?' she demanded of her husband who was leaning against the door jamb, nursing his swelling forehead and kicking the outside of the door with the sole of his foot.

The cat seized its opportunity to escape further conflict and dashed past the man to reach the sanctuary of the house. The man saw the flash of black fur and made a vicious kick, hopelessly late, at the animal and smacked his small toe along the faded paint of the door.

'Fuck me!' he roared and doubled over to grab the tortured foot.

'Stop that filthy language!' his wife shouted.

'You brought that bloody cat here in the first place,' the man snarled, 'stinkin' the place out with its piss. I'm goin' t'kick its balls off!'

'You'll do no such thing...' the woman began.

'Will you two stop that squabblin' and let us get some sleep!' the voice of their nextdoor neighbour shouted from his bedroom window.

'Now look what ye've done!' the woman hissed at her husband. 'I'm goin' back to bed.'

'That's bloody typical!' the man shouted after her and then limped to the kitchen sink. He squinted into the small round mirror on the window frame and inspected the damage to his forehead.

'I will,' he vowed. 'I'll kick its balls off!'

The dog sat behind the garden shed, one hind leg cocked, tongue licking furiously at the claw wounds on the soft covering of the testicle sack. As he worked, the animal howled softly and hoarsely, self-pity giving way to anger and frustra-

91

tion. He had to fight again, to strike at someone or something. His emotions rose inside his jumbled brain and were vented by increasing the speed of his tongue. But soon even that was insufficient and he began nibbling with his teeth at the torn skin. The cat and the fight were now only hazy recollections at some distant time. The irritating pain was now his enemy and must be eliminated decisively. The hoarse howl in his chest rose to a crescendo and changed tone as he opened his mouth wide and bared his teeth, a small trail of saliva snaking from his lower jaw onto his belly. He fixed his dilated eyes on the target, his fuddled reasoning telling him that this was a prey which must be approached with caution and despatched with savage sureness. His head moved slightly back, muscles braced, and then snapped forward, the powerful jaws closing and locking the teeth through the mangled tissue, fat and viens of his testicles.

Strangely, he felt no pain, only a sensation of triumph. He growled satisfaction and he jerked his head from side to side to loosen the fibres, then wrenched his head back, tearing the testicles from their delicate hold on his belly and severing the femoral artery. He bit and chewed frantically before swallowing and renewing his attack on the gaping hole and seeping flesh. The pain gave way to dull ache and quickly to merely torpid consciousness. His fury left him with the arrival of the new sensation. He felt suddenly tired and weak. His supporting foreleg trembled and slid away. He rolled onto his back and settled slowly to his full length, back legs jerking and trembling in response to the torn nerves. Soon the movement stopped.

The following morning the man found the dog and buried it sorrowfully in the rough ground behind the small vegetable patch. He had never seen such mutilation. The cat snuggled comfortably on the sill behind the window of the upstairs bedroom and watched the burial with no outward sign of satisfaction. The man's wife stood behind the animal and gently stroked its head. The cat purred its pleasure.

The man felt the eyes on him but resisted the temptation to look towards the window until he had completed his task. He patted the final piece of earth into place and mumbled softly, 'Poor bastard.'

Peter Phelan slid open the big door of the garage in Rathmines three hours later and admitted the American.

'Didn't expect to see you here,' he said, pulling the door shut again. 'I thought you were going to see Casswell and Coates this morning.'

'I've just come from there,' said Stolford. 'The Voice has been in touch again.'

'Oh?' said Phelan, turning again to the engine on the workshop trolley. 'What did he want this time?'

Stolford walked around to face the engineer. He seemed unsure for the first time since they had met. Phelan lifted his eyes and then straightened.

'Something wrong?'

'Well, look Peter,' Stolford began. 'He says it wouldn't be wise, y'know, for you to... well...' his voice trailed into embarrassed silence.

'To what?' Phelan prompted, uneasy now.

'Well,' said Stolford hesitantly, 'to see Betty.'

Phelan stiffened and the American added quickly, 'At least for the time being. Until this is all over.'

'I see,' said Phelan, bending to the engine again. The words were toneless and gave no indication of consent or disagreement.

'I suppose he has a point,' said Stolford, still probing for a definite reaction. 'Like if Betty got mixed up in it. Well, y'wouldn't like that now, would you?'

Phelan stood upright and smiled. 'Sure, I understand. Tell him he's got nothing to worry about. I'll leave her alone. For ever.'

Stolford was unconvinced about the sincerity of the promise but there was nothing more he could do about it. And he could not tell Phelan that the real fear was that Betty might talk him out of the operation. Without him there would be no operation.

On a personal level, Stolford was sure the threat to kill anyone who tried to pull out was not an idle one. Phelan might nurture the belief that he could hide from The Voice and his organisation, but they would get him wherever he went and however long it took. None of them had shown their faces and he doubted they would. The young man would be chased by

93

shadows until reality caught up with him. He hoped Phelan realised how real the threat was.

Phelan broke into his thoughts. 'Did The Voice give any idea about the target?'

'No. Just to expect two new helpers. From France.'

'France?'

'That's what he said.'

'Did you ask him what was in that bottle?'

'Yeah,' said Stolford and shrugged. 'Said we didn't need to know.'

'Any ideas?'

'Oh yeah, sure,' said Stolford smiling. 'But non that makes sense right now.'

The *Marie* had made good time because of the relatively calm seas and Edouard Dufour's calculations.

After taking Adrien D'Albe on board at Cherbourg, he took his first real rest of the journey, leaving the landlubber at the wheel with specific instructions in navigation, simplified sufficiently for the basic course set. D'Albe woke the diver at two-hour intervals to check their position but, as predicted, the drift was slight and required only a minimum of correction.

D'Albe made a good sailor, much to his own surprise, and enjoyed the new responsibility. He kept calm despite the ever-present threat of being rammed by much bigger vessels in this the busiest sea lane in the world.

The dangers of the English Channel seemed less daunting with the comforting presence of the supremely confident and competent Dufour nearby. Only twice was the experienced seaman called to the bridge, when approaching ships seemed to make collision inevitable.

Dufour's detailed planning of the trip paid handsomely on the approach to Penzance near the south-west tip of England. He had timed it perfectly to round Land's End and catch the six-hour flood tide northwards. He would head directly to St David's Head in Wales before turning west to pick up the Tusker Rock lighthouse after passing through the Rusk Channel below Carnsore Point on the south-eastern tip of Ireland. From there he would take the boat along the coast and inside the sprawling sandbank which runs from Dublin to

94

Wexford about a mile off the shore and parallel to the land. For security reasons he would have preferred to move outside the bank, but that would have meant having to pick his way across the bank with the risk of grounding the boat.

'Will we get get there on time?' asked D'Albe for the first time since he came on board at Cherbourg.

'I hope so,' said Dufour who was crouching at the tiny chart table to the right of the wheel. He looked up at the chronometer and back to the chart.

'Well, anyway,' D'Albe said, 'they'll be at the rendezvous point for three nights in succession.'

'Yes,' said Dufour, 'so you've told me several times.'

He stood and patted his friend on the shoulder. 'Relax, Adrien,' he said kindly. 'We'll make it.'

Lutz Feldmann rode the elevator to the penthouse suite of the luxury New York hotel favoured by broker Robert Melchoir for entertaining clients and his numerous female acquaintances.

The interests of Feldmann and Melchoir met only in the shared ambition of increasing their individual wealth. The ambition bonded the two men sufficiently to pass for close friendship. It was the closest either would experience in personal relationships. Yet it was, at best, acquaintance. Commercial and therefore necessary.

Melchoir greeted the little procurer and motioned him towards one of the armchairs in the over-furnished apartment. Inwardly, as on every previous visit, Feldmann grimaced. But his smile never faltered.

'Just thought you'd like to know everything is on schedule,' he said, accepting the proffered glass of sherry. 'Heard from Dublin again. No problems.'

The broker smiled his relief. 'Well, here's to us then.' he said, lifting his glass.

Both men drank silently, unhurried. Melchoir sat down on the arm of the settee facing Feldmann's armchair and leaned forward, forearms resting on his knees, rolling the cut-glass tumbler through his palms.

'There's just one thing I would love to know, Lutz.' he said slowly, selecting his words with care. 'How are the items going to get out of Ireland to their new owners?'

Feldmann looked into Melchoir's face, his expression one of mock surprise.

'Why, with the assistance of the Irish Arts Council, of course.'

For a moment his expression held and then he laughed loudly.

'Of course,' Melchoir chuckled. But he did not, of course, understand.

Melchoir was clearly anxious but Feldmann knew he would not push the subject. The next move was his.

'Alright, Robert,' said Feldmann placatingly, 'I'll satisfy your curiosity.'

Robert Melchoir smiled his gratitude.

'You see,' Feldmann said, 'we're bringing over some sculptures and other works by Irish artists for exhibition here. The art treasures will be inside the sculptures.'

The broker's smile wavered and then vanished entirely.

Feldmann went on, 'The sculptures have to travel many miles by road to Shannon where they'll be flown out to San Francisco. Now, on that journey in Ireland, which will be undertaken by our handlers, the sculptures will be pulled into a warehouse and opened. The Irish treasures will be put inside them and the sculptures resealed.'

He grinned mischievously. 'Simple.'

'But what about the possibility of damage to the treasures?'

'The handlers are experts, jewellers and craftsmen in their own right. They'll use electron beam and laser welding. The treasures, most of them gold, will be wrapped in several layers of asbestos towelling with specially designed cold bags over those.'

Melchoir exhaled thinly and took Feldmann's glass to refill it.

'Still, it would be the louse-up of the century if the heat damaged the goods after all this trouble,' he said, pouring sherry.

'With two hundred and forty-eight million dollars at stake there'll be no mistakes.'

Robert Melchoir returned his glass. 'Still...'

'Look, my friend,' said Feldmann, 'they'll be using fifty-

fifty solder. That means fifty per cent lead, fifty per cent tin. It melts at four hundred and twenty-one degrees Fahrenheit, not much more than the boiling point of water. Gold takes almost two thousand degrees to melt, bronze slightly less, and silver less than that again. So, no danger. OK?'

'OK'

This time Melchoir laughed.

In the following days in Dublin, the garage in Rathmines became a mechanical and electronic workshop under the direction of Peter Phelan.

Carl Stolford noticed that the engineer's drinking had eased to a few whiskeys at the end of each working day and that he made no apparent attempt to see his wife, Betty. But the telltale signs were often obvious to them all. Phelan worked harder than any of the others on the team, punishing himself or trying to obliterate the hurt of his previous punishment. At times the effort was far greater than necessary for the task. But, Stolford knew, it was necessary for the man.

More than any of them, Peter Phelan needed success, any success. The operation was, in effect, life.

Today the group stood watching Phelan demonstrating an elaborate concrete-cutting machine.

'*Very* impressive, dear boy,' said Casswell from the back of the truck.

'And bloody dangerous,' Simon Coates muttered.

'And too goddam bulky,' Stolford said despondently, 'for our needs.'

Phelan pushed the goggles up onto his forehead to reveal eyes narrowed in defensive aggression. His voice matched the facial challenge.

'If you told us more, gave us some information, we'd save ourselves a lot of time and avoid this kind of fuckology.'

Stolford understood Phelan's frustration and ignored the challenge.

'For all our sakes,' he said quietly and slowly, 'I can only tell each man what he needs to know for his part in the operation. If any one man is caught he can't know enough to tell the cops the overall plan.'

'Except you, that is,' Phelan retorted, walking away.

'Someone has to know,' said Stolford to the retreating back, 'but at least that's an acceptable risk. OK?'

Phelan had stopped at the workbench. He looked over his shoulder and stared hard at the American for a long moment before his head dipped in an almost imperceptible nod.

'So what do you want?'

'Something small, for a confined space,' said Stolford. 'Powerful but small. And something any one of us can use.'

'I won't be the operator?' Phelan turned to face him.

Stolford shook his head slowly. 'That much I can tell you.'

Phelan seemed poised for another confrontation but, instead, shrugged and said, 'There's an ordinary stone-grinder. A bit slower but compact.'

'Right,' said Stolford, 'that's what we need.'

Casswell cleared his throat. 'So there's no point asking what this diver chap is going to do?'

Stolford smiled: 'You're right, Charles, no point.'

They drifted back to their chores, each with his thoughts.

By the following morning work on the truck had almost been completed. Its original red paint had been replaced by orange. Four tubular steel hoops had been fitted into sleeves welded upright inside the sideboards of the vehicle. Over this was placed a canopy of sheet aluminium forming sides and a roof, similar to the principle of an American covered wagon. The bottom sections of the covering were held in place with bolts and wing nuts for quick easy removal. Thus, the vehicle was now both a truck and a van, depending on need. A rear aluminium section was added, with wide doors which opened outwards, allowing the tailboard to drop downwards as usual.

From the second hoop hung a twenty-four volt Wreckers International winch fitted with chains. The winch, with a lifting capacity of eight thousand pounds, would be supported by two heavy steel rails which would be swung into place beneath it. Spring-loaded clips to hold three rifles and one pistol were attached to the underside of the aluminium roof.

A square section of the floor of the truck, on one side and near the tailboard, was cut away to make a trapdoor down through the chassis girders. A wooden chest of drawers to hold tools and cables was built to slide over the cut-away area. Narrow shelves were placed against the opposite side of the vehicle. Two twelve-inch-wide steel runners without side lips were hung above the sideboards inside the truck. At first glance these fourteen-feet-long runners would appear to be part of the reinforced construction of the truck. Immediately behind the cabin of the vehicle and to one side another chest of drawers and a series of shelves had been fitted to conceal tape-recording equipment and twin eight-inch speakers.

Black lettering on both doors spelt 'Matthews Pressure Cleaners'. During the operation this would be covered with two white adhesive squares with large black Posts and Telegraphs initials. Above the initials would be the fleet number of the 'van'. The vehicle's registration plates would also be replaced with false numbers made by Phelan.

Coates had received four parcels from a south-side printing firm. They contained letterheads, invoices and visiting cards, all bearing the name of the bogus pressure-cleaning business. To further substantiate the 'legitimate' firm they placed advertisements in selected trade magazines and newspapers offering their services to factories. Replies would receive courteous letters, quoting figures gleaned by Casswell in a series of telephone calls to established cleaning firms in the Dublin area. Any serious offer of a contract could be delayed with excuses or completion dates which would be deliberately unsatisfactory for the prospective customers. The company apologised for having, as yet, no telephone installed.

Phelan travelled to Belfast and Cork to purchase radio and telephone equipment. He paid cash and was careful to spread his buys over a number of shops. In some he gave the impression that he was a radio ham, in others that he owned a television and radio repair business and in yet others that he was a trawler skipper.

He bought a Midland VHF forty-five-channel marine transceiver, a high-impedence voltage meter, a Vega Selena domestic radio receiver, a digital-readout frequency counter, special radio crystals, alligator clips and leads and two pairs of ex-Army rubber-cupped earphones. In a shop dealing in new and second-hand recording equipment he purchased an Uher 4000 Report-L tape-recorder and a Sony Electret condenser microphone to suit Stolford's cassette recorder. He also found a Mark 2 Tele 250 'tapper' used by telephone engineers to check lines. The green box, about the size of a workman's large lunchbox, contained terminals, a telephone handset, a dial and a small cranking handle. The tapper was in need of some minor repairs but, back in Dublin, Phelan had it working perfectly after two hours' work.

While the engineer worked, Carl Stolford drove south in Casswell's hired Fiat to Kilcoole Strand in County Wicklow. It was here the diver would rendezvous with them on one of the next three nights. Exactly when would depend on what progress the Frenchman could make with the tides and weather.

Stolford drove to Bray, along the Wexford road as far as Newtownmountkennedy, Ireland's longest place-name, and then turned left for the small village of Kilcoole. When he reached it, he followed the signpost which read simply 'Strand' and drove slowly along the road which narrowed rapidly to the size of a lane. It was bordered by hedgerows and occasional clumps of trees. There were few houses. The lane led to a six-barred steel gate with a small pedestrian gate alongside. The larger gate was closed but unlocked. Beyond this was a railway line, level with the laneway, and across this was the Strand, separated from the tracks by a low concrete wall. A plaque on a boulder told of a landing here in 1914 when guns were brought ashore for the Irish Volunteers. Stolford smiled as he read the inscription.

He crossed the railway line and walked onto the Strand. He walked slowly southwards along the wide expanse of sand, towards the only other person in sight: a man walking with a small dog by the water's edge. The wind blew the sand in scurries and tumbled the small waves onto the Strand. The dog barked at every one.

Stolford was tempted to question the man about the tides and depths, but changed his mind and walked back to the car. He drove back to Kilcoole, a picturesque village of brightly painted terraced houses and shops with newer housing developments on the outskirts. In a telephone kiosk he checked the addresses of police stations in the area. The nearest was at Newtownmountkennedy. He returned to the Strand gate, zeroed the milometer on the dashboard and the chronometer on his wrist, and drove directly to Newtownmountkennedy,

100

trying to maintain the car at a steady thirty miles an hour. The journey took eight minutes. At night, with no other traffic on the road, it would be marginally quicker.

He noted the situation of the police station and then headed back to Bray. From there he drove to Kilcoole, this time along the coast road through Greystones.

Happier, he swung around and forty minutes later was back at the garage in Dublin.

Aboard the converted lifeboat *Marie*, Edouard Dufour and Adrien D'Albe had left the Tusker Rock lighthouse behind some hours previously and were now moving up along the east coast of Ireland, having negotiated the Rusk Channel on the south-east tip of the country. They were inside the long sandbank and had no difficulty identifying the numerous light buoys as evening drew in around the boat.

Since mid-afternoon they had seen only five other vessels, all of them some distance off and sailing outside the bank. The weather should hold out and, unless they had mechanical problems, they would make the Kilcoole rendezvous on time. The *Marie* chugged effortlessly through the rough-water area inside the Arklow Bank and left the Wicklow lighthouse on her port, its group flashes splashing every fifteen seconds. Since he had come on board, D'Albe had proved to be a good crewman despite his lack of sea experience. His willingness and quick grasp of the fundamentals of navigation had eased the burden on Dufour.

Inside the South Ridge and India Bank they could see the red group flashes of the Breaches Shoal buoy ahead and knew they were on course and on time. By late evening they had taken their final three-point fix from the Breaches, Moulditch and Kish lights and had moved to take station just inside the Codling Bank, five miles off Kilcoole.

On land, Carl Stolford, Simon Coates and Charles Casswell drove out of the garage in Rathmines in the hired Fiat.

The Avon inflatable boat was tied to the roof-rack and the Chrysler engine was in the boot. The three men had anoraks and pullovers, and if stopped at a police checkpoint could indicate the three suitcases and the fishing tackle on the rear seat and say they were heading south for a boating holiday. With luck, they would not encounter any curious policemen on the journey.

Their luck held: the drunken drivers and car thieves had the roads to themselves on this night. Stolford moved the car through the quiet streets of Greystones almost unseen; the few who did notice gave it scant attention. Such obvious boating expeditions were commonplace in this area. They arrived at Kilcoole shortly after midnight and eased down the main street before turning onto the Strand road. Even here, especially here, Stolford kept the car in top gear, the engine only just able to cope with the low revolutions. Most of the houses were in darkness and the road was empty.

At the six-barred gate he switched off the lights while Coates stepped out, looking for others who might be around. The place was deserted. He opened the gate and the car passed through and swung to the right. Here it would be hidden behind the wall and hedge. Coates moved across the railway line and onto the beach, the slight breeze only audible between the wavebreaks on the shoreline. It too was deserted. He walked quickly back to the car and nodded to the waiting men.

All three donned anoraks and quickly unloaded the inflatable and brought it to the water's edge, then returned for the engine and fuel tank. A third journey brought the fishing rods and an electric torch. Two of the rods were placed on board the inflatable along with the torch. Then they lifted the boat into the shallows and mounted the Chrysler engine on the stern fittings. Casswell and Stolford climbed aboard and paddled the craft out to sea. Coates watched until they had disappeared into the night and then busied himself with the fishing line. He made four elaborate casts with the long fibreglass rod before satisfying himself that he would not improve on distance. The fifth cast went badly wrong, the line released before he completed the arc and the weight taking the hook and feather snaking back across the beach behind him. He found himself facing the sea with the line trailing back from the rod high above his head.

Frantically, he began to reel in the line, looking left and right, his eyes meeting those of the imagined audience of thousands staring, unspeaking, at the man who fished backwards and on dry land. But he was alone with his blushes. The nylon tightened and the reel stopped as the feathered hook, far behind him, snagged itself. The faint splutter of the inflatable's outboard engine coughing into life turned his eyes towards the sea, but there was only darkness and soon the waves swallowed the sound as the boat moved further away from the shore. A glance above his head assured him that if he could not see the fishing line then a chance visitor might also be deceived. He huddled down on the sand, knees against his chest, the handle of the rod between his feet, feeling only slightly less than ridiculous.

At sea, Carl Stolford kept the engine on minimum revolutions and the boat on a due easterly heading, the inflatable rising and sliding on the gentle swell. After forty minutes he knew they must be near the western edge of the Codling Bank. Charles Casswell, in the bow, narrowed his eyes to penetrate the ink of the night, pretending not to notice the increased consultations by Stolford of wrist-watch and compass. They turned south.

For another seven minutes they kept that course, a line roughly parallel with the distant shore. Suddenly, Casswell, looking back, pointed excitedly. Stolford turned and saw them too: the red and green navigation lights of the *Marie*, switched on when Edouard Dufour heard the chugging engine of the inflatable passing three quarters of a mile off the port bow of his anchored boat. Stolford swung the tiller and headed for the beacons.

Fifty minutes later a cold and cramped Simon Coates, chin buried in the neck of his anorak, lifted his head and listened to the engine sound, barely discernible above the surf. Then it was gone again. He fumbled for the cigarette packet in his pocket and then the box of matches. A non-smoker, he had difficulty lighting the cigarette, each match extinguished by the breeze before he could suck the flame onto the tobacco. At last it caught and he sucked, possessed, until the end glowed furiously red, his tongue and throat raw from the smoke, his breath gulped and exhaled between coughs. He stood, still holding the fishing rod anchored to the top of the beach, sucking on the cigarette. He glanced upwards and stretched towards the nylon line. It parted, melted by the burning tobacco, and he stepped towards the sea, free at last from his embarrassment.

In the rubber boat, the three men saw the red glow and paddled towards the pinpoint. Shadow eventually took form, the dark anorak of Coates moving across the light contrast of sand. The young man, shivering in the thigh-deep waves, clutched the side of the inflatable and forced a smile at the beaming Charles Casswell. The actor swept a hand at the newcomer beside him and boomed, 'May I introduce Monsieur Adrien D'Albe. Monsieur D'Albe, this is...'

'Fuck the formalities,' Stolford interrupted sharply, jumping down from the boat. 'Haul ass.'

In less than six minutes they had transferred the weapons and equipment from the boat to the car. Stolford taped the electric torch to the bow of the inflatable and, with Coates, turned the craft around to face the open sea and the waiting *Marie*. The tiller was taped to keep the rudder midship. Stolford started the engine and wrapped tape around the throttle in the quarter-speed position while Coates held the craft back. When the torch had been switched on, both men stepped clear and watched the rubber boat head out to sea.

Casswell had already moved the Fiat out through the gate when Coates and Stolford joined him. D'Albe was sitting in the back seat, his face blank. It was the face of a veteran. To the uninitiated it would seem to reflect boredom, but to Carl Stolford it showed the acquired control of a man who had experienced the gut-gnawing tension and fear of combat. The expression on the handsome face of the Frenchman was one he had seen countless times on seasoned troops moving into the front line in Vietnam. How often had he heard war correspondents describe their look as one of 'battle-numbness'? They were as wrong as the recruits, who feared the zombie-like veterans almost as much as the Viet Cong. The fear was greater for the veteran than the rookie because the veteran *knew*. The expression was just part of the veteran's flimsy lifeline: camouflage of the mind and its terror.

Stolford sat in the back of the car beside D'Albe. Coates, beside Casswell, fidgeted anxiously as the actor drove slowly away from the beach and made no attempt to increase speed.

'Can't you drive a little faster, Charles?' Coates urged.

'No, he can't,' Stolford interrupted sharply, too sharply, he realised. 'Not without attractin' attention,' he added, tone modulated.

He glanced quickly sideways at D'Albe. He saw, or imagined he saw, a smile. The Frenchman turned away to look out of the side window.

At the Codling Bank, Edouard Dufour spotted the approaching dot of white light. It would pass a quarter of a mile north. He started the *Marie's* engine and moved the boat ahead, roping the wheel on interception course. He left the wheelhouse and, clutching a harpoon gun, walked forward along the deck to the bow. He waited until the inflatable had passed in front of the converted lifeboat before firing the harpoon. The barbed spear struck one of the forward inflation compartments in the rubber boat, the sudden hiss of escaping air inaudible above the engine noises of both craft. He reloaded quickly and fired again. Another hit, but the inflatable moved on. He returned to the wheelhouse and altered course to give chase. Twice more the powerful gun recoiled in the diver's strong hands before the rubber boat crumpled in deflation and under the drive of the outboard engine. The propeller rose suddenly from the water and almost somersaulted before the weight of the remainder of the engine pulled it sidways and down into the rumpled rubber that had been the inflatable, chewing at the material like a hungry wolf with fresh meat. After only seconds, the rubber fouled the drive shaft, and the whirling blades hesitated and stopped before the tangled mess sank beneath the surface. The electric torch shone upwards through the water, white, then green and finally blue as it went deeper.

Dufour stared until the phosphorescence vanished, then he went back to the wheel to steer up along the coast again, to Dun Laoghaire, south of Dublin. He arrived just before dawn, yellow 'Q' flag flying to inform the harbour authorities that there was no disease on board. He was given a mooring inside the west pier. The harbourmaster and the customs officials were satisfied with his papers and the explanation for his visit, and kept the formalities to the minimum.

Too tired to cook breakfast, the French diver fell onto his bunk for the first deep sleep since he left Brest.

Chapter Seven

In the terraced house on the north side of Dublin, the man glared at the cat sitting in the weak sunshine seeping through the grimy kitchen window.

His wife, as usual, was still in bed, leaving him to prepare his own breakfast. She would only lift her head after he had left the house. The ritual never varied: first the cat would be fed and then she would brew the first of the numerous pots of strong tea. Breakfast and lunch were combined after chain-smoking ten cheap and throat-burning cigarettes. The food, prepared during a lengthy discourse with the cat, inevitably contained a not inconsiderable quantity of cigarette ash, but this was fortunately unnoticeable in a meal of such mammoth proportions. In contrast, the supper, which she shared with her husband, would consist of toast and beans, or toast and jam, or toast and boiled egg, or just toast. It wasn't her fault, she would pout, that her husband couldn't be home at midday when her culinary skills were on show. Out of the question, she emphasised repeatedly, for her to cook two full meals in one day. The logic, if there was any, and the food, escaped the husband.

He had found some consolation in recent days in that the cat had shown less affection to his wife. It had taken to sleeping in the kitchen more frequently, rather than curled up alongside the flesh mountain in the bed. It had also shown signs of irritability and listlessness. Food had only been picked at during the last four days. This morning he noticed that the cold sausages and milk-soaked bread had not been touched since the previous day. When was the last time *he* had been offered sausages?

The man walked to the cupboard and pulled out the sliced loaf packet. It contained the heel and one half slice, both hard. Disgusted but hardly surprised, he went to the bottom of the staircase and roared upwards, 'There's no bloody bread!'

'Stop that cursin',' the wife countered immediately and predictably.

The man mimed a repetition of the words and tapped his fingers and thumb together in a parody of her mouth. He shook his head resignedly and walked back into the kitchen, crumpling the bread packet in his fist. He stopped inside the doorway and stared at the cat. The cat, attracted by the rustle of the paper, looked sleepily at him for just a moment and then turned to face the sun again. The man drew his arm back and hurled the crushed paper and bread at the animal. The thump on the shoulder pushed the cat against the yellowing lace curtains and brought it onto its feet, back arched and fur upright as it growled its fright and anger. The sound came from deep within the body, the eyes wide and staring, ears flat on the skull. The long curved claws were moving in and out on the front feet.

Suddenly the man was afraid, remembering the death of his dog. He stood unmoving but aware of the creeping of his skin on the back of his neck. The cat's growl decreased and gave way to a silent half-yawn. It looked away and walked the length of the window sill to drop gently onto the cracked linoleum. It looked back to the man who stood transfixed, and then padded silently and unhurried out of the door and up the stairs. The man relaxed, only then aware that he had been holding his breath, his fear giving way to relief and the beginnings of temper.

His wife's voice, seconds later, was both anxious and accusing. 'What've ye done to the poor cat?'

The man snatched his coat angrily from the chair and walked to the front door. He opened it, paused undecided, and then walked back to the foot of the stairs.

'I stuffed the bread up its arse,' he bellowed up the staircase, 'and it shaggin' well loved it!'

The woman flinched as the slamming front door vibrated the building. She closed her eyes in pious self-control and then reopened them to address the cat.

'And to think I wasted my best years on that...that *thing*,' she said with practised martyrdom, stroking the animal's head. 'Never you mind, puss. The bad man's gone now...'

She broke off as a sudden suspicious thought came to her. Almost fearfully, she gently lifted the cat's tail and peered underneath. Relieved, she returned the appendage to its former position.

'No, of course you wouldn't like it,' she said smugly, again stroking the animal's head.

Outside, the clink of bottles, the whirring electric motor and a tuneless whistling heralded the arrival of the day's milk supply.

'There's the milkman,' she said to the cat. 'Mammy'll make you a nice, warm drink. You'd like that, mmm? Yes, of course, you would.'

The milkman walked to the hall door and bent to place the bottles on the step. The scream, long and agonised, jerked him upright again. The door was thrown open suddenly and the fat women staggered and stumbled into his arms. The bottles fell from his hands and smashed on the concrete but he was aware only of the woman's horrific injuries and his own mute howl of fright.

Her left eye hung down onto her cheekbone, blood and clear liquid oozing from the gaping socket, the eyelid twitching with the action of the tortured nerve-ends. Four narrow, bleeding tracks stretched from the empty socket, across her face and neck and onto the bulbous left breast.

She was only vaguely aware of the milkman's voice. 'Jaysus, missus, wha' happened?'

The woman reached up to her cheek and felt the slippery knob. She lifted it to the tip of her nose and tried to focus through the red, shimmering haze.

Slowly she moved it backwards and forwards, trying to clear the blur. And then, in a sudden screeching moment of clarity before unconsciousness, she recognised it.

Later that morning, the husband returned to the house with a uniformed police sergeant and two policemen. En route, they called at the police kennels to collect one of the force's dog handlers.

In silent procession, they followed the handler, who was wearing heavy leather gauntlets and sleeves, towards the kitchen. They jumped, startled, when the front door, caught by the draught, slammed noisily behind them.

The kitchen was empty.

They moved to the stairs, the handlers still leading. As they reached the landing, they noticed spots of dried blood on the thin stair-carpeting. The handler stopped suddenly, holding up a warning hand. They listened, each aware of his own heartbeat and then the other sound. It was pleading, pitiful, and with no hint of aggression. The handler stepped slowly across the creaking landing to the doorway of the bedroom facing the stairs. The others followed, gathering closely behind in a herd-like protective instinct.

The black cat was huddled in the centre of the bloodstained clothes on the dishevelled double bed. It was looking back over its shoulder at the handler, the whining now dropped to a low growl.

'Nice kitty,' said the handler gently. Then in a whisper from the corner of his mouth, 'What's it called?'

The husband swallowed and muttered.

'What? asked the handler, cocking his ear.

'Cleopatra,' the man blurted, self-consciously.

'Oh, Christ,' the sergeant winced.

'Thought you said it was a tom-cat?' The handler was puzzled.

'It is,' the man answered miserably. 'Didn't find out for five months. Wife wouldn't let me look. Said it wasn't right. By the time we found out, the name had stuck.'

'Ah, well,' the handler sighed resignedly, 'here kitty, nice *Cleopatra*. Good...*boy*, Cleopatra.'

The whining had stopped, the animal's attention fully on the advancing man. The handler's left arm was extended but bent at the elbow, offering the leather sleeve to the cat as he inched forward. He stopped instantly when a new sound rose from the animal, a low growl which continued even as the cat lifted itself slowly onto its feet and turned its body to face the stranger. The leather sleeve was advanced another few inches to within a couple of feet of the cat's nose and immediately the growl changed to an open snarl, the lower jaw falling away to

110

reveal the jagged pinnacles of teeth. A long, thin trickle of white spittle trailed down from the lower lip and hung, suspended, between the cat's forelegs. The claws had moved out between the pads on the feet and the ears had almost disappeared into the fur on the animal's head.

The handler looked into its blazing eyes and felt his flesh creep, tingling and tightening along his spine and neck. He had faced angry dogs many times and had known fear, but this was new to him. A good fighting cat would beat the best dog, he had heard oldtimers say. Until now, he could never believe them for, in the past, he had seen cats fight only defensively. Here before him was fearless, naked aggression.

'Oh, shit...' he breathed, as the animal launched itself at his head, a strangled drone wheezing between the bared teeth.

Instinctively, the handler rose to protect his face as he pulled back against those behind him, pushing the youngest officer off balance. The cat hit the leather sleeve in mid-flight and was carried onwards by the rising arm over the handler's ducking head to land on the young policeman's face and neck. As the barbs sank in and took hold, the policeman tore frantically at the fur to free himself from the pain. The animal, growling its hatred and vindictiveness, snapped at the clawing hand, teeth ensnaring the soft flesh between finger and thumb, back feet kicking and lacerating the throat.

The officer stepped backwards off the landing, the hands of his colleagues snatching at his uniform in a useless attempt to prevent his fall. He bounced, shoulder first, on the fourth step down and somersaulted once, legs jack-knifing and straightening again to wedge his body sideways across the stairs, his face pressed between the banister rails. Only the cat moved, tugging hard to free one of its claws from the bleeding neck. The officer lay still, eyes peering intently at the faded wallpaper across the hall, head rolling slightly with each pull by the captured paw.

Only seconds had passed since the cat had launched its initial attack but it seemed like long minutes to the other men, stumbling down the stairs to the injured officer. As the sergeant reached the still form, the cat pulled free and bolted down the stairs and along the hall to the kitchen.

'Get that bastard,' he roared at the others and dropped down

111

beside his young charge.

He turned to the house-owner who was now crouching beside him, white-faced. 'Stay with this lad. I'll radio for an ambulance.'

'I think his neck is broke,' said the house-owner. 'I told ye that shaggin' cat was mad.'

The sergeant ignored the comments and stamped down the stairs. A screech drew his eyes to the kitchen. The handler knelt in the doorway, the cat pressed flat on the floor under the weight of the leather-clad arms. The animal was hissing and growling, claws scratching tracks in the linoleum. The other policeman hovered, frightened and uncertain, behind the handler, a small steel cage in his hand.

'If you let that bastard loose again,' the sergeant began, but turned away quickly, leaving the warning unfinished.

He strode out to the patrol car, the handler's muttered retort lost in the noise of the struggling cat.

Early in the afternoon the woman had recovered sufficiently to tell the surgeons what had happened that morning. They questioned her about the cat's behaviour during the previous seven or eight days. She remembered the fatal fight with her husband's dog.

Across the city in another hospital, Jervis Street, the young policeman lay, unconscious. He would live but it was too soon to tell what permanent effects the broken neck would cause. That would depend on which nerves, if any, had been permanently damaged. The possibility of paralysis was strong.

Journalists making routine check calls to the ambulance service and the police had been given details of the incident. Combined with the earlier attack, and with interviews with the neighbour, it would make a welcome lead or off-lead for the late editions of the evening newspapers and the early television and radio bulletins. Only the injuries sustained by the three people would keep the story out of the category of amusing variation on 'dog bites man'. But only just.

After telepone calls to the Department of Agriculture, the police had taken the captured cat to the microbiology department of University College Dublin. It was in an almost continuous rage, attacking the bars of its cage with teeth and

112

claws. During these paroxysms, the cat drooled thick, white saliva, its eyes wide and staring. The professor and doctor studying the behaviour had little doubt about the cause and confirmed it with tests on samples of the spittle. They telephoned the Department of Justice. Communication in all cases was at the highest level and in strictest confidence. The handler and sergeant had stayed with the cat in the microbiology laboratory at the request of the professor. No explanation was offered for their detention but the reason was fearfully obvious to both men. In less than twenty minutes the other uniformed officer had been sent to join them. In the meantime, the microbiologists waited impatiently for the bureaucratic gears to engage. On this day they were, not surprisingly, quick. Sanction came initially by telephone and later, as requested, in writing from the Secretary to the Minister for Health, the buff-coloured envelope delivered by uniformed messenger. Before the latter had arrived, the inoculations had been given and arrangements made for the transfer of the sergeant, handler and policeman to the isolation unit of Cherry Orchard Fever Hospital on the western outskirts of the city.

The professor, James Morrissey, telephoned the casualty officer at Jervis Street even before he inoculated the policemen in his laboratory. He also called the senior surgeon at the Royal Victoria eye and Ear Hospital. In both cases he recommended that the patients involved in the cat attack be transferred immediately to Cherry Orchard for isolation.

'And what about the staff who came in contact with him?' the casualty officer asked. 'Including me?'

'We'll send vaccine across to you,' Morrissey answered. 'And to the Royal Victoria. Whether you inoculate or not, of course, must be your decision.'

'Your recommendation?'

'Well, as you know,' the professor said, 'the virus usually makes entry only through a cut or abrasion, but not necessarily. So if any of the doctors or nurses, even the ambulance attendants, have cuts on their hands, then I would strongly advise immediate vaccination.'

'What's the vaccine?' asked the casualty officer.

'The Mérieux human diploid,' said Morrissey. It's extremely safe and usually effective. There may be some slight discomfort

113

around the injection site during the twenty-four to forty-eight hours. Otherwise, nothing.'

'Anything else we should do?'

'Yes,' Morrissey said positively. 'Get everyone who has had contact with the patient to wash their hands thoroughly in soap or detergent. Then apply alcohol, iodine or a quaternary ammonium salts solution.'

'Very well.'

'And re-sterilise the rooms he's been in. Burn the bedclothes he's used 'til now.'

The professor terminated the call and turned to his colleague, Doctor Elizabeth Farrelly.

'Royal Victoria?'

'Yes,' she answered flatly. 'They treated the woman for tetanus but, understandably, didn't consider the other possibility. I've sent some vaccine across to them.'

'Where were the wounds?'

'That's the big problem,' she answered. 'Face, neck and breast.'

'Sutured?'

'Yes. They'll reopen and instil before transferring her to Cherry Orchard.'

The professor's secretary walked into the room. 'The Minister for Health wants you both to go to his office immediately. Or as soon as you can.'

'Tell him we're on our way,' Morrissey instructed. 'And ask the police to pick up the woman's husband again and take him to Cherry Orchard.'

The sergeant, sitting at the back of the room, smiled pleasurably at the thought of further harassment of the house-owner who, as far as he was concerned, was the root cause of the whole mess.

When the microbiologists arrived at the office block near the city centre, they were taken to the upper floor by a uniformed security man. At the end of a long, carpeted corridor they were shown into an outer office and had to wait only a few moments before being taken into the minister's wood-panelled room.

The minister, a tall, angular and affable man, was not alone. Seated before the large desk at the picture window overlooking the River Liffey were the Ministers for Justice and Agriculture, and the Deputy Commissioner of the Garda Siochana, the police force.

'What's the situation exactly, Professor Morrissey?' he asked, rising to shake hands with the newcomers. His smile was strained.

Morrissey was too experienced for that opening. 'Too soon to be exact, Minister,' he answered, exchanging nods of greeting with the other visitors and accepting a seat at the end of the line of poker-faced men who stood dutifully until Elizabeth Farrelly had also been seated.

'We've taken what immediate steps we can for the patients and those who've come into contact with them,' the professor went on. 'Too soon to be definite about anything except our findings with the saliva samples.'

'No doubt about those?'

'None, I'm afraid. Have there been any more attacks?'

'Not so far,' the deputy commissioner answered for the minister.

The Minister for Agriculture, ruddy-faced, rotund, and universally disliked outside the farming community, sat forward in his chair, planting his shapeless hands firmly on the knees of his baggy trousers.

'Will this thing hit the farming industry?' he demanded gruffly.

'It can be contracted by *any* warm-blooded animal,' Professor Morrissey answered.

'Quite,' the health minister responded, trying to maintain his chairmanship of the meeting. 'So, let's be quite clear what we're dealing with here.'

Professor Morrissey nodded to his colleague. Farrelly would not sugar the pill.

'Rabies is a virus,' she began carefully. 'It's usually contracted by means of a bite from an infected animal. In the domestic environment, such as city or town, this would be a dog or cat, obviously. In rural areas, foxes are often the prime carriers.'

The agriculture minister grunted knowingly. His background dictated a natural and deep hatred for the fox.

'But they're not the only known carriers,' Farrelly added

115

hastily. 'Pigs, horses, cows, even sheep can pass it on. As Professor Morrissey has said, any warm-blooded animal, either domestic or wild.'

'How, exactly, is it passed on?' the justice minister asked. His tone and manner were the most disturbing of all the speakers so far, Farrelly thought. His reputation as the toughest of the government members was understood in the quiet delivery of his speech, measured and unhurried. A calculating man, respected only by hardliners, feared by most.

Farrelly faced him and had difficulty matching his stare. She resorted to glancing from face to face while answering the question. The minister realised her discomfort but took little pleasure in his power on this occasion. He knew her background and her lack of interest in politics. She would have no bearing or influence on his eventual rise to the leadership of his political party.

'The bite injects the saliva and virus into the other animal,' she said briskly.

'Or human being,' Professor Morrissey added.

'Yes,' she confirmed. 'Or human being. Once in the body, it travels through a peripheral nerve to the brain. There the virus–under a microscope it looks like a rifle bullet–multiplies in the nerve cells.'

She paused to look at Professor Morrissey but he gave no indication of wanting to add to anything she had said.

'Well, anyway,' she went on, 'because all the cells are infected, it follows that the limbic system of the brain is affected. This system is believed to control our emotions, so if the balance of that system is upset it changes people's behaviour, their personality even. A usually friendly animal or person can suddenly become aggressive and violent. A brave dog, for instance, can change to a timid, nervous animal, cowering in a corner.'

The room was still, almost afraid that the slightest sound or movement would cause an interruption. They were absorbed, even stunned by the enormity of the potentially terrible outbreak.

'In rages,' Doctor Farrelly continued, 'they will savagely attack other animals, human beings. Even themselves. They've no fear and seemingly no sensation of hurt or pain.'

116

Professor Morrissey cleared his throat. 'There are *two* forms of the disease. The best known is called *furious* rabies which Doctor Farrelly has just described. The other is *paralytic* which attacks the spinal cord.'

'And in human beings?' the agriculture minister asked.

'I was referring to both, Minister,' the professor answered softly.

The Minister for Health stood and walked to the window to stare at the grey River Liffey a quarter of a mile away. Even the seagulls, usually therapeutic in times of crisis, hovering gracefully or diving steeply for titbits, seemed to offer little support today. They stood in groups on the low granite river wall above the water, bracing themselves, like old men huddled inside the collars of overcoats, against the stiff breeze sniping up from the mouth of the port.

'And the mortality rate?' he asked quietly.

'Practically one hundred per cent,' Morrissey replied equally quietly. 'The problem is that once the disease becomes obvious in a patient it is usually too late to save him. There are only about three people in the world who have had rabies and survived.'

The other men stirred unhappily, wanting an end to the morbid lecture. The minister turned, expecting questions. As Minister for Health, he must have known the answers to all the previous questions, but he obviously wanted the others to hear them answered by recognised experts.

There were no questions from the group. Farrelly broke the silence. 'One expert has put the total of annual deaths in India alone at fifteen thousand,' she said. 'And we know that in the United States...'

The telephone buzzed on the minister's desk. He lifted the receiver and listened, then held it towards Professor Morrissey. The professor stood and took the telephone. After a few short seconds he thanked the caller and hung up.

'That was one of our assistants at the laboratory,' he said, straightening. 'It's confirmed. He carried out an immuno-fluorescent microscopy of a small section of the cat's skin and this provided positive identification of the virus antigen.'

'God almighty,' was the only audible reaction. It came from the agriculture minister.

'But only in the cat, yes?' the health minister asked hopefully. 'I mean, there's no evidence yet of the woman or the police officer having rabies, is there?'

'No,' the professor answered. 'Too soon. The virus has to incubate.'

'And how long does *that* take?' the justice minister prompted, tired now of the student-teacher atmosphere of the meeting.

'Generally,' the professor replied, unruffled, 'between two and eight weeks, sometimes far less. But it *can* take more than two years.'

'Ye gods!' the minister exploded, 'you mean we may have to wait around, wondering, for *two bloody years*?'

He was on his feet now, hands on hips, challenging but not disbelieving.

Doctor Farrelly intervened hastily. 'I don't believe we'll have to wait that long in these cases. You see, a lot depends on the point of initial contact. For instance, bites on the face and neck are more serious because they give less time for vaccine to combat the rabies before the virion reaches the brain. The woman and the policeman were both bitten or scratched on the head.'

'It's still a wait, though,' the agriculture minister grumbled, slumping back onto his chair.

The health minister also sat down again, noisily turning pages in a desk pad and taking a pen from the inside of his jacket. It was a blatant but understandable attempt to avoid further confrontation.

'You mentioned vaccine, Doctor Farrelly,' he said, pen poised.

'Yes, Minister. The type we would recommend is manufactured by a French company, Institute Mérieux International at Lyon. But...'

She smiled.

'Yes?' the minister prompted, looking up from the desk pad.

'...It's not yet licensed in this country.'

'Ah, yes,' the minister said slightly embarrassed, 'well, I'm sure we can take care of that, Doctor Farrelly. Have we sufficient quantities, despite the licensing problems?'

He tried a smile of conspiratorial confidentiality but only

managed to look, and feel, slightly silly.

Doctor Farrelly ignored the gesture. 'Enough for the moment,' she said. 'But we should have more flown in, just in case this is the first sign of a major outbreak.'

The agriculture minister groaned at the last words.

'Right,' said the health minister. 'I'll have my people liaise with the French about transport immediately.'

Deputy Commissioner George Swann turned to the professor. 'Is there anything my men can do?'

'Not really, Mr Swann,' Professor Morrissey answered, 'except rush anyone bitten by a dog or cat to the isolation unit at Cherry Orchard.'

'Wait now,' the health minister said, holding up a restraining hand. 'Let's not get too melodramatic about this. Treatment yes, but no panic.'

'Exactly,' the justice minister agreed. 'Do that and you'll have vigilantes out on the streets shooting every dog and cat in the city. Or worse, even people.'

The deputy commissioner nodded agreement.

Doctor Farrelly now read different warning signs, here in the room.

'You mean we shouldn't warn the public?' she asked incredulously. 'About the signs, at least?' she added.

'Signs?' the justice minister asked.

'Changes in behaviour of their pets. Restlessness or excessive friendliness. Drooling. Persistant licking of the hands and faces of their owners.'

The health minister could see another confrontation looming.

'All in good time, Doctor,' he said placatingly. 'Let's first be absolutely sure this isn't just an isolated case.'

The doctor would not concede this argument. 'According to the husband of the injured woman, his dog had a fight with the cat. Later the dog was found with massive stomach wounds which means the dog savaged himself. Classic symptoms of furious rabies.'

'Yes,' the justice minister smiled, 'but the dog is buried and no longer a danger.'

'But,' the doctor persisted, 'did the dog infect the cat or vice versa? Either way, one off them was a vector, a carrier. So, one of them contracted the disease from another animal. Where is *that* animal? Maybe there's more than *one* infected animal on the loose.'

The professor hastened to support his colleague. 'Doctor Farrelly has a point, Minister,' he said quietly. 'Rabies just doesn't appear in a country; it has to be imported. And there could be animals out there right now incubating the disease or developing symptoms.

The agriculture minister glanced at the health minister who studiously ignored the implied challenge. The health minister knew the microbiologists were right, but there were other considerations, not least his own career. A decision now, either way, would be on record and would show it was his alone.

'I can appreciate the problem, of course,' he said, voice laced with sympathy and understanding, ' but I don't want to cause panic among the population. A few days and we may have more evidence. In the meantime, I'll discuss the problem with my colleagues here to see what course of action is necessary.'

The agriculture minister was waiting for that sidestep. 'Yes, indeed,' he agreed, too readily, 'we should know exactly what we're facing. My department, while not responsible for counteracting an outbreak such as this, will gladly lend what assistance the health minister may decide is necessary.'

If the disease is shown to have come from agricultural animals, the health minister thought grimly, I'll have his balls for squash practice.

'Very well, then,' he rose, smiling, signifying the termination of the meeting, 'we'll be in touch with each other constantly during the coming hours and days. And I'll get that vaccine flown in.'

'There's just one other question,' the deputy commissioner halted the exodus. 'What signs would a human show if he'd been infected but didn't know it himself?'

Doctor Farrelly, still chafing from her defeat at the hands of the patronising ministers, turned to face the policeman.

'A *man* might be *very* easy to spot,' she said smugly.

The words and their form of delivery stopped all movement in the room, all except the agriculture minister's. He was halfway off his chair when the doctor spoke. Slowly, as if controlled by a hydraulic hoist, he sat down again, his eyes never leaving the woman's face as he lowered himself noiselessly onto the seat.

Doctor Farrelly took in all the faces with her gaze, which panned the room rapidly yet which seemed to dwell on each of them in a perfectly timed sequence of individual study.

'You see,' she said evenly, her mouth twitching in a mocking smile, 'he may be walking around with an uncontrollable erection.'

The deputy commissioner, who thought he had been the butt of a crude joke, chuckled but the sound died abruptly under the withering stare.

'Yes, gentlemen,' Doctor Farrelly went on, enjoying their discomfort, 'he may even ejaculate in his trousers.'

Again the panning gaze. This time they felt naked, felt she could see every inch of their flesh and that she was scoffing at their physical claims to manhood. The urge, although resisted, was to clamp their hands tightly over their groins to prevent further humiliation.

'The condition is known as priapism,' she went on, unhurried. 'It occurs if the rabies virus affects the libido area of the brain.'

She turned and walked to the door, her carriage and deportment akin to a schoolteacher leaving a class of juniors: undisputed monarch. At the door she turned to face them again, as countless film stars had done through decades of celluloid exits, to deliver her parting shot.

'*Some* men even have an uncontrollable urge to show their equipment in public,' she smiled coldly. 'Others just get a very severe *pain* in it.'

Suddenly the smile was gone and so was she.

No one moved, waiting perhaps for a reappearance and further verbal chastisement. The professor smiled inwardly. He should not be pleased with the petulant and unprofessional conduct of his colleague. But he could not help delighting in the moment.

He walked after her and, without looking back, said, 'It's true, gentlemen, absolutely true.'

Chapter Eight

Charles Casswell greeted the last of the arrivals at his apartment, Edouard Dufour, and then sat expectantly as Carl Stolford unfolded the eight pages of typing and two of drawings.

It took Stolford eleven minutes to read them aloud. For seconds after he had finished the men stared in silence at the sheets of paper.

Casswell broke the spell. 'Well,' he began with noticeable control, 'it sounds splendid, of course, put like that in writing. But will it work in practice?'

'And why Dublin?' asked Dufour. 'This could have been done in any city the treasures visited, yes?'

'Presumably because The Voice initiated the idea,' said Stolford. 'And he would plan it for the city he knows.'

'So,' Dufour said, 'he's Irish or has lived here a long time.'

'Obviously someone with access to the necessary information,' Simon Coates said.

'Not so difficult to come by, though,' said Peter Phelan.

'But probably a policeman or a soldier?' suggested Stolford.

Phelan nodded. 'Could even be a politician.'

'Well, gentlemen,' said Casswell, again breaking the spell. 'To get back to my original question: will it *work*?'

Stolford smiled at the actor. The expression was a challenge in itself.

'If you're as good as you're supposed to be.'

The actor opened his mouth to answer the taunt but stopped himself and looked away.

'I'll need more equipment,' said Peter Phelan, without

taking his eyes from the pages, 'in view of this complete plan.'

'So?' Stolford prompted.

'I reckon it can be done, my side of it anyway,' said the engineer thoughtfully, running spread fingers through his fair hair, 'but we're going to need an awful lot of luck.'

'You, Edouard?'

'If the figures are correct...flow and measurements,' he began, 'and we only have the word of The Voice for them...' He tapped the pages, '...well, anyway, I also will need more equipment.'

The French diver paused and then grinned at the faces around him. 'And you, my friends, will need a lot of training.'

Simon Coates grimaced. 'I don't even know how to *swim*,' he moaned.

Dufour held out his huge hands. 'Put yourself in these, mon chéri,' he said comfortingly but grinning hugely.

Coates was not amused. All except Carl Stolford laughed at the set expression on the youngster's face.

'What's wrong, Carl?' asked Phelan, eyes narrowed behind his spectacles.

'The bottle,' Stolford muttered, turning the pages of the instructions. 'No mention of it. Not a word.'

'So we still don't know what was in it,' Phelan said quietly, 'or what it was for,'

Adrien D'Albe would brazen this out, the moment he had been waiting for since his arrival in Ireland.

'Bottle?' he asked, mystified. 'What is this about a bottle?'

Stolford turned to the Frenchman. 'You know nothing about it, huh?'

D'Albe shook his head.

'But you fixed up the weapons and explosive yeah?'

D'Albe nodded.

'Were you asked t'get or organise anything else, something that would fit a small bottle?'

'Nothing at all,' said D'Albe, 'except what Edouard brought with him. What is this about a bottle?'

Stolford ignored the question. He was unconvinced by D'Albe's performance, but a confrontation now would cause a rift and might jeopardise the whole operation.

Phelan, too, ignored the question. 'Maybe it *was* just Milk of

Magnesia, after all,' he said. 'Just a test, to see if you'd do what you were told without asking questions?'

'Expensive test, though,' Stolford grumbled.

'Anyway,' said Casswell with ill timed cheerfulness, 'it obviously had nothing to do with the operation or it would have been mentioned in here.'

He tapped the pages of the plan with well manicured nails. But his smile wilted under the baleful glare from Stolford.

The Minister for Health was an angry man the following morning.

He peered across the desk at Deputy Commissioner Swann, who had waited for twenty minutes for the minister's arrival from his meeting with the Prime Minister. The policeman had expected this kind of reaction. He could, however, console himself with the knowledge that the problem had not been caused by anyone in the Force and especially by anyone in his department, C Branch, Serious Crime and National Security.

'Damn woman,' the minister snarled, his fingers whitening as their entwined grasp was tightened. 'What right had she to communicate with the World Health Organisation without clearance from me?'

The experienced detective had learned the crude skills of jungle politics the hard way, fighting his way up the ranks; with each promotion, he had encountered increasing webs of in-fighting between government and civil service, reaching out to draw him in, alternately opponent and ally. He had had to fill both roles during his twenty-nine years in the Garda Siochana, the requisite acuity increasing with every step up the ladder. At this penultimate position in the Force's hierarchy he found his political and diplomatic acumen tested almost daily. Today was going to be one of those days.

'It may well be, Minister,' he began carefully, 'that Doctor Farrelly will claim that she was merely performing her rightful duty in informing them. After all, she is their representative in this country...'

'She is responsible to me and my department for her actions, first and foremost,' the minister interrupted angrily. 'And I...'

'Indeed so, Minister,' said Swann placatingly. 'What I was going to say was that in this case, and especially in view of its delicate nature, it might have been wiser to inform you, or me, of her intentions.'

He had scored well. The sharp look from the politician with the mention of the words 'or me' indicated that the barbed reminder of Swann's importance in matters of national security had struck home. The professional politicians needed occasional jolts but the timing was critical. Today, the policeman knew, he would encounter no backlash. This minister might need the support and allegiance of C Branch at the end of the episode.

The health minister nodded; the movement was acknowledgement of both agreement and mutual understanding.

'Exactly, Mr Swann,' he said, voice calmer than before, friendship licking at, but not encroaching upon, the words. 'I mean, we were trying to keep this low-key, weren't we?'

Swann, face impassive but smiling inwardly, pushed the bait back. 'Well, sir,' he said, 'if that is still your wish, perhaps we can manage it.'

The minister swivelled his chair parallel to the desk. He stared out at, but did not see, the grey skyline of the city. Damn woman, now this smartass policeman playing politics. He turned again to the deputy commissioner, his dark thoughts hidden in the furrowed expression on his face.

'Let's see what my colleagues say after this visit,' he said. 'What time are the other people arriving?'

Swann reached inside his jacket for a black notebook, the only visible link with his past as an investigative detective, though he would argue otherwise.

'British Airways eleven fifty-five from Heathrow,' he said, reading from the top page. 'Arrives one o'clock, so they could be here in your office at about one-thirty.'

'Right,' said the minister, reaching for the intercom. 'I'll have the other ministers here then.'

Charles Casswell looked impressive, and Simon Coates told him so. The others in the Rathmines garage broke off from their respective chores to add their expressions of admiration for the uniformed 'army officer'. The actor, carrying a swagger stick, strutted up and down the concrete floor to the muted applause of the onlookers, stroking an imaginary moustache and picking spots of distasteful fluff from the shoulders of his 'troops'.

Stolford, dressed again in the priest's clothing, smiled his satisfaction and slapped Adrien D'Albe on the shoulder. 'OK, let's you and me go play tourists and see a church.'

The two men left the garage and followed their street-map route to St Michan's Church on the north bank of the River Liffey. A few miles distant on the same side of the city, a small unmarked van pulled up outside a terraced house. A saloon car parked immediately behind the van. Neighbours stared blatantly from windows as the vehicles disgorged their occupants, including the owner of the house.

At the door he hesitated, turning to the woman behind him. 'Jasus, the neighbours'll think we've got fleas or somethin',' he moaned.

'It has to be done,' said Doctor Farrelly.

'Everything?'

'Everthing,' she said emphatically.

He turned the key and pushed open the door, glancing down at the bloodstains, now browned, on the granite step. The group walked into the hall, the three men bringing up the rear carrying a large steel box and two industrial carpet shampoo machines.

'We'll begin upstairs,' said Farrelly, leading the way to the bedroom.

The steel box was placed at the end of the bed and opened. While one of the men took cloths and bottles of solution from it, the others busied themselves removing the bed clothing and pushing it into plastic sacks.

'Curtains and everythin'?' the house-owner asked, unnecessarily.

'For the sake of your neighbours as much as for you,' the doctor answered.

The safety of his ever-complaining neighbours was not uppermost in the man's thoughts as the powerful-smelling liquid was poured from the bottles into the shampoo machines.

Carl Stolford and Adrien D'Albe joined the procession of tourists around the internationally famous St Michan's Church in Church Street, and listened to the guide describing its

127

features and potting its centuries of history.

Built in 1095, it was for many centuries afterwards the only church north of the River Liffey. Another claim to fame was the playing of the church's organ by the composer Handel when he visited Dublin for the first-ever performance of his *Messiah*. But for Stolford and D'Albe the interest was in the vaults beneath the weathered building.

They followed the tourist group through one of the several steel double doors set into the bottom of the outside walls. Ancient and worn stone steps led down to the flint and clay floor of the vaults; both sides of the passageway had burial chambers, each containing the stacked coffins of a single family. The guide recalled that one family had requested that their chamber remain unopened after the last burial in it. A later, and curious, generation had cut two holes in the wooden door as a compromise between honouring the family's wish and satisfying their own interest in the vault. They found that, although subjected to the same conditions as the other chambers, it was the only one which had not gathered dust down through the centuries. This phenomenon had never been explained despite numerous investigations.

Stolford and D'Albe followed the tourist party down the passage. Huge cobwebs waved gently in the air displaced by the passing men and women, shuffling quietly after the guide who explained that the temperature in the vaults never varied, summer or winter. It was this, combined with the dryness of the atmosphere, that kept the coffins and bodies partially preserved. Some years ago, flowers had been brought into one of the chambers and their moisture had rotted the wood of the coffins inside.

Near the end of the passage, in a chamber on the left, were four open coffins, each containing a body. Several women in the party gasped when they saw the brown-grey remains. The bodies were largely skeletal but, despite the time they had lain beneath the church, still had finger-nails, skin, noses and ears. Under the chest covering of one of the bodies could be seen the lungs and heart. At the back of the chamber was the most famous of St Michan's mummies: a huge man, measuring about seven feet in length, and believed to have been a crusader. His right hand, extended on his almost perpendicular forearm, was shiny black in contrast to the greyness of his body. The hand had turned that colour from generations of handshakes by visitors to the vaults.

While the guide talked, Stolford and D'Albe stole glances at the end of the vault passage which petered out in a pile of tumbled stone and earth. The guide noticed their interest and pointed out that it was believed to be another tunnel, as yet unexplored. As they left the vaults, D'Albe was able to look closely at the double locking system on the steel doors: one lock set into the doors and activated with a large, old fashioned key; the second was a padlock which secured a steel bar across the outside of the doors.

The party moved down the church path towards the street.

'No problem,' D'Albe whispered to Stolford.

Deputy Commissioner George Swann was waiting in the outer office when the two men from London arrived.

'Hello George,' beamed Chief Superintendent Bob MacIntyre. 'Congratulations on the promotion to deputy.'

'Yeah, thanks,' Swann smiled. 'Long apprenticeship, though.'

The chief superintendent turned to the bespectacled man at his side. 'This is Doctor Timothy Dunstan.'

The small man shook hands and stepped back again. There was no warmth in the handshake or in the weak smile which barely registered on his pale and pinched face.

A secretary announced their arrival and all three were shown in immediately to the minister's office. Six men were already seated at the long boardroom table, including the Ministers for Defence, Justice, Agriculture and the Environment. The other two were Professor Morrissey and the Army's chief-of-staff, Lieutenant-General Thomas McHugh. The health minister stood before his desk while the introductions were made.

'You're from New Scotland Yard, Chief Superintendent?' as he shook hands with the English policeman. Only the minister would have used the word 'new', thought Swann, and would have asked a superfluous question.

'Yes, Minister,' the Englishman answered patiently. 'Deputy head of the Anti-Terrorist Squad.'

'And you, Doctor Dunstan,' the minister smiled at the

policeman's companion, 'you're also with New Scotland Yard?'

'Yes and no, Minister.' The clipped voice was cold, the accent Northern-English. 'I work closely with the Yard from time to time but my pay cheque is signed at the Ministry of Defence.'

'I see,' said the minister, puzzled. 'So, where *are* you employed?'

The little man hesitated for a second and then said quietly, 'Porton Down in Wiltshire.'

The defence minister and chief-of-staff exchanged glances and looked more closely at the doctor. Everyone called to the meeting had expected to meet two senior English policemen. Their surprise was tinged with annoyance at what verged on blatant deception. Their annoyance was voiced, badly, by the agriculture minister.

'Ye mean, all them funny-bugs and germ things?' he blurted, ruddy face reflected in the glossed surface of the table.

'That might be how a layman would describe it,' the doctor answered voice calm, delivery noticeably slowed to chill each syllable.

The health minister tried to avert confrontation by ushering the newcomers to seats at the table, but it merely postponed the inevitable. Chief Superintendent MacIntyre also tried to defuse the situation.

'As you know, Minister,' he said quietly, 'rabies has to be imported...it can't cross water, for instance...it had to be transported...'

'So, some silly bugger has brought in an infected animal,' interrupted the agriculture minister testily, still smarting from the put-down. 'What's that got to do with you lot in Scotland Yard and the funny-bugs place?'

MacIntyre directed his reply at the health minister. 'I was just coming to that, Minister,' he said, as quietly as before. 'My section, the Anti-Terrorist Squad, have been concerned for some time about new developments in terrorism. Not just political but criminal terrorism...'

'One and the bloody same, as far as we're concerned,' the agriculture minister interrupted again.

'Tom,' the health minister reproved and soothed, 'let the

130

chief superintendent have his say. We all know what he means by the two words.'

The agriculture minister stared hard at his colleague and sucked in a deep breath which turned his complexion a deeper shade of red, but he said nothing.

The policeman turned this time to the angry minister. 'Introducing nuclear-powered generating stations and submarines brought with them the possibility of theft of fissile materials such as plutonium and uranium. With readily available commercial equipment and five kilos of plutonium, for instance, a terrorist could make himself an atom bomb about the size of the one that obliterated Hiroshima.'

'What, in God's name, has that got to do with rabies?' the farming man demanded, unimpressed by the figures and their potential.

'On the face of it, nothing,' MacIntyre replied evenly. 'But I...my people, that is, have to consider every possibility, however remote.'

'And this rabies business here,' the minister pressed, seizing the obvious opportunity to ruffle the feathers of the policeman, 'you have any evidence that this could be anything other than an accident, caused by some...?'

'No evidence whatsoever,' the policeman interrupted, flatly and noticeably unruffled.

A silence fell on the room, a void the others expected to be filled by a continuation. MacIntyre held the agriculture minister's eyes, unblinkingly, tempting and almost taunting. The ruddy-faced man could not resist for long.

'Well?' the minister blurted, conceding.

The policeman spread his hands, palms upwards, a shrugging gesture which drew an exasperated and dismissive snort from the minister.

The chief-of-staff, however, was caught in the net which had been cast by the Scotland Yard expert.

'You did say the possibility was remote, Chief Superintendent?'

'It has never...' the policeman began, then paused, choosing his words more carefully. 'We have no knowledge of any outbreak of this disease having been caused by anything other than carelessness or thoughtlessness.'

The courtroom-like wording had, as intended, a pile-driving effect and it brought another silence, broken after some moments by the Porton Down scientist, Doctor Dunstan.

'I think I too should emphasise the remoteness of this possibility,' he said with measured assurance. 'But personal dangers would be as great, if not greater, than someone handling the fissile materials necessary for making an atomic bomb.'

The others in the room studied his face intently for any sign of untruth, a hint of exaggeration. There was none.

'The medical knowledge required would be the greatest barrier to personal safety,' the doctor added. 'This is, after all, one of the most specialised fields in medicine.'

He opened his briefcase and produced a cardboard folder of colour and monochrome photographs which he passed around the table.

'These photographs,' he explained, 'are of men, women and children in various stages of the two forms of the disease: furious and paralytic. They're not very pleasant.'

The pictures slid clockwise around the group, the swishing sound of paper on polish now the only sound in the office. Some pushed the photos quickly to their neighbours, others seemed mesmerised by the horror of the deathbed pictures. A slip of paper on the back of each photograph detailed the patient's name, age, date of known or assumed contraction of rabies and date of death.

The environment minister spoke for the first time. 'Well, Doctor Dunstan, you've certainly made your point about the consequences of an outbreak. But why exactly are you here? Are you suggesting...'

'We're just suggesting a possibility,' the chief superintendent said quietly. 'No more than that, Minister.'

'Ireland hasn't had an outbreak of rabies before,' said Dunstan, gathering the photographs. 'Now it's here, out of nowhere. If it came from the continent, it jumped neatly across England and Wales.'

'Well, surely if someone smuggled a cat or dog or something from the continent directly to Ireland then it *wouldn't* involve England or Wales,' the health minister reasoned.

'More than likely that is what *did* happen, Minister,'

Dunstan said. 'The other is a possibility which must, I would respectfully suggest, be considered.'

He stood, shutting his briefcase, and pushed back his chair.

'We'll be staying overnight, Minister,' said MacIntyre, 'if there's anything we can do…'

'I'll be in touch,' said the deputy commissioner quietly to the Englishman as he closed the door on the visiting duo.

'Well,' said the health minister, resuming his seat at the table, 'all that seems to confirm my opinion that we should keep this thing under wraps for as long as possible. Nothing to be gained by spreading fear.'

'I'm inclined to agree,' said the defence minister, speaking for the first time. 'Last thing we want is troops out on the streets. Agreed, General?'

The chief-of-staff nodded readily.

'At the same time,' said the health minister, halting the moments of unanimity instantly, 'some presence might be advisable. Patrols of some kind. When this does hit the newspapers we can show that we have been providing protection.'

He looked at the deputy commissioner. 'What do you think, Mr Swann?'

'Certainly protection should be provided, sir,' said Swann affably, the words bringing instant expressions of relief to the faces of military men, but the slight elation was short-lived.

'However,' the deputy commissioner went on, 'the Garda Siochana is already stretched in all sections.' He paused to glance at his own superior, the justice minister. 'As you know too well, Minister,' he added with suitable emphasis, the minister dipping his chin in acknowledgement and absolute support.

'In view of that, Minister,' Swann went on, turning again to the health minister, 'and in view of your suggestion of providing immediate suitable protection, I think perhaps that army sniper units might be deployed as part of roving patrols.'

The blatant but successful manoeuvring by the wily policeman was secretly admired by everyone in the room, except the representatives of the Department of Defence. The stories about George Swann's political in-fighting were legion in government circles. Today, some of those present were

133

experiencing his honed proficiency for the first time.

Grateful for the lead, the justice minister took his cue. 'Yes, wasn't there a special sniper unit formed when that Dutch industrialist was held by terrorists here some years ago?'

Cornered, the defence minister mumbled, 'mmm'.

'Well, what was done before can be done again, surely?' the justice minister said, pressing home his victory. 'The Army has the men, equipment and the know-how.'

The last words had left no option.

'General?' the health minister prompted, leaning forward, eyes boring into the soldier's.

The army chief looked to his own minister for some escape. The glowering face said it all.

'How *many* patrols, Minister,' the lieutenant-general asked resignedly.

Peter Phelan studied the rough diagram drawn by the diver, Edouard Dufour. It showed two tubes sliding together telescopically, the larger of the two measuring approximately six centimetres in diameter. Fitted into each other but fully extended, they would cover six feet in length. On the larger tube, near its junction with the other, there was a flanged nipple rising one and half centimetres from the surface. Alongside was a second nipple with a small hole in its side. The extremities of the tubes were fitted with rubber pads, four centimetres deep and twelve in circumference.

'How many of these telescope things would you need?' Phelan asked.

'Two,' said Dufour.

'Aluminium?'

'Not strong enough,' the diver said. 'You will have to use steel, my friend.'

'And the junctions?' Phelan tapped the diagram with his pencil. 'How should they be sleeved?'

'Rubber, preferably. A certain amount of leakage would be acceptable, but very little,' Dufour said, holding his finger and thumb together.

In another corner of the lockup garage, Carl Stolford sat before a workbench, watched by the second Frenchman, Adrien D'Albe. On the workbench, two plastic-covered wires were connected to a battery at one end and a torch bulb at the other. Between the battery and bulb, one of the wires had been cut and wound around itself. The other wire, in a much heavier plastic covering, was intact. Both wires lay in a kitchen saucer. The American pulled on heavy gloves and opened a metal flask to pour a precise amount of clear liquid into a measuring cup. D'Albe watched, fascinated, thumb poised on the start button of his wrist chronometer.

'Ready?' asked Stolford.

D'Albe nodded.

Stolford poured the acid into the saucer and D'Albe activated the chronometer's sweep hand. As soon as the liquid touched the plastic coverings, a tiny wisp of black smoke spiralled upwards, the acid burning its way though to the wire inside. After several minutes it seemed the acid had stopped acting but then, suddenly, the torch bulb flickered once and lit fully as the thinner wire, now stripped of its insulation, completed the electric circuit, the acid itself acting as conductor.

The Frenchman smiled, stabbing the chronometer button. 'Three minutes, forty-two seconds,' he said. 'Now what?'

'Now we do it again and again,' said Stolford, 'until we're sure of the average time it takes.'

The next four experiments showed widely differing times, the earlier elation of D'Albe dissipating more with each one.

'No good,' said Stolford. 'We have t'be sure of the burning time. Too quick or too slow and we're all in the shit bucket.'

He produced a packet of condoms and laid one on the workbench. He cut several one-inch sections from the extended sheath and then bared a similar length of the thinner wires, wrapping a strip of rubber around the naked copper as insulation. Again the measured amount of acid was applied and its working time counted. Six times with single layers of rubber and four times with double layers produced the necessary consistencies on the chronometer.

Now it was Stolford's turn to smile. 'I was just thinkin',' he chuckled, 'it's the first time I had a light bulb on one.'

The following morning the government ministers and selected officials, including the principal officers of the Departments of

Agriculture, Health, Defence and Justice, together with the Director of the Veterinary Section, gathered. The venue was Mornington House in Merrion Street, birthplace of the Duke of Wellington and now headquarters of the Land Commissioner. The house, separate from government buildings in the same street, gave necessary cover for today's secret Cabinet meeting.

Prime Minister James Donovan was the last to climb the wide, carpeted staircase. He nodded cursorily to the gathering. For a moment, his eyes caught those of Professor Morrissey and Doctor Farrelly but there was no outward indication of their mood.

For almost twenty minutes the impatient Taoiseach listened to the suggestions and the arguments. Recommendations ranged from mass vaccination to mass extermination. Then, as most of those present knew he would, he declined both extremes. He opted, instead, for a carefully worded public warning to be issued through the media. But he covered himself against political attack from his opponents by involving the Army in an ostentatious display of public protection.

'The military patrols are ready?' he asked the defence minister.

'They'll be on the streets tonight, Taoiseach,' the minister replied. 'They've been drawn from the Curragh where the sniper nucleus is based.'

'Good.'

Three hours after the meeting ended, another sheet of typed instructions slipped into the mailbox of Charles Casswell's apartment.

It was just five hours after the meeting that the mucus-covered and yellowing teeth of the large black dog crunched into the jaws, gums and tongue of the football-playing boy in the public park...

Deputy Commissioner George Swann replaced the receiver and sat back in the high-backed leather armchair. His office overlooked a military square, now part of the headquarters of the Garda Siochana.

He lifted his long frame wearily and walked to the window. The room, with a simple teak desk, three chairs and a small bookcase, was carpeted in plain light green and was as neat and unadorned as its occupier. No one in the Force could remember seeing the greying, black hair untidy or the charcoal-grey suit rumpled. Swann seldom wore uniform.

Swann's C Branch was the most politically sensitive section of the Force, being responsible for the investigation of political terrorism and other serious crime. This branch, commonly known as C3 or the Special Branch, was the elite of the Garda Siochana and included control of the forty-two hand-picked men known as the Task Force. These men, mostly in their late twenties and early thirties, were adept in the use of handguns, automatic rifles, sub-machine guns and all kinds of explosives and detonating devices. They also operated the most sophisticated bugging and surveillance equipment.

George Swann was the most respected–and sometimes feared and hated–man in the police force.

Much of this hatred had its origin in jealousy. Men who wanted his job and who would fight and destroy to achieve it. But, Swann could have told them honestly, the glamour and the excitement were illusory. They would not have believed him.

His wife had seen his promotion through the ranks, her loneliness increasing with each year, her friends fewer and her husband more distant, emotionally and often physically. Their son and daughter, now married, lived abroad. This completed the desolation in the big suburban house, whose constantly ringing telephone indicated only further disruption or suspension of the few precious hours with the man she had married and once known.

His office window overlooked the Dublin Zoological Gardens, through the trees across the road, and he occasionally had glimpses of the giraffes, torsoless heads gliding through the early-morning and evening mists that drifted across the expanse of the Phoenix Park, the largest enclosed park in Europe. The spring and summer scents and sounds compensated in some measure for the darker months of autumn and winter, when the damp coldness seeped into his middle-aged bones with depressing questions and equally depressing answers. And at the end of it all, what would he show for all these years? At best, an inadequate pension and a presentation record-player; at worst, the gnawing knowledge that he had

had a son and daughter he never knew and now never would, a wife who had suffered the loneliness and unnecessary doubt of his often secretive profession, and the recurring fear of physical retaliation by some crackpot grudge-harbourer. But at the end of this year he would be out of it all, on early retirement and living in Spain. Meanwhile...

He returned to his armchair and lifted the receiver, flicking open a small desk directory at a selected letter. He dialled slowly, holding the last digit to clear his throat. The direct-line number was answered immediately. Swann pressed the scrambler button on the top of the telephone cradle.

'Hello, Minister,' he said with contrived flatness, 'Swann here. We've just had another attack. Ten-year-old boy in Herbert Park. Pretty bad...alive but only just...the dog tore his tongue out.'

The policeman listened to the expected expressions of revulsion and sympathy before the questioning.

'Yes, sir, positive diagnosis...yes, I'm afraid. The animal ran into the road and was killed by a car...No, sir...no doubt. Definitely rabid. They've given the boy some jabs and done what they can, but it's just a matter of time...'

Peter Phelan sat before the maze of coils, wires and transistors, his tuneless humming indicating awareness of the audience which had gathered at the workbench.

'The Russians make good radios, anyway,' he said to the onlookers with muted enthusiasm.

He had removed the casing from the Vega Selena domestic radio receiver and was now gently prodding the innards with a screwdriver. This was the inexplicable and irresistible gesture of the professional engineer, as mystifying to the layman as a car salesman kicking the tyre of a vehicle while appraising its trade-in value. A desire, perhaps, to make physical contact while the brain computed.

'What are you going to do?' asked the actor, Charles Casswell.

'I'm going to listen to some soldier-boys making small talk,' said Phelan, smiling and without lifting his eyes. He began whistling again.

'How, precisely, will you do that?'

Phelan stopped whistling and turned to look into the face of the Englishman. He sighed with exaggerated patience and said, mockingly, 'Precisely, Charles, I'm going to utilise an IF trimmer after I break into the coils, and tweak them to a central frequency of fifty-five megahertz with a digital readout counter. Any better suggestions?'

All but the embarrassed actor laughed at the teasing put-down.

'I'll wager you're not so damn conversant with the works of Shakespeare,' the actor retorted huffily. He moved away, set-faced, to the jars and tubes of theatrical make-up on the driving seat of the truck.

In the seaside village of Dalkey, south of the city, the actor's friend, Simon Coates, walked into the shop of the diving and watersport specialists, Marine Sales. The shop assistant would remember the unusual purchase of four full-face diving masks with spider retaining straps. He would also recall that the young man spoke with an English accent and that he had long, red hair and a generous beard and moustache. The Englishman's disguise reflected the skill of Charles Casswell. Coates told the assistant that he was opening a diving school in Belfast where, he said, delivery of this kind of mask had been delayed by an unofficial labour dispute at the dockside warehouse. On his return to the garage in Rathmines, he stopped at three pharmacies to purchase two pairs of surgical gloves in each.

'No problem,' he told Casswell, pulling off the wig and easing the irritating moustache from his lip.

'Hello Zero. This is Rosebud. Over.'

The crackling voice brought everyone to Peter Phelan's workbench. The speaker in the radio receiver hissed for a few moments before the voice broke in again.

'Hello Zero. This is Rosebud. Over Zero.'

'Hello Rosebud.' The second voice was noticeably less urgent.

'Hello Zero,' the first voice said. 'Our ETA at point seven is seventeen-fifty hours. Over Zero.'

'Zero. Roger Out.'

Grinning with unashamed pride, Phelan switched off the set and swivelled to face the others. Carl Stolford winked and patted him on the shoulder.

'What was all that?' asked Coates.

'An army mobile patrol or section, possibly on escort duty for a payroll or bank shipment, speaking to headquarters to give their estimated time of arrival at their destination or next point in their journey.'

'Like to give it a try, Charles?' Stolford asked the actor.

'May I hear it once more?'

Phelan turned back to the workbench. A Sony cassette recorder lay alongside the radio receiver. He pressed the rewind button and then the play knob. The same exchange of words came across on the small speaker in the recorder. Casswell closed his eyes tightly, absorbing the words and tones. The taped words ended but Casswell's eyes remained closed for some seconds afterwards. Then he opened them slowly and nodded. Phelan handed him the recorder's microphone. The actor hesitated for just a moment after Phelan put the machine into recording mode, then he spoke carefully.

'Hello Zero. This is Rosebud. Our ETA at point seven is seventeen-fifty hours. Over Zero.'

'Shit,' drawled Stolford in head-shaking admiration for the perfect impersonation of the army radio operator.

Phelan rewound the tape and they listened to both voices: the real operator and Casswell's. The accents and intonations were practically identical. With the hiss of normal transmission sound in the background, Charles Casswell's would be a duplicate of the genuine voice.

Edouard Dufour was the first to speak. 'Bravo, my friend,' he said in an awed whisper.

'*Fucking* bravo,' said a delighted Phelan, slapping the actor on the upper arm.

The others broke into spontaneous applause which they sustained while Casswell, grinning, took one pace back and bowed low from the waist, rising and dipping again and again.

'My beloved public,' he beamed, waving a limp hand in mock humility.

Chapter Nine

The woman was resting now, her exhaustion laden with sadness; her bandaged breast rising and falling beneath the hospital gown, her remaining eye peering mistily at the face behind the glass observation window. Her husband forced a smile and waved, briefly and self-consciously, at the unblinking eye and the wrinkled mouth. A white trail of saliva trickled from the corner of the orifice onto the pillow. A nurse in goggles, mask and rubber gloves stepped quickly from the end of the bed to wipe away the spit and the tear globule.

The room was tidy now, the bedside locker and cloth screen upright, the bedclothes smooth and tucked neatly. The husband would not be told what had happened two hours before his visit.

'Come along now,' the ward sister urged, taking his arm to shepherd him from the dispensary.

He nodded meek obedience and turned to leave. At the door, he stopped and looked back to smile encouragement and sympathy. The eye stared, unseeing. He walked out quickly, the ward sister steering his course. He could not hear the whining gurgle in the other room or see the clear plastic tube beneath the sheet, inserted earlier in the woman's windpipe in a hasty tracheotomy to prevent her suffocating.

Since ten o'clock that morning, the glass jug and tumbler had been removed from the bedside locker. By then, the woman had been sedated after her first attack of hydrophobia. Her mouth and tongue had felt parched but as soon as the water touched her lips she had been overcome with a terrifying fear of choking on, or drowning in, the liquid. She had spat it onto the

141

nurse's mask and threw her head back to escape what seemed inevitable death. The violence of the struggle was as frightening as it was short-lived for those in the single-bed ward. While the nurse held the patient on the bed, she plunged a needle into the woman's arm. The struggling gave way rapidly to a brief period of shivering and then sleep.

There had been several spasms during the afternoon, although no attempt had been made to give the woman water or any other liquid. Care had also to be taken now in opening the door to the ward, because the slightest draught on her face or neck would induce another desperate attempt to escape from the room and those trying to 'harm' her. During these spasms she would flail her arms around to ward off those she imagined were attacking her, arching her back from heels to neck and trembling uncontrollably. The classic symptoms of furious rabies were anticipated by those in the ward but were still frightening for the medical staff. They had never had to nurse a rabid patient before.

The rabies had done its work, inflaming the brain stem which controls breathing, the heart and the swallowing muscles. The hypothalamus was also affected now, causing her eye to 'cry' continuously and her mouth to secrete thick saliva. Her vocal chords were swollen and the system in her brain for controlling her body temperature would soon be destroyed. Already, thermometer readings were beginning to show fluctuations. But between spasms she was able to talk to those in the room about how she felt and what she feared during the attacks of tremors.

She lay, quiet now, her head still turned to the window separating the ward from the dispensary. The tears which ran from her eye blurred her vision but it did not matter. Perhaps she would sleep. But the eyelid wouldn't close. She tried again. The harsh whiteness of the neon lighting beyond the window stayed. She didn't like that whiteness. Nor the funny bubbling sound deep in her throat. She didn't like any of this. Her clothes? She would dress and go home to her own bed, away from this bare white room and its white sheets and white light. God was angry with her for something. He had sent that white light to punish her. It wasn't light; it was lightning. A long, searing sheet of lightning reaching out to burn her. She must get away from here, to her own house away from the lightning. The woman turned her head and sat upright, startling the nurse at the small table near the end of the bed. The young girl stood and walked to the woman. 'There now, relax, you're all right,' she said through the white mask.

The frog had returned. But this time it was red, vivid red all over. Even its wide eyes were red. The huge featureless mouth was pulsing in and out, its arms raised to attack.

A sudden bark stopped the nurse in her tracks. The swollen vocal chords had distorted the woman's voice so that her scream of aggression and fear sounded like a dog barking. The woman herself was aware of the peculiar sound. She had distinctly said 'Stay away.' But that was not what her ears had heard. Her mouth hung open, the white saliva forming a motionless waterfall between her upper and lower teeth, the dilated pupil half-mooned by the drooping lid, tears streaming down her cheek, matting a strand of her hair that had fallen forward. Her body trembled, lungs fighting to cope with the irregular and shallow breathing.

The nurse felt the hair creep on the back of her neck. If only the ward sister would return. The alarm bell was at the top of the bed and to get to it she would have to pass the patient. If she left the room to get help the patient might kill herself. Tranquilliser. It was her only hope. Slowly, very slowly, she lowered her arms and felt behind her back for the syringe in the aluminium kidney dish on the table. She smiled reassurance to the demented woman, then realised the stupidity of the gesture behind the mask and goggles. Her rubber-gloved hands touched the dish and fumbled with the cloth covering the syringe. The dish rattled on the table surface, the sudden noise startling both women. The nurse desperately wanted to empty her bladder, fear sweeping over her in trembling waves.

She found the syringe and felt for the plunger, the plastic body of the instrument beating a rhythm against the dish. Her fingers and thumb in position, she brought her right hand slowly up into the small of her back, wrist pressed hard against her spine to minimise the shaking. Her left hand eased down by her side as she took a slow step towards the woman. She tried to repeat her original words of gentle assurance but succeeded only in croaking at the back of her dry throat. She coughed and

143

automatically brought her hand before her mouth. The sudden sound, movement and sight of the liquid squirting from the needle sent the patient into a paroxysm of terror, throwing herself back against the steel rails above the pillows.

'Jesus, help me,' the nurse screamed and jumped forward.

In two steps she was alongside the top of the bed and full length across the heaving mass of the woman, who growled and barked in a pitiful attempt to form words to frighten the attacker. The needle stabbed into the shivering white acreage of her upper arm and would kill her unless she could fight her off. The woman wrenched her right arm free of the frog's heavy body and clawed at the side of its head, her fingers slipping under the rubber band holding the nurse's goggles in place. She pulled hard on the band and snapped the girl's head and shoulders back, twisting her body for extra leverage. The nurse instinctively gripped the woman's left shoulder with both hands as she felt herself being thrown backwards off the bed. Both women crashed onto the floor, the weight of the patient knocking the wind out of the nurse's body and the impact snapping the needle of the syringe still embedded in the fleshy arm.

The nurse became hysterical in her frantic efforts to free herself of the weight which was denying her oxygen. The patient, equally terrified by the clawing and kicking of the frog, tried to free her arm pinioned against the floor and her left hand now gripped by the attacker's fingers. She would not be killed by this monster and she had only one weapon left at her disposal.

Sister Dempsey, returning to the dispensary, heard the crash of the falling bodies as she walked along the corridor with the duty doctor. They ran into the outer room just as the rabid patient coughed and vomited clawing inside her own mouth and throat to remove the moist, stringy particles which threatened to choke her. She would live, comatose, for another eighteen hours, slipping gently and quietly into death. Nurse Maureen McGlinchey would be buried in her native village five days later in the full glare of international television and newspaper publicity.

The two bodies would be washed completely by masked and rubber-suited mortuary attendants using dilutions of benzalkonium chloride and cetrimonium bromide before the under-takers would be allowed to handle the corpses.

An hour after the nurse died, the first army sniper patrols moved out to begin their box-pattern sweeps of Dublin. Sixteen tight-lipped young men, armed with semi-automatic rifles fitted with Trilite telescopic night-sights, to protect a city of three quarters of a million people.

That same night Dufour slipped the *Marie* quietly out of Dun Laoghaire under cover of darkness and steered south for two miles, to the smaller of the two islands off Dalkey.

This small hump of rock and coarse grass, The Muglins, served a grim purpose during the reign of Elizabeth I and for several decades later. It was here that pirates were hanged on gibbets and left to rot as a warning to others who might be considering the plunder of merchant ships sheltering in Dalkey Sound. For many years only the hangman would set foot on this haunted island; even the families of the executed men were loath to try to recover the bodies of their kin. Crews of visiting ships slipped quietly past, the only sound being the sighing of the breeze and the creaking of the steel chains suspending the skeletons.

Dufour anchored the converted lifeboat half a mile seawards of the island and turned to the other three men with him. Casswell, Coates and Stolford watched as the diver assembled the equipment and then explained the purpose of each item and how it functioned. The lecture lasted forty minutes and was followed by another ten minutes of question-and-answer. Only then were they allowed to don the diving suits, lifejackets, masks, fins and tanks. Another ten minutes of explanation and demonstration of safety techniques. Each listened with respect for the dangers and for the experience of the Frenchman.

Carl Stolford volunteered to be the first over the side. Dufour attached a two-metre length of nylon rope to the front of the American's weighted belt, checked the valves, mask and pressure gauge on the air tank and nodded his approval. Stolford moved out of the wheelhouse before slipping the fins onto his feet. Dufour glanced around for other boats, but the sea was dark and empty. He tapped the ex-marine on the shoulder and stood back to avoid the splash, holding the other end of the nylon rope. When Stolford surfaced, the Frenchman attached the rope to a cleat on the gunwhale near the stern and handed the coils of excess to Casswell to feed out.

'Ready, mon ami?' he asked Stolford, who waved briefly and braced himself.

Back in the wheelhouse, Dufour started the engine and eased the boat forward, watching Casswell slipping the nylon rope through his hands until they were empty. The actor glanced back at the barely visible American and turned to Dufour to give him a thumbs-up sign. The engine gradually increased its speed to four knots, pulling Stolford deeper into the water.

Stolford found increasing difficulty in breathing with the pressure of water around his face, neck and chest. He had to fight to resist grabbing the rope in what would have been a futile attempt to ease the drag. But he remembered the diver's instructions and tried to use his fins and legs to keep himself stomach downwards in the water. For a while it worked. Then he flipped over onto his back, flailing uselessly to try to right himself. Only when Dufour eased off the throttle did he succeed. Again the boat increased its speed and again Stolford spun onto his back, only the strong spider strap keeping the full-face mask in position.

When the boat finally stopped, Stolford swam slowly to the side and was hauled on board, exhausted but exhilarated.

'Christ almighty,' he panted to Dufour, 'that was wild!'

Dufour's face was set. 'It was also very sad my friend. Get it wrong on the night and you could die.'

The American sighed and heaved himself to his feet. 'So, where was I going wrong?'

Ten minutes later Stolford was back in the water, more confident and proficient this time, flipping over only once when he momentarily lost concentration and forgot the expert's instructions.

Charles Casswell spent thirty minutes in the water, realising his lack of fitness despite his all-year-round tan and care for his weight and diet. An average swimmer, he was, however, unprepared for the strain of the four-knot drag and the clawing fingers of the strong undercurrents in the Sound. He knew that if the rope had not been tied to his weighted waist-belt he would have panicked into releasing himself from the immediate and future ordeal.

Lying panting and shivering on the deck, he gasped, 'There must be an easier way to become rich, dear boy!'

Stolford, aware of the frightened Simon Coates, who was hanging on every word and reaction, said quickly, 'You're just out of condition, Charles.'

The actor looked towards Coates, standing beside the wheelhouse and dressed now in a rubber suit.

'Not for *some* things, dear boy,' he said with more feeling than he had intended to reveal. Coates turned, embarrassed and annoyed.

'I'll take your word for that, Charles,' said Stolford, moving away.

'Oh, believe me, you'll have to,' said Casswell caustically. 'Not my type at all.'

'Thank Christ,' Stolford muttered to Edouard Dufour.

Coates trembled as he prepared himself to go over the side. Dufour had to almost prise the young man's teeth apart to relax him enough to carry out his routine check of the breathing equipment. A non-swimmer, Coates had to be assured several times that, with the rope attached to his belt and with a lifejacket partly inflated, he would not sink to the sea bed. Stolford had to suppress a laugh when he listened to the sound of the racing and shallow breathing through the regulator. If he doesn't get in the water soon, he thought, he'll drown in his own sweat, or worse.

Dufour took special care with the actors's friend, recruiting the other two to lower him gently into the sea and to hold his arms until he got used to the change of temperature and overcame his initial panic. First one arm was released, then the second, Coates gripping the gunwhale of the boat with white knuckles. Gradually with Dufour's quiet encouragement, he released his grip and floated free except for the tight rein of rope held by Stolford. A quarter of an hour passed before Coates would allow the first attempt to be made to pull him through the water, almost an hour before Dufour eased the boat to four knots.

'That's enough for tonight,' the Frenchman announced when Coates was back on board. 'Another lesson tomorrow night.'

When they eventually arrived back at the lockup garage in Rathmines they found Adrien D'Albe trying to revive a very drunk Peter Phelan who was lying in the back of the converted truck.

'What the hell happened?' Stolford demanded angrily. 'I told you to keep him away from the booze.'

'I just slipped out for an hour or so,' said D'Albe defensively. 'When I got back I found the radio gear all switched off and Phelan like this.'

'You were supposed to stay with him to monitor the army broadcasts,' Stolford snapped. 'And to keep him off the hootch.'

'Look,' D'Albe blazed, 'when I took on this job I did not expect to be a babysitter.'

'You were told to take your orders from me,' Stolford retorted.

'Gentlemen, gentlemen,' said Casswell soothingly, 'this will get us nowhere. Argy-bargies and tiffs. Well, I mean, really…'

Stolford swung around but Edouard Dufour stepped quickly between the two men. Casswell retreated hastily, remembering what the American had done to Simon Coates in the apartment.

'Enough, Carl,' Dufour said softly. 'You have made your point, no?'

The threat was there. It was there in the stance of the blocky diver, his quiet words a challenge recognisable to fighting men everywhere. Stolford could probably take the Frenchman but he, and the operation, would be damaged. For just a moment they stared hard into each other's eyes and then Stolford turned back to the slumbering engineer.

'Help me get him into the car,' he said to the others. 'We all meet here tomorrow morning at the usual time. One more fuck-up and someone gets hurt.'

The final message from The Voice was waiting in the mail box at Charles Casswell's apartment, addressed to Carl Stolford.

Phelan sipped the strong coffee and pulled deeply on the cigarette. His head hurt and his mouth tasted foul. He reached across to the bedside chair for his spectacles. Stolford, sitting

148

on the edge of the bed, came into focus. He sipped more coffee and replaced the mug with an ashtray which balanced on his stomach.

'Well?'

'I went to see my wife, Betty.'

The statement, although bold, was laced with noticeable apology. A bond had developed between the two men, quickly and surprisingly, based on an understanding of each other's past. They had deserved better from life; each had been hurt by lesser men. Both had been forced to adopt a new morality to compete, to claw something from a future which otherwise seemed to hold little hope.

'It's really over this time,' Phelan added with conviction. He went on, 'Took off with some bloke, according to the neighbours. The bastard even collected some of her clothes for her.'

'D'ya know who?'

'No, but he wasn't the first, anyway,' said Phelan dispraisingly, thinking of his brother. 'This guy must be loaded. Left most of her things behind.'

'Whyd'd ya go back?' The question was a gentle challenge.

Phelan could have lied but saw no point in that. He pulled on the cigarette and exhaled slowly. 'I suppose I was having second thoughts about this operation of ours. Maybe there was another way...' He paused and smiled ruefully. 'Like I said before, we're losers. Last night just confirmed it.'

Stolford shook his head. 'No,' he said grimly, 'this time we *win*.'

The engineer studied the American's face for just a moment, then smiled.

'Yeah. Fuck her, anyway.'

'For Chrissake,' Stolford moaned, 'try t'act like *soldiers*. Ya look like a bunch of new whores at a tea party.'

Charles Casswell held onto the front of the truck with one hand and held up the other to call a temporary halt. His chest was heaving with the exertion.

'A moment, dear boy,' he panted. 'Pray tell me why it is so necessary to wear this dreadful thing beneath the uniforms?'

He pulled open the battledress jacket to reveal the black rubber of the diving suit.

'Because, *dear boy,*' Stolford mimicked, there won't be time to put it on at that stage of the operation.'

Peter Phelan, sitting cross-legged on the workbench in jeans and shirt, said teasingly, 'I think you look *frightfully* fetching, Charles. Rubber is definitely *you*.'

Even Casswell's friend Coates smirked at the annoyed and miserable expression on the actor's face.

'It's alright for you,' said Casswell sulkily. 'All you have to do during this thing is pull a few wires and things.'

'Envious, dear boy?'

Everyone laughed at that one, even the actor, who reluctantly allowed his face to crease into a smile.

'Alright,' said Stolford, holding up a hand, 'we'll take a break.'

The American moved across to Adrien D'Albe who was standing at the end of three planks of wood laid across two boxes to form a platform. The marine radio and cassette player, now encased in a steel cabinet and painted matt green, stood at one side on the outermost plank. Two small metal shields, bearing the colours and markings of the 3rd Infantry Battalion, Curragh Command, were propped against the boxes supporting the planks.

'So when do we get a *real* Land-rover?' Stolford asked, nodding towards the platform.

'Whenever you need it,' said D'Albe in his French accent. 'There is one at a farm on the northside, near Dublin airport.'

'And it's the right model?'

'That is where I went last night. Looking for a vehicle. There were plenty at various farms but only a few of the correct size, with the right wheelbase.'

Stolford faced Phelan. 'And you? Everything set?'

'Well we've got the foam and the concrete. And the Draeger meter,' said Phelan, glancing at the equipment on the workbench.

The ex-marine took off his beret and ran a hand through his black hair. It was something he had noticed many times before, the tingling of his scalp just before action. With other soldiers it was sweaty palms or cold shivers. With Stolford it was always the need to scratch.

'Well,' he said with a casualness belied by his eyes, 'I

suppose there's no excuse for us to postpone it for another week.'

The others were all hanging on his words now. Somehow it always seemed remote, the moment of decision. Always a reason for delay. Equipment, training, insufficient knowledge, practice. Now there was really nothing anyone could invent to postpone the inevitable.

Glancing around the group but not holding anyone's gaze for more than a second or two, he smiled and rubbed his hands briskly together.

'Right,' he said, as businesslike as his dry throat would allow, 'we go Friday, like The Voice said.'

The late city editions of the Dublin newspapers carried the story of the attack on the baby and her mother.

Television pictures of the scene, together with interviews with eyewitnesses, were being edited for satellite transmission to the rest of Europe and to the United States. No one had pictures of the actual attack but cameramen had had time to get to the dockland warehouse where the rabid dog had taken refuge from his pursuers. A detective arrived before army and police sharpshooters reached the scene, and killed the animal with his pistol.

There were grapic descriptions of how the dog, foaming at the mouth, had taken the baby from her pram and torn pieces from her face and body, shaking her like a rag doll, her mother frantically trying to pull the animal's jaws away. The incident, after the morning's calm performance by the health minister, was a bonus for journalists national and international. It was also an ideal opportunity for Opposition politicians to make themselves available to reporters and register their 'shock and horror' and condemn the 'government's handling of the whole affair'. Doctor Farrelly announced her resignation 'in protest', adding fuel to an already raging fire. 'Innocent people,' she said in a statement, 'have had to pay the price of the government's inactivity.'

Stolford sat with Casswell in the garage, reading the newspaper accounts of the developments. The others in the group listened to the six-thirty radio bulletin. D'Albe was aware of the unspoken speculation, but there was not evidence to link him to the introduction of the disease. And, after all, it was Stolford who had brought the blue bottle from France.

Stolford felt sick. Innocent civilians, again. The guilt was as great as before and the anger burned with the almost-certain knowledge that once more he had been duped by adhering to the cardinal rule of a soldier's life: obedience. He felt the shame of guilt and yet the anger of the cheated.

'The bottle,' he said numbly. 'It must have been in that bottle. How else could The Voice have known with certainty that army patrols would be put on the streets? And without the patrols there'd be no operation.'

'Now, now, dear boy,' Casswell soothed. 'There's nothing to prove that, at all,' he reasoned, unconvincingly. 'Probably some fool smuggled in an animal from the continent and The Voice altered his original plan to grasp this opportunity.'

He placed a hand on Stolford's shoulder and smiled kind assurance. 'Nothing to do with *us*, dear boy.'

'Christ,' Stolford sneered into his face, 'where've we heard *those* fuckin' words before!'

The Friday-morning radio bulletins carried an interview with the health minister, outlining the government's plans to deal with the rabies outbreak. More important to many listeners was the weather forecast for the next twenty-four hours. No surprises, continuing cold and dull with scattered outbreaks of rain in most areas.

Peter Phelan lay resting on one arm, smoking his second cigarette of the day. The American stood at the tiny shaving mirror, the razor scraping through the foam and stubble. He had a small scar on his shoulder above the powerful bicep of his right arm. Phelan wondered how it had been caused.

Stolford waited for the forecast to end and, splashing water onto his face, spoke into the sink, 'Tonight's the night, looks like.'

'Looks like,' said Phelan, his stomach churning.

In the Sandymount apartment, Simon Coates giggled delightedly at the result his efforts with the soapy sponge had instantly produced.

'Not this morning, Simon,' Casswell chuckled. 'I'm too

bruised after last night's training...'

They both turned as the door opened. Edouard Dufour, already dressed, took one quick glance at the couple standing under the shower and at the protruberance from the soap suds. He had seen similar behaviour on some oil rigs.

The Frenchman shook his head slowly and smirked at the shamefaced duo.

'How is that expression, my friends, boys will be girls?'

He turned and walked out, snapping over his shoulder, 'Come on, we have a busy day ahead.'

The other Frenchman was tired. He had acquired the Land-rover from the north-Dublin farm and had spent the night washing it down in the Rathmines lockup garage and fitting it with its military markings and equipment. This morning, while Peter Phelan transformed the truck into a van, he would give both engines a much needed tuning.

Like the others, Adrien D'Albe found that this morning he was excited to the point of being on a 'high'. The ex-marine Stolford would have recognised it as the familiar exhilaration of a trained man at last having the opportunity to put his learning into practice.

Later, much nearer the time, the mood would give way to one of almost overwhelming fear.

Part Three

The Execution

Chapter Ten

A cold wind had dried the remaining traces of the early showers. Peter Phelan shivered slightly but shrugged away the tremor and, with another glance at the sky, shut the garage door and turned back to the other men gathered in a loose circle around the actor, Charles Casswell.

Phelan was dressed in dark blue overalls and a black 'donkey' jacket with leather shoulder-pieces and elbow patches. Edouard Dufour was similarly attired. The others wore army uniforms, and waited patiently in turn for Casswell to apply an assortment of theatrical make-up, altering their colouring and features.

Carl Stolford's black hair was turning dark red under the puffs from the aerosol can which Casswell was weaving backwards and forwards. On the back of both wrists he now had 'tattoos'. Casswell's own silver hair was now dark, with a matching moustache. One of his front teeth sported a gold cap, and two brown contact lenses would later cover his grey irises.

Adrien D'Albe's sharply bridged nose had been rounded and widened by Naturo mortician's wax. His ears had been broadened with the same putty-like material. The colour of his eyes had also been changed with contact lenses.

Simon Coates' long fair hair had been cut short and tinted dark brown. In addition, he now had a small scar running just below the left cheek-bone. This had been achieved by pouring a small quantity of Collodion flexible liquid plastic onto his cheek to form a thin line which pulled the flesh on each side towards the centre of the line as the mixture hardened.

'That should do it,' Casswell said, tapping the American on the shoulder.

Stolford looked into the mirror and smiled, admiring the new hair colour and baring his teeth to show the two front teeth which, half an hour ago, had been sound but now looked darkened and in need of filling.

'Want to hear my soldier bit?' Casswell asked Stolford.

'Why not?'

Casswell placed his military peaked cap on his head, turned briefly to check the angle in the mirror and then swung around sharply, face stern.

'Alright, sergeant,' he snapped brusquely to Stolford. 'Get the men fell in.'

'Sir,' the American growled obediently. 'Right, you lot, Get fell in.'

Peter Phelan smiled broadly at the Irish accents. There was no trace of American or English pronunciation.

Deputy Commissioner George Swann had been working late but had remained elusive, frustrating the many calls he had received during the day from officials of the Departments of Health and Defence. Several requests had also been made by journalists to interview him on the rabies situation. Stock excuses were drawn from the hat of the superintendent in charge of the Press office, while his sergeants released up-to-date casualty reports. At times like these theirs was the most unenviable position, unable to answer questions which were routine to the reporters but politically sensitive in the overall situation.

The scrambler telephone buzzed at Swann's elbow. He reached across to the narrow shelved telephone cabinet alongside his desk and lifted the receiver. This was the only telephone he would answer tonight; even the direct line to his office had remained ignored. His wife would not be pleased when he finally arrived home.

He pressed the button on the top of the instrument to activate the scrambler and said, 'Hello. George Swann.'

'Hello, George,' said the familiar voice of Chief Superintendent John Frampton of New Scotland Yard's Anti-Terrorist Squad. 'How is it?'

'Well, John,' said Swann wearily, 'we're in the politics game. Have been since this morning. I'm keeping low.'

Frampton chuckled understandingly. 'Any indications that the terrorist theory is a runner?'

'Not a whisper, thank God,' said Swann with feeling. 'Why, have you heard something?'

'No, no,' Frampton hastily assured Swann, 'but the heavies here, the *Times*, *Telegraph* and *Guardian*, have been sniffing among our lot along those lines. You know the kind of thing: could it happen here, how could it be done and so on.'

Swann rubbed his eyes through closed lids and sighed. 'What did your people tell them?'

'That we'd be prepared for such an eventuality, of course,' Frampton replied ruefully. 'They know we're talking through our arses, but what the hell could we say? We tried the smoke screen of it being unwise to reveal what our contingency plans were. Christ, they were laughing in our faces.'

'Any idea what line they're using?'

'Oh, yeah. No secret about *that*. How easy it'd be for a madman or terrorist outfit to get hold of rabies virus and plant it.'

'And?'

'And nothing,' said Frampton sourly. 'What the hell could we say to that! They even pointed out that a television crew proved how easy it was to get into the Central Veterinary Laboratory at Weybridge. They just drove into the place in their car and walked through the swing doors of the 'Pathogen A' laboratory itself, where they're carrying out tests on rabid animals and on the various strains of virus, for God's sake.'

Both men fell silent for some moments, digesting the enormity of the possibilities and their own helplessness.

'Anyway,' Frampton broke the silence, tone altered, 'to get away from *our* problems here, what's the score there in Dublin?'

'Oh, just as you can imagine,' said Swann ironically. 'Every dog or cat that farts is a sure rabies case. In fact the score is fairly low and seems to be in the Dublin area only. The 'deliberate' theory seems to be a non-runner but...'

'Yeah?'

'...I just got a gut feeling that *something's* on.'

Phelan opened the doors of the garage and gave the 'all-clear' signal.

159

The Land-Rover, with Adrien D'Albe at the wheel and Charles Casswell beside him, moved quietly out. Carl Stolford sat beneath the green canvas roof of the vehicle with Simon Coates crouching beside the radio apparatus, earphones over his black beret and microphone at his lips. The military shield markings and long swishing aerial completed the picture of an army patrol.

Stolford gave Phelan a thumbs-up as the Land-Rover disappeared around the corner. The young engineer smiled tightly and turned back to the garage where Edouard Dufour was waiting beside the converted truck, hands on the hips of his overalls.

'OK, my friend?' the Frenchman asked.

Again the tight smile. 'OK,' he said resignedly.

Dufour closed and locked the garage doors after the truck had moved out and stopped. Then he climbed up into the passenger seat of the cabin and slapped Phelan's knee. 'Let us go and get rich, my friend,' he grinned.

It was eleven minutes past eleven.

'There is no way through or around the systems,' The Voice had said. 'The only method is to make use of those systems.'

In the National Museum, the uniformed security man nodded to the young policeman peering through the glass panelling in the double wooden doors of the building. It was the final check for those involved in protecting the nation's treasures.

Locked inside, the security man would switch off all but a few of the building's lights and make his way to the staff-room and the waiting camp bed. Unless he was called on the telephone linking the staff-room with the glass-walled hut on the forecourt, there would be no contact between him and the outer security ring. This outer ring comprised another uniformed guard and a corporal of the military police who was armed with a Browning automatic pistol. Beyond the hut were the high steel railings fronting the complex, with two uniformed civil policemen, unarmed except for batons but each carrying a walkie-talkie for communication with the Garda Central Control Room at Dublin Castle.

The museum is one of three buildings forming three sides of

a rectangle facing onto Kildare Street near the city centre. In the middle and set back from the street is Leinster House where the parliament sits. Originally the home of the Earls of Kildare, the grey-stone building was built in 1745. Later it was sold to the Royal Dublin Society, and in 1922 the newly founded Irish Free State took it over to house the government. On the right and nearer the street is the National Museum, built in 1857. Directly opposite the museum across the concrete 'lawn' of Leinster House and forming the other side of the rectangle is the National Gallery. Architecturally in keeping with the museum, stone pillars supporting a high rotunda, it is the baby of the three, opened in 1864.

Leinster House is guarded by a detachment of troops, as well as the security men under the command of a 'Captain of the Guard'. The troops occupy basement quarters linked by direct line to their barracks headquarters. They are infantrymen, armed with semi-automatic rifles and submachine guns, who make periodic patrols of the entire complex during their hours of duty.

Inside the museum and gallery are ultra-sonic and 'passive red' alarm systems. Based on the Doppler principle, the ultra-sonic system is a progression of a Second World War device for detecting submarines. A high-frequency signal is transmitted when the alarm is operative and is monitored at a central receiver. The slightest disturbance of air inside the building, such as a draught from an opening door or a human body passing through a room, would alter the frequency and activate an alarm.

The 'passive red' is based on the radiation of every item in a room. The alarm is tuned to accept only the total amount of radiation emitted by those items. Any increase in the amount of radiation, like that from a human body, would activate the alarm.

In both instances however, there would be no bells or lights in the buildings. The intruders would be unaware that they had triggered the alarms until the police and soldiers surrounded them. Until now, only one pathetic attempt had been made to break into the complex. The security was rightly considered to be impenetrable.

Other premises around the city also have these systems

installed, each linked to a security firm's control room or 'police station' as it is known. Windowless, green-painted, concrete rooms, such as that owned by a company a mile from Leinster House, manned twenty-four hours a day by two-men shifts. Each alarm is represented on a panel by three lights—green, red-yellow and blue. On each panel there are twenty such sets.

Reporting for duty, the two duty men look up into a tiny television lens mounted above an inconspicuous shop doorway to identify themselves to the men in the upstairs control room and be admitted through the electronically operated door. The upstairs steel door is also electronically controlled. On hand-over, the newcomers check the alarms by flicking a spring-loaded switch on each set. A green light will show it is functioning. In the event of an alarm being triggered the blue light will come on, a bell will sound and the red-yellow light will flash. Having identified the alarm, one of the duty men will cancel the bell and flashing light and lift the direct-line telephone to the Garda Communications Room in Dublin Castle and give the relevant information.

The security room itself is protected from attack. Apart from gas masks and their own manual alarms to Dublin Castle, the men inside know that the direct lines to and from the room are protected in their underground pipes. Any attempt to cut them will trigger the Garda alarm. Should there be an electrical power failure the system automatically switches itself to emergency batteries, with enough power to sustain it for eight hours. The only furniture is a couple of straight-backed chairs, and the only comfort a small washroom in which the men can brew coffee or tea and cook snacks during their twelve-hour shift.

The Land-Rover slipped quietly through the streets, Simon Coates monitoring the radio reports of the army rabies patrols and pinpointing their positions on the street map spread on his knees.

He relayed the positions of the patrols to Adrien D'Albe at the wheel and gave diversionary instructions to avoid visual contact with genuine army patrols. The sudden appearance of another patrol would cause curiosity, and the reporting of this phantom unit to the Security Network Headquarters at Cathal Brugha Barracks would bring military reinforcements and the police anti-terrorist squad, forty-two sharpshooters armed with pistols, rifles and submachine guns.

The three addresses given in the detailed instructions by The Voice were all in the same district on the north side of the Liffey and extending westwards towards the Phoenix Park. D'Albe pulled into the dark alleyway alongside the jewellery shop, the city's late-night pedestrians paying the vehicle scant attention. Stolford checked his wrist-watch. It was eleven-forty. He reached into a steel box on the floor and brought out a small package of explosive taped to a glassless wrist-watch. He moved the hour hand to eleven o'clock on the watch. There was no minute hand. He carefully made the final connections between the timepiece and the detonator and wound the spring. Then he stepped carefully from the Land-Rover and placed the complete package behind the jeweller's storeroom window-sill. It rested behind the protective bars and against the glass.

In exactly one hour from now the hour hand would reach the top of the watch-face and make contact between the battery and detonator. Similar explosions would be caused at the rear of a large furriers and a bank. All three were connected to the control room of the security firm a mile from Leinster House.

By the time Stolford had planted all three devices, Peter Phelan and Edouard Dufour were in position on the south side of the river. The converted truck, with its post office markings and false number plates, was parked some two hundred yards from the Electricity Supply Board's generating station on Pigeon House Road, the south wall of Dublin Port which extends finger-like out into the bay. Captain Bligh of The Bounty visited Dublin to advise on this extension and other developments to the port. The Pigeon House itself got its name from John Pigeon, the superintendent of equipment during the construction of the south wall. The house, a large rambling grey-stone building, became a hotel, a military barracks and, finally, offices for the generating station.

In the back of the truck, Dufour shoved the chest of tools away to reveal the cut-away section of the floor near the tailboard. Phelan lowered himself through the opening and inserted the clasps of the Wreckers winch into the steel manhole cover set into the roadway. Dufour put the winch into reverse and the cable lifted the manhole cover clear of its recess. Phelan pushed the cover to one side as the Frenchman lowered the cable again to put the cover on the ground. Phelan took the tools and shielded torch from Dufour and stepped down into the rectangular opening, legs straddling the sausage-shaped lead housing which joined the two pipes extending into the soil on both sides of the manhole. It took him nine minutes with a blowtorch to open the housing. Dufour, kneeling at the edge of the opening in the truck's floor, whistled softly when he saw the maze of multi-coloured plastic wires.

Phelan reached up and took the telephone tapper box and the pair of headphones from Dufour and began uncovering the waxed paper connections on each pair of wires, attaching crocodile clips to each joint and listening on the telephone handpiece of the tapper. The work was methodical and, of necessity, slow. Many of the lines, connected to factories and warehouses along the road and the adjoining reclaimed land, were 'dead'; the switchboards had closed down for the night and only a few open lines were still purring. Dufour began to fidget and glance at his wrist-watch as the engineer worked.

But suddenly Phelan looked up and smiled. He reached into the breast pocket of his overalls and brought out a small square of paper. The six-digit number on the paper was the one listed in the telephone directory as the 'after office hours' number of the generating station. He pushed the switch on the top of the tapper box to the left and dialled the number. After two rings a voice answered, 'Hello. Control Room.'

'Post Office engineers here,' said Phelan into his mouth-piece, accent heavily Dublin. 'Just doin' a line check. Bit o' trouble wi' the Ballsbridge exchange. Could y'just hold your line open for a few minutes while we check our pairings at this end, please?'

'Sure,' said the control room engineer.

Phelan cradled the handpiece against his shoulder and began a frantic search for the same line with the headphones. These headphones were also fitted with crocodile clips, a microfarad blocking capacitor attached to one of them to prevent interruption to the current running along the line. After four minutes he found it, thanked the engineer for his help and ended the call by flicking the tapper switch back into the central position and replacing the telephone handpiece on its cradle.

He handed the tapper set to the Frenchman, playing out the leads carefully behind him to avoid breaking the crocodile clip connections to the generating station control room line.

Dufour glanced at his watch again. 'Where are they?' he asked anxiously.

'They'll be along,' Phelan answered with more hope than conviction. 'Probably avoiding the army patrols.'

Moments later the Land-Rover pulled up in front of the truck and Casswell slid out of the front passenger seat. He was joined by Carl Stolford at the back doors of the truck. The American looked up into Phelan's enquiring face and nodded affirmation.

'When?' asked Phelan.

Stolford looked at his watch and said, 'Seventeen minutes from now.'

'We're cutting it a bit fine, aren't we?'

'Better this way than to be seen hanging around here getting people curious.' Stolford smiled.

He turned to Casswell and slapped him on the shoulder. 'Better get ready, Charles.'

The actor nodded and extended a hand to be helped up into the back of the truck. He sat before the tapper set now resting on a shelf of the tool chest, and glanced around at the tape-recorder and speakers to his right near the front of the temporary cabin.

'Set?' asked Phelan.

Casswell swallowed and said tightly, 'Set.'

Stolford slapped one gloved fist into the open palm of the other glove and said abruptly, 'Right, we're on our way.'

He went back quickly to the Land-Rover and jumped into the back. The vehicle moved off quietly towards the generating station. They drove past the gates and, a hundred yards beyond, swung around and stopped. In the back, Stolford lifted the powerful Technisub Reefmaster harpoon gun and slid the specially made harpoon into the breech. Originally the harpoon had a barbed tip. This tip had now been built up into a spearhead of pewter. Further back an Ever-Ready three-volt

165

battery had been taped to the shaft to give balance to the harpoon in flight and to supply the required power when it reached its target. Two wires, leading from the head to the battery, were also taped to the shaft.

He pulled back the heavy double rubbers of the sling action to cock the gun, and tapped Adrien D'Albe on the shoulder. The Frenchman moved the Land-Rover slowly towards the gates of the generating station. Just before it drew abreast, Stolford leaned out over the low tailgate, clutching the twin pistol grips of the weapon and aiming carefully over the boundary railings. He squeezed the trigger and felt the sharp slap as the rubber sling whipped the harpoon up into the darkness, the light from the street lamps and the building glinting on the steel when it reached the top of its arc and began its swift descent. The target was not a difficult one: rows of transformer units and insulators in a huge wire-mesh enclosure to the right of the main building and behind the security cabin. They heard it drop with a metallic ring.

'Go,' Stolford ordered, and the Land-Rover moved slowly and quietly back to the parked truck on the deserted road.

The American glanced at his watch and hoped the special harpoon would perform as it had done during the lonely morning he had spent in the Wicklow mountains. The soft pewter should crumple on impact, smashing the fragile hyperdermic syringe body inside and allowing its chemical mixture to spill onto the condom rubber insulation around the bare wires. The mixture should corrode the rubber in about ten minutes, give or take a minute, allowing the wires to come in contact and complete the circuit to the battery. The three volts would be sufficient to power the small detonator and explode the small quantity of black C-4 plastic explosive.

No one spoke as the minutes ticked away. Charles Casswell sat before the telephone tapper as if mesmerised by the silent instrument. Peter Phelan stood near the tape-recording equipment, fingers pressing the rubber cups of the earphones to his ears. Simon Coates crouched in the back of the Land-Rover listening for something to interrupt the wind-rustled sound of the canvas canopy. Adrien D'Albe, hunched in the driving seat, tapped the steering wheel in a rhythmless finger tattoo. Edouard Dufour stared down into the darkness of the manhole, a focal point and excuse for avoiding the strained faces around him.

Only Carl Stolford looked back through the cold night at the lights of the generating station, his wrist-watch before his face, urging the sweep-hand to increase its speed yet dreading the moment which would signify success or failure. The others might forgive failure but he would not.

The moment passed. Just the sound of the breeze and the sudden, distant barking of a dog. The barking stopped.

Stolford turned to Phelan and shrugged. 'Almost a minute over,' he said helplessly and apologetically.

'It still…' Phelan's encouragement was interrupted by the soft thump, felt more than heard.

The American snapped his eyes back to the station. A thin spiral of dark smoke rose vertically and was blown away as it left the shelter of the building. Seconds later a blue and yellow flame shot into the trail of smoke as the oil in the blast-damaged transformer unit ignited.

'We're in business,' said Stolford with relieved satisfaction.

In the station's control room, the much practised fire drill was about to go into operation. First indication of the explosion some distance from the large sound-proofed room came as the duty engineer was reaching for his cup of tea. The meters in the pale green fascia of the circular desk flickered and dropped below the normal level. Moments later, while he was still checking for possible mechanical faults, the intercom telephone buzzed. The security guard at the main gate told him breathlessly that one of the transformers in the yard had blown up. At that point the engineer grabbed the desk microphone and yelled over the station's loudspeaker system that there was a fire at the transformer compound and that this was not an exercise.

The shift workers rushed to their fire points and donned the necessary gear before following their leaders to the fire. Meanwhile the duty engineer and his control room colleagues took that section of the transformer compound out of the system. Then the engineer reached for the external telephone to summon help from the city's fire brigade. In the truck, Peter Phelan monitored the call on his headphones and held up a finger to signify to the others that this was the first one from the station.

The duty engineer terminated the brief call and dialled another number. This was to the central control room of the national grid. They had noticed the drop in power from the Pigeon House station but had resisted the natural impulse to contact the station and thus clog communication. Besides, they had their own adjustments to make to level out the power to avoid blackouts. Phelan listened to this call and held up a second finger. The line went dead again. Seconds passed.

'Come on, you stupid bastard,' Phelan urged the unhearing duty engineer. 'Make the third call.'

The engineer obliged as soon as he heard the first damage report from the fire scene. Transformers just don't blow up. Not here. Not with so many regular checks on their condition and performance. The city fire brigade would probably tell the police about the outbreak as a matter of routine, especially a fire at an installation as important as a generating station. But, better cover himself. He lifted the telephone and dialled the Dublin Castle Communications Room.

'This must be it,' Phelan warned as he monitored the dialling clicks. He pressed the 'play' button on the tape equipment in the truck. The speakers replayed the recording prepared the previous day in the Rathmines garage. It was the sound of men talking in the measured tones of those permanently employed in radio communications.

He whipped off the pair of wires leading from the tapper box to the outside world and flicked the switch to the 'LB' position on the left. As he did, Charles Casswell lifted the handpiece to his ear and said in a provincial Irish accent, 'Hello, Control.'

'Hello,' said the duty engineer. 'Pigeon House Power Station here. Duty engineer. We've had a bit of a bang here in one of our transformers and...'

'Yes,' said Casswell. 'We were told by the fire brigade. How bad is it?'

'Well we have it more or less under control, but I thought you'd better be prepared for some flickering of power in one section of the city.'

'Will there be blackouts?'

'No. At least there shouldn't be,' said the duty engineer. 'Actually by now the national grid should have compensated for the drop and the flickering should have stopped.'

'Right,' Casswell said. 'Thanks for the call. Some of our lads should be with you in a few minutes, anyway.'

Both men replaced their receivers. Phelan reconnected the wires to the tapper box and flicked the switch to the position on the right marked 'CB'. He put the recording spools into fast forward motion to find the next prepared band, separated from the previous recording by a yellow leader tape. The sound from the speakers was now a hum like a distant electric carpet cleaner, but heavier and more resonant. Casswell lifted the receiver from the tapper. Phelan took the piece of paper from his breast pocket again and dialled a six-digit number. It rang four times before a voice answered with the words Casswell had used to the duty engineer.

'Hello, this is the Pigeon House. Have the fire brigade been on to you about our little outbreak?' The accent was now a fair likeness to that of the duty engineer.

'They have,' the communications inspector confirmed. 'How bad is it?'

'Ah, not as bad as we first thought,' said Casswell with a smile in his voice. 'One of our transformers popped. Overload probably, caused by a defect in our by-pass unit in the second stage of overlay.'

The technical gibberish was sufficient to impress the policeman, unwilling to be drawn into areas beyond his knowledge. 'Ah, yes,' he said, with as much conviction as he could manage. Phelan, listening on the headphones, smiled and gave a thumbs-up to Carl Stolford.

The inspector would try to bring the conversation back into his area of expertise. 'No indication that it was deliberate?'

'Sabotage, you mean?' Casswell asked with just the right measure of incredulity.

'Well,' the inspector replied defensively, 'it's something we here always have to consider. Especially at a generating station.'

'Yes, I understand,' Casswell acknowledged more seriously. 'No, it's our problem I'm afraid.'

'OK'

'Oh, but there is one thing you ought to know,' Casswell said as if the thought had just occurred, 'especially with all those army patrols out on the streets because of the rabies scare...'

169

'Yes?' the inspector prompted, sensing drama.

'...well, because of the power drop from us to the national grid system, there will be a flickering of domestic and public lighting. Probably in a rough line westwards from Sean McDermott Street up through the city centre area as far as the Phoenix Park.'

'Yes, our lights were flickering for a while. But they're alright now. The drop didn't trip our emergency generator.'

'No,' Casswell went on in the voice of the duty engineer, 'with a bit of luck it won't. But the alternating power could resume until we can get ourselves sorted out here. Problem is, it might start tripping alarm systems around the city-centre area.'

'Ah, yes,' said the inspector, comprehending this unexpected complication. 'I see what you mean.'

'Wouldn't like yourselves or the army chasing ghost burglars,' said Casswell with a chuckle.

'Right.' the inspector agreed. 'I'd better give the soldier-boys the word.'

Casswell finished the call, thanking the policeman for his promised help.

Phelan sat back in the van and glanced at his watch. 'Maybe he won't,' he said to Casswell, 'but we have to be sure.'

The actor nodded his understanding but made no effort to hide his nervousness. 'Opening night was never as bad as this,' he said with veracity, as distant whines became audible above the gentle breeze, announcing the departure of fire brigade tenders from a city station. Forty seconds ticked by, a lifetime to the waiting men, before the handpiece against Phelan's ear buzzed and brought a rueful smile to his lips. 'Crafty bastard,' he muttered, and activated the tape-recording of the simulated generating station again.

Casswell took the handpiece and watched Phelan flick the switch on the tapper box. 'Pigeon House, duty engineer,' said Casswell in perfect imitation of the man he had spoken to before.

'Garda Control here again,' said the duty inspector at Dublin Castle. 'Just want to confirm your call...in case of a hoax.'

'Yes, of course,' said Casswell understandingly. 'I called a few minutes ago to warn you about the possibility of triggered alarms. OK?'

'Fine, Pigeon House,' the inspector answered, relieved. 'I'll get on to the Army. Goodbye.'

Casswell nodded to Phelan to disconnect the line. Stolford punched the smiling engineer on the shoulder affectionately. '*You're* the crafty bastard,' he said, admiringly.

Phelan jumped back into the manhole and reconnected the wires before replacing the lead casing over the jumble of plastic coverings. In less than a minute the manhole cover was back in place and the truck was moving back down the street towards the centre of the city. The first fire tender rushed past them towards the station, followed by a police patrol car. The policemen ignored the Post Office van but waved briefly at the army Land-Rover following close behind it. Before they swung off Pigeon House Road, a second fire tender with a turntable ladder hee-hawed towards the station, its twin blue lights flashing.

'So far, so good,' said Phelan to Edouard Dufour beside him. Behind them the flames had disappeared and the black smoke was thinning its veil over the lights of the generating station.

On the other side of the River Liffey there were three sharp slaps as the hour hands of the pocket watches reached twelve and completed the detonator circuits. The sounds, heard only in an area of less than a hundred yards' radius of each explosion, were indistinguishable.

The actual time was twelve-forty.

In the green control room of Abel Alarms, other colours were added to the subdued lighting.

'Jim,' the shirt-sleeved duty man called to his companion in the washroom. 'We've got three together,' he roared above the noise of the bell.

The other man hobbled into the control room, clutching his trousers and underpants at half-mast. He mouthed something to the desk man.

'What?'

'I said, turn off the...'

The bell died.

'...shaggin' *bell*,' he roared into the sudden silence.

The first man cancelled the flashing red-yellow light and reached for the telephone.

'I'll do that,' the second duty man said, hobbling up to the desk.

'Control,' the duty inspector in Dublin Castle intoned.

'Hello, Abel Control here. We've got three simultaneous.'

'Where?'

The inspector traced the addresses on the wall map as the Abel man spoke.

'Yeah,' he confirmed. 'That ties in with what the ESB people said might happen.'

'What's that?' The Abel man was slightly annoyed at the smugness in the policeman's voice.

The inspector explained the warning he had had from the duty engineer at the generating station.

'We'll check them out anyway,' he said calmly, further deflating the excitement of the man in the alarm room. 'Thanks for the call.'

The duty man slammed down the phone. 'Stupid prune,' he snarled at the receiver. 'Why the hell couldn't he have told *us* we might get false alarms.'

The two men had worked together for four years and the desk man knew his companion would offer an explanation in his own good time. To question him directly would be useless. He waited patiently.

'Fire at the Pigeon House. Triggering the alarm systems,' he muttered as he turned and hobbled back towards the wash room. 'Christ, I was just about to go,' he rumbled disgustedly. 'After four bloody days.'

His companion stifled a giggle at the sight of the flapping shirt tail and rumpled trousers.

The converted truck pulled onto the pavement and stopped near the junction of Leinster Street and Lincoln Place. The Land-Rover turned off St Stephen's Green and into Kildare Street, its heavy-treaded tyres protesting sharply. Its passenger door was already open before the vehicle nose-dived to a halt, wheels locked, in front of the two startled policemen standing side by side outside the high railings. Both men kept their lighted cigarettes hidden in cupped hands behind their backs.

Charles Casswell walked briskly around the front of the vehicle as Adrien D'Albe killed the headlights and motor.

The actor adjusted his cap and tugged unnecessarily at the wrists of his leather gloves as he confronted the two open-mouthed gardai. 'Which end of the building are they in?' he demanded briskly.

The two bemused men looked at the demanding face of the army officer and at the stern sergeant standing just behind him with a rifle held across his chest. The driver had jumped from the vehicle and was now crouched against the tailboard, rifle aimed generally at the Leinster House complex, eyes scanning the buildings. A fourth soldier appeared briefly around the canvas side covering, headphones covering his ears and a rubber-cupped microphone over his mouth.

'Eh, who do you mean by "*they*", sir?' the older of the two asked. His companion shifted uncomfortably and looked anxiously towards the complex and back to the moustachioed 'captain' with the West of Ireland accent.

'The intruders, of course,' Casswell snapped irritably.

The policeman looked even more bemused and wished to God someone would tell them what had happened or what to do next. Their walkie-talkies crackled only routine patrol messages, none of them relating to this area.

'Well,' Casswell sighed, looking at both men in turn, 'I only hope for all our sakes that this is a hoax.' He turned to Carl Stolford. 'Sergeant, eyes peeled,' he barked, thumbing towards Leinster House.

'Yes, sir,' said Stolford with appropriate obedience. The sergeant moved to the railings and went down on one knee, rifle barrel poked through the bars. Inside, the military policeman and the security man peered curiously and uncertainly through the glass of the hut. Casswell looked back at the policemen and crooked a finger at them. They followed immediately, discreetly dropping their cigarettes in their footsteps. The 'captain' led them to the rear of the Land-Rover and past the vigilant Adrien D'Albe.

Simon Coates was fiddling busily with the controls of the radio equipment and seemed not to notice the approaching trio. Casswell touched him on the shoulder and the 'radio operator' lifted one earphone to hear his commanding officer.

173

'Is this business still on?' Casswell asked.

'Yes, sir,'

'Check again.'

'*Again*, sir?'

'That's what I said,' Casswell sighed with heavy patience. 'These guards,' he said, glancing at the policemen, 'seem to know nothing about it.'

'Yes, sir.'

'And put it up on the speaker so we can all hear it.'

Coates flicked a few switches and pressed the microphone to his mouth.

'Hello Zero. Hello Zero. This is Blackbird. We're still in position. Verify original report. Over.'

The accent, stage Irish, was not impressive. But fortunately the rubber cup of the microphone muffled Coates' voice sufficiently. The policemen were too concerned anyway with the return message. Coates flicked a switch immediately he finished speaking and pointed to the speaker set into the matt-green console before him. The switch, in fact, operated the cassette tape machine hidden behind the fascia and wired to the speaker.

Peter Phelan's recorded voice broke through the hiss. It had taken several attempts during the recording session in the Rathmines garage to emulate the sing-song of the typical army control voices they had monitored on the doctored Vega radio receiver.

'Hello Blackbird. This is Zero. We still have a confirmation from Garda Control. Museum alarm has been activated. But may be due to voltage drop. Investigate. Other units are on the way. Over.'

'Wilco. Roger. Out,' Coates murmured, and flicked the switch to its original position.

'Right, that's it,' said Casswell, pushing past the two policemen and walking through the narrow side gate towards the glass-walled hut. The military policeman stepped quickly outside and threw up a smart salute. Casswell touched the peak of his own cap in an impatient dismissal of formality and looked beyond him to the uniformed security guard standing in the doorway.

'Get on to your man inside the museum. If you can wake

174

him,' he added sarcastically. 'And get him to cut the alarm. Then tell him to open the door for us.'

'What's wrong, sir?' asked the military policeman.

'The alarm has been activated. Could be a false alarm. Might not, though.'

The security man moved back into the hut quickly and telephoned his colleague inside the building. Casswell beckoned to Stolford and D'Albe to join him at the entrance to the museum. Coates stepped down from the Land-Rover and watched the group moving towards the double doors beyond the stone pillars. The two gardai hovered uncertainly between the street and the hut.

'Tell our Control what's happening,' the older man told his companion.

Garda Control confirmed that alarms were being tripped in different parts of the city because of the power station fire.

In the hut, the military policeman also checked by telephone with his controller.

'Yes,' he was told, 'Dublin Castle warned us this kind of thing might happen. Come back on to us when you've checked it out.'

The group waited for only a few moments before a dishevelled figure appeared beyond the glass doors, peering warily at the unfamiliar faces and then relaxing visibly at the sight of some of his colleagues. A jangle of keys and the group moved through the double spring-loaded doors, led by Stolford and Casswell.

The actor brought them to a halt just inside the doors and beneath the high rotunda. He beckoned to the military policeman who had now drawn his pistol from its white webbing holster.

'Corporal, get back to the telephone and get the Leinster House guard here on the double.'

The order, Casswell knew, was superfluous. Army control would already have alerted its detachment in the basement of the complex. As the non-commissioned officer turned to leave, running rubber-soled boots could be heard approaching. A sergeant and three private soldiers rushed through the door and bunched to a halt before the 'captain'.

'Better late than never, Sergeant,' Casswell reproached the NCO.

'Sorry, sir. HQ just told us.'

'Right,' Casswell hissed in a stage whisper, making elaborate checks of his own Browning pistol. 'Get your men around to the Merrion Street end of the building. They may make their break there.'

'Do we shoot to kill, sir?'

'Standing orders, Sergeant. Standing orders.' Casswell's voice contained just the right level of patronising patience, Stolford thought admiringly. He was superb in the role of condescending officer.

'Corporal,' Casswell turned to the military policeman. 'You go with the guard. And Guard,' he beckoned to one of the gardai, 'you go too. That way we'll be in touch by walkie-talkie. Your colleague can stay with us. Tell us when you're in position, then we'll comb the place systematically towards you in Merrion Street.'

'*Are* there intruders, sir?'

'That's what we're going to find out, Sergeant. It may be just a false alarm. Let's hope so.'

'Yes, sir.'

The sergeant and his detachment hurried from the building and Casswell ordered the museum security man to lock the doors again.

'Murphy,' he said, addressing Adrien D'Albe, 'you stay here in case they come this way past us.'

D'Albe moved to the reception desk beside the door and crouched beside it while Casswell led the rest of the party into the main hall. The guards and policemen scanned the huge room with its glass cases and cabinets of coins, costumes, antique watches, pottery and silver. Casswell and Stolford stared across to the door which, they knew, led to the specially reconstructed wing housing the treasures. The two men looked briefly at each other, understanding, supporting.

'Right,' Casswell whispered to the group, 'this way.'

He moved along the broad balcony circling the recessed mosaic flooring of the hall, the others tiptoeing behind him. The walkie-talkie crackled into life, startling them.

'We're in position now. Over.' The words reverberated around the hall.

'Turn it down,' Casswell hissed to the policeman. 'Tell him we're moving towards him slowly. No sign yet. And tell him not to speak again until we do.'

The policeman repeated the words quietly into the mouth-piece. Casswell waited until he had finished and then levelled the pistol at his head. The young policeman's mouth slackened and then froze, partly open.

'Fuck *me*,' the museum guard whispered. 'I thought...' The words died in his throat when he felt the hard steel of Stolford's rifle barrel nudging him gently behind the ear.

The actor motioned with his left hand for the group to sit on the floor, side by side. The policeman turned to look at Stolford and beyond him for any possibility. The 'sergeant' knew the thoughts in the young man's mind and slowly shook his head. He looked back at Casswell who held out his open hand. The policeman stood motionless and defiant. For the first time Casswell was unsure and it showed on his face.

Stolford broke the impasse. He moved his right hand to the cocking handle on the side of the rifle and worked the mechanism quickly and sharply. The sudden noise made the museum guard jolt. 'For God's sake, do as he says,' he pleaded with the policeman. The other guard nodded agreement. The policeman's body loosened in sudden resignation. He lifted the walkie-talkie off his shoulder and slapped it into Casswell's hand. The three men sat on the marble floor, obeying the gesture of the rifle barrel. Stolford produced a roll of insulating tape from inside his combat jacket and taped their hands and legs, then the mouths and eyes.

Casswell walked quickly back to the entrance to the reception rotunda and slid the keys along the floor to Adrien D'Albe at the front doors. In moments, the Frenchman and Simon Coates had taken the necessary equipment from the Land-Rover and were back inside the museum, the doors locked behind them. Stolford took the keys from D'Albe and tried several times before one fitted and opened the lock on the treasure-wing door; he pushed the tall, wooden door open to reveal a black, felt-lined cave. The treasures, in perspex boxes on concealed stands, glittered in the light from the tiny, hidden spotlights in the ceiling. The four men moved silently through the door and into the first of the five interconnecting rooms, the sheer magnificence of the workmanship of the Bronze Age and Early Christian metalsmiths and jewellers mesmerising and dazzling them. Before, they had moved with haste; now they stepped slowly past each box, unspeaking, hushed in awe of the brilliance and beauty of the pieces.

D'Albe brought them from their reverie. 'We should not delay too long, my friends, no?'

Stolford cleared his throat and bent to the equipment at D'Albe's feet. He took a Black and Decker electric saw from one of the bags and a reeled extension lead. When D'Albe had found a wall socket, he switched on the saw and moved from case to case, carving rectangular slices from the perspex of each. Casswell and Coates laid plastic waste-disposal sacks on the floor and then prepared a special mixture from two cans of chemicals. One contained a clear liquid, Caradol. The second chemical, black and thicker, was Caradate.

'Ready,' Coates said to D'Albe.

The Frenchman went to the first case and waited for Stolford to join him. The American reached into the case and gently lifted the silver and gold Ardagh Chalice from its perch. This eighth-century work of art was uncovered just over a hundred years previously by a young boy working in a potato patch. The silver bowl, studded with precious blue and red stones, was sumptuously decorated with bands of beautifully interlaced and plaited gold.

For just a moment Stolford hesitated, aware of the unique workmanship he now held in his gloved hands. D'Albe and Coates were also entranced by the chalice and what it represented in the worlds of religion, history and art. How many years had it taken to complete? And how many craftsmen painstakingly worked its metals those many centuries ago, casting, engraving, enamelling? Who owned it originally? And why was it buried?

Adrien D'Albe slowly reached out and gently touched the chalice with the tips of his glove. The gesture brought a smile to Stolford's face and the Frenchman grinned self-consciously and moved his hand away quickly. 'Better get on with it,' Stolford whispered hoarsely.

Simon Coates lifted one of the cans and poured a small quantity of the liquid into the plastic sacks held open by D'Albe. Liquid from the second can was added and immediately the mixture began foaming and bubbling in a softly hissing ferment. Stolford pushed the chalice deep into the honey-brown foam and watched it disappear in the rising mixture. D'Albe closed the neck of the sack and fastened it tightly with a length of wire as the foam reached its maximum expansion.

He patted the swollen sack with satisfaction and grinned at Stolford. 'Not bad, eh? Ninety seconds to set and we have a waterproof and shockproof parcel.'

They worked in silence from then on, moving from case to case, putting several items in each sack of expanding foam: brooches, shrines, bells, crosses, torcs, rings, bracelets, sword hilts and scabbards, cups, bowls and collars. Only two processional crosses, with the shafts too long to fit the plastic sacks, were left in the cases.

One item was kept loose: the Tara Brooch. Stolford wrapped this carefully in a square of flannel and then put it into a small, flat padded box. He placed the box inside his combat jacket against his chest.

'Our insurance policy,' he grinned at D'Albe. Behind him, Casswell was on the walkie-talkie, assuring the police and soldiers outside the building that the search of the museum had so far proved fruitless.

Finally they removed the Stowe Missal and the Books of Kells, Dimma and Armagh. Even greater care had to be taken in placing them in the sacks. Each was wrapped in plastic sheeting before immersion in the foam. The most famous and beautiful of the quartet, the Book of Kells, was the work of monks of Saint Columba in the eighth and ninth centuries. The skins of a hundred and fifty calves produced the vellum leaves, and it had taken four principal artists and several other monks a lifetime to complete the four illuminated gospels in Old Latin. Oliver Cromwell's scoutmaster-general, Henry Jones, presented the book to Trinity College in Dublin in 1661 where it had remained on permanent exhibition ever since. In 1953, to safeguard it, the book was bound into four volumes. Two of the volumes had been on a tour of American cities. These would now disappear into the private museums of two of Lutz Feldmann's buyers.

Carl Stolford took a final glance around the exhibition cases while Casswell again radioed the waiting soldiers to ease their impatience. It had taken only eleven minutes to remove a span of history stretching back to fifteen hundred years before the birth of Christ. He stood at the six bulging sacks and then to Adrien D'Albe who stood over the prisoners in the gallery. Again the enormity of what they were doing struck him. He was shaken from his thoughts by Simon Coates who lifted his wrist to the American's face and tapped his watch.

'Right,' said Stolford. 'Let's get it out.'

Charles Casswell walked cautiously to the locked double doors, clutching the security man's keys. D'Albe and Coates moved the six sacks up to the rotunda entrance hall behind him and waited for Stolford, who had gone to a position at the back of the main hall with the three FN rifles. With the insulating tape he secured the weapons to the balustrade, their muzzles pointed towards the high ceiling. He then produced a small coil of nylon fishing line and attached it in small interconnecting loops to the triggers of the weapons, checking that each was cocked and in the 'automatic' mode. Carefully, he moved towards his three companions, feeding the line through his gloved fingers. When he reached the others he nodded readiness. Casswell gently unlocked the doors and stepped cautiously outside. He could see no one but, as he turned to signal all clear, a hoarse voice snapped, 'What's up?'

The actor jumped with fright and swung his gun arm instinctively towards the sound, finger clicking the trigger of the empty pistol, his momentum stumbling him over the uniformed figure ducking defensively under his arm. Behind the glass-panelled doors, the others threw themselves flat when they saw Casswell and the stranger drop to the ground.

'For Chrissake,' the man complained to Casswell as he pulled himself to his feet, rubbing a bruised knee, 'I only asked what was up, not to shoot me arse off!'

'Sorry,' Casswell mumbled, retrieving the fallen pistol and walkie-talkie. 'Who are you?'

From the corner of his eye he could see the faces of the other three peering through the glass panels of the doors.

'I'm from the main buildin',' the middle-aged man replied, standing up and adjusting his uniform. 'I saw yiz all goin' in an' I was wonderin' what was up.'

'Ah, yes,' said Casswell, quickly regaining his composure, 'I'm glad you're here. We've got armed intruders in there. We also found some inflammable material which we're removing in sacks.'

'Jasus,' mused the security man, 'I never thought anyone'd wanna set fire to a museum. The world's gone bloody mad altogether.'

'Yes, well, now that you're here, you can help us.'

'Oh, yeah?' the man was not sure he wanted to be near this trigger-happy officer.

'Yes,' Casswell confirmed, placing a hand on the man's shoulder and directing him away from the doors. 'Slip back to your phone and check with Dublin Castle. See if the reinforcements we asked for are on the way.'

Relief showed on the man's face and he hurried before the officer changed his mind. Casswell released a long sigh through his clenched teeth and turned to wave the others out of the museum.

Stolford was the last to leave. After switching off all the lights. He looped the nylon line through the inside handle of one of the double doors and, holding the other door slightly ajar, he pulled up the slack and tied the end around the second handle.

'That'll get their heads down,' he said with satisfaction, easing the door shut.

'All loaded,' said D'Albe, returning with Coates from the Land-Rover.

'Right,' Stolford said to Casswell, 'do your stuff.'

The actor lifted the walkie-talkie microphone to his mouth and pressed the transmit button. 'Hello, guard. Can you hear me?' The instrument stayed silent. Casswell tried again, with no success.

Shrugging, he said to Stolford, 'Oh, well. It doesn't really matter, does it?'

'It *does* matter. We want all their attention on this building.'

Simon Coates looked closely at the walkie-talkie and tapped Casswell on the shoulder. 'Might help, Charles, if you turned it on,' he said, pointing at the small switch on the transmitter.

'Ah, yes. Quite so, dear boy,' said the unperturbed actor.

Stolford looked skyward and shook his head in disbelief.

'Hello, Guard,' Casswell whispered into the walkie-talkie.

'Hello, sir,' the policeman at the other side of the building immediately replied.

'We've located intruders. They're in a central room beyond the main exhibition hall. We may need help. They're armed. So you lads get back around this side of the building and follow us inside.'

'Right,' the young policeman answered eagerly.

Casswell switched off the small transmitter and followed the others quickly to the Land-Rover. D'Albe took the wheel with Stolford beside him. Casswell climbed into the back with Coates and reached for the microphone on the radio equipment.

'It's set?' he asked Coates. His friend glanced at the dials and nodded.

'What call signs?'

'Take your pick,' said Coates, shrugging. 'There's a patrol calling itself Magpie. Or there's Wolfhound. Or...'

'Hello Zero. Hello Zero. This is Wolfhound. Over.'

'Hello Wolfhound,' the army controller in Cathal Brugha Barracks replied.

'Hello Zero. We're at the National Museum in Kildare Street, assisting the Leinster House detachment. There are armed intruders, dressed as troops. We need assistance. Over.'

'Wait, Wolfhound.'

Seconds passed, the four men sitting motionless in the Land-Rover, its engine ticking over. Less than half a mile away, Peter Phelan and Edouard Dufour sat in the back of the converted truck wondering if the operation had stalled. Phelan glanced again at the silent walkie-talkie beside the modified Vega domestic radio, which was chattering at regular intervals with the voices of the various army patrols giving their current positions around the city. Both men stiffened when they heard Charles Casswell's voice. Now they also waited for the army controller to answer.

Instead a different voice broke the silence. 'Hello Zero. *This* is Wolfhound and we're nowhere near the museum. We're at Drumcondra.'

In the Land-Rover Charles Casswell smiled. Simon Coates said smirkingly, 'Blackbird.'

Casswell pressed the transmit button on the microphone.

'Hello Zero. This is Blackbird. We confirm that report. We had visual contact with Wolfhound at Drumcondra a few minutes ago. Over.

Now another perplexed voice joined the exchange. 'Hello Zero. That report is inaccurate. *We're* Blackbird and we're at Ballsbridge. Over.'

Casswell spoke again, this time with a measure of annoyance.

'Hello Zero. This is Wolfhound. Repeat *Wolfhound*. And we're at the museum. Verify with Garda Control. Over.'

The actor leaned forward and tapped Carl Stolford on the shoulder. The American extended the walkie-talkie aerial upwards through the open side window and whispered, 'Green.'

D'Albe gunned the engine and pulled sharply away from the kerb. Casswell and Coates grinned broadly at each other, imagining the confusion at the Army's Security Network Headquarters.

At the junction of Kildare Street and Leinster Street the operation almost came to an abrupt end. A second Land-Rover rounded the corner and into the one-way street the wrong way. D'Albe jerked the steering wheel to the left and mounted the pavement, bouncing onto the roadway again beyond the apex of the corner. Casswell and Coates were thrown up against the canvas roofing and landed among the plastic sacks in a tangle of arms and legs, then crashed forward into the partition behind the front compartment as D'Albe hit the brakes.

'Typical French...!' Casswell snapped, his indignation cut short as the vehicle went into reverse, throwing the actor and his friend into the partition again.

In Kildare Street, the other Land-Rover had slid to a halt, one front wheel on the pavement. Its sergeant commander, pale-faced and shaken, resisted the obvious complaint. It was he who had told the driver to ignore the one-way regulations.

He pointed a finger towards the museum building. The driver reversed the vehicle off the pavement and moved away, mouthing silent condemnation of NCOs in general and sergeants in particular. Behind him, a soldier pressed a microphone to his mouth.

'Hello Zero. This is Rosebud. We're in Kildare Street. Another military vehicle has just mis…has just passed us…'

In the army control room, the duty officer instructed the operator to put every patrol on 'hold'. He lifted the telephone and asked the switchboard operator to connect him to the commanding officer.

A sleepy and annoyed voice growled from a south-city bungalow.

'Hello, sir. Lieutenant Brady here at HQ. Bit of a problem, I'm afraid…'

In the converted truck, Phelan and Dufour had heard the word 'green' and had thrown open the rear doors. Then they slid out the steel ramps and listened to the sound of the approaching vehicle, its engine revolutions rising and falling with each harsh gear change. The headlights lit the sides of the buildings in the narrow street before the vehicle appeared around the final corner, moving fast, too fast.

D'Albe tried to correct the line of approach but knew even as he hauled on the wheel and jammed his foot on the brake pedal that he had screwed it. The Land-Rover straddled the outermost ramp and ran screeching up along it, sparks cascading from the chassis and the engine cutting out.

Casswell pulled himself upright for the third time in ninety seconds and gripped the tailboard grimly. Coates, wide-eyed, licked his lips and decided to stay prone beneath the plastic sacks.

As D'Albe feverishly tried to restart the engine, the actor drawled sarcastically, 'Tell you what, dear boy. You stay *here* and *we'll* bring the truck to *you*.'

The engine restarted, preventing a reply; the Land-Rover backed off the ramp and D'Albe ran it harshly up into the truck, Phelan and Dufour disconnecting the ramps and sliding them up along the right side of the floor before closing the rear doors again. Phelan repeated the operation he had carried out at the power station, the roof-mounted winch lifting the three-quarters-of-a-ton steel cover set into the pavement. This time Dufour squatted beneath the truck, guiding the weight to one side. With the aid of a torch, he peered down into the deep hole and the rushing water at the bottom. He pulled himself up into the truck where the others had already discarded their army uniforms to reveal the black wetsuits beneath.

'It's alright, my friends,' said the Frenchman. 'No flooding.'

Carl Stolford nodded and turned back to the radio equipment in the Land-Rover. The radio messages were jamming the airwaves as Charles Casswell repeated his spurious messages to the army controller. Peter Phelan had guessed correctly: only some of the Army's patrols had scramblers fitted to their radios. Consequently, a call by headquarters to switch to scrambled transmissions as a means of isolating the bogus caller left many of the soldiers just as powerless as before in protesting their authenticity.

At the front doors of the National Museum, the Leinster House detachment had smiled with relief at the arrival of the mobile patrol. But the smiles faded when they were disarmed and held at gunpoint until their identity was established through their pocketbooks and by verification with headquarters. By now, two more patrols had arrived and leapt from their vehicles and repeated the identification process on the earlier arrivals. But worse was yet to come, in the form of two car-loads of uniformed and Special Branch civil policemen who crouched behind the railing and trained Uzi submachine guns on the soldiers and demanded their surrender.

It was, in the words of the inspector who roused Deputy Commissioner George Swann from his sleep, a 'bloody shambles of cowboys and Indians'.

It would get worse.

Chapter Eleven

Edouard Dufour and Simon Coates stood at the foot of the thirteen iron rungs at the bottom of the manhole, and assembled the bags and sacks of equipment lowered to them from the trapdoor in the floor of the truck high above their heads.

The sewer water flowed gently around the ankles of their rubber wetsuits as they worked in the tunnel, stacking the gear and mentally checking the list for possible omissions. Above them Peter Phelan prepared the final loads for Carl Stolford to transfer. The treasures, in their protective covering of hardened foam and plastic bags, were tied at two-foot intervals onto a nylon line and eased gently into the waiting hands seven and a half feet below street level.

Charles Casswell had made five radio transmissions since the Land-Rover had been driven up into the truck. Each was made with a differing accent and each claimed the identity of any army patrol, denying its true geographical position or moving it from its last reported position. It was not a good night for the officers and men of the Signals Corps at the Security Network Headquarters.

The actor joined Stolford in the descent of the manhole and stood watching as the steel cover moved back into place and shut out the faint light from the street. They had a long way to go in the coming hours.

Phelan started the truck and moved away, D'Albe in the passenger seat beside him, the Tara Brooch hidden behind the dashboard panel. The men in the tunnel heard the murmur of the engine and waited until the sound faded. Then they began moving north-westwards with their load, beneath Leinster Street and Nassau Street. Stolford led the procession, followed by Coates and Casswell. Dufour brought up the rear.

The smell in the sewer, although strong, was not as bad as they had anticipated, but several times weird sounds echoing down the black tunnel froze them to statues. It seemed they were not alone. With each sound they switched off their flashlights and strained their hearing above the water to identify the reverberating booms and clangs in the darkness ahead.

'Traffic running over manhole covers in the streets,' Stolford said to Coates reassuringly. 'The sound carries for miles down here.'

Coates relayed the explanation to the others but progress was still slow and slippery. Casswell was the first to fall face first into the sewage, his rubber-encased feet skidding backwards on the sediment beneath the water. He rose, spluttering and nauseated, and with the help of Dufour.

'OK, my English rose?' the diver smirked. Casswell shrugged off the steadying hand and moved on again, coughing and spitting in a vain attempt to rid his throat of the foul taste. The others would suffer similar indignities in the next few minutes.

Everything down here was exaggerated: sound, sight, smell. And it brought each man's phobia to the fore. Edouard Dufour, at the rear of the column, shone his flashlight around the walls in wide arcs, searching. Whenever he found a crevice or hole he held his breath and stole past, pressing himself against the opposite wall. It was during one of these evasive moves that his nerve broke and erupted in hysteria.

He had pushed himself against the left wall, hip and shoulder scraping along the brickwork and one gloved hand sliding forward, palm flat, along the masonry, flashlight beam fixed on a dark gap in the bricks of the opposite wall. As he took another sidestep, his left foot slid out into the centre of the tunnel, bringing him down on his backside. Instinctively, he grabbed for the wall behind him. His fingers wedged in a crevice, suspending him by one arm, rubber feet flailing to regain his footing.

The brown rat, one and half pounds in weight and sixteen inches from nose to tip of tail, had been crouching in the crevice, frightened by the noise of the passing humans. Suddenly the rubber fingers appeared in the entrance, threatening, attacking. The rodent, terrified, made a bolt for safety, along the rubber fingers of the diver and up along his arm, behind his neck and down into the running water beyond the screaming man.

Stolford turned and splashed back along the tunnel, discarding his equipment and pushing past Coates and Casswell who stood mesmerised by the screams of the Frenchman. Dufour was shouting obscenities at the darkness and smashing his flashlight into the shallow water, its beam catching the wide-eyed stare of Casswell, transfixed by the demented action.

'It's gone, Edouard,' Stolford shouted at Dufour, grabbing his thrashing wrist from behind and pulling him back against his chest. 'Alright, Edouard. It's gone.'

The Frenchman's blocky body was quivering. Stolford held it until the trembling eased.

The Leinster House complex was now in a state of siege, cordoned off from the rest of the city by army and garda vehicles. Blue roof lights diluted the white glare of spotlamp beams on the windows and stonework of the National Museum. Behind the lights young soldiers in black berets and flak jackets crouched, fingers extended along trigger guards, set faces betraying excitement and uncertainty. Behind the troops, Special Branch and Central Detective Unit detectives stood in a loose group listening to the descriptions being given to the detective chief superintendent and the two senior army officers.

'The so-called sergeant had tattoos on both wrists, sir,' the military policeman said.

'And the captain had a black moustache...and a gold filling in his front tooth,' the garda added.

'The soldier with them had a kind of broad nose, like a boxer...'

The voice of the guard commander sergeant faded and died when he caught the unforgiving stare of the lieutenant-colonel behind the chief superintendent. Tomorrow would be a long day for a sergeant who had taken orders from an imposter and left the museum defenceless.

Conversation stopped abruptly with the arrival of the fast-moving black Ford Granada. The passenger door swung open before the vehicle had stopped and a squat figure in civilian clothing emerged. Assistant Commissioner Tom O'Malley, his square face beneath the neat silver hair set in an expression of challenging belligerence, hands dug deep in his overcoat pockets, strode towards the waiting group.

'So?' The question, to Chief Superintendent Dan Sullivan, was both enquiry and dare. Sullivan, who was O'Malley's assistant, was used to the brusque manner of his senior officer on such occasions and was no longer awed by the irascibility of the man.

'We have it sealed off, sir,' he said calmly. 'We don't yet know how many are still in there.'

'Armed?'

'Yes, sir, but no shooting yet.'

'And our uniformed man, and the museum staff?'

'No sign.'

'So, we really don't know if there *is* anyone still inside or whether they all took off in that Land-Rover. Right?'

The question was pointless. Both men knew it. Sullivan made no reply. O'Malley moved to the edge of the group and glanced at the museum and its surrounding and eager fire-power. The chief superintendent, at his side, voiced his own thoughts.

'Real smart-asses, sir,' he said with feeling. 'Ballsed-up the army radio network, the electricity grid, security firms...'

'And *our* lot,' the assistant commissioner reminded him.

Sullivan nodded grimly.

'Right, Dan,' said O'Malley, folding his arms tightly across his chest. 'I want this lot. And I want them soon.'

'No chitchat?'

'Look,' he said, taking the chief superintendent by the elbow and moving him further from earshot, 'the Press are already at the barricades down the road. By tomorrow morning the world's television will be here. We can't even guard government buildings, they'll be saying.'

'I know,' Sullivan agreed despondently.

'I'll sign the forms, Dan,' O'Malley assured him.

'Right.'

The chief superintendent turned to move back to his men but was stopped by a neatly dressed man who stepped before him.

'Chief Superintendent Sullivan?'

'Yes.'

'I'm Robert Nugent, Director of the National Museum.

'Ah, yes, Mr Nugent. Thanks for getting here so quickly.'

Tom O'Malley turned to hear what the director would say. The little man nodded to the assistant commissioner and smiled briefly. He looked back to the detective and asked anxiously, 'Are the treasures safe?'

'We honestly don't know, Mr Nugent,' Sullivan answered flatly, 'we haven't been inside yet...'

'Not *yet*?' Nugent asked incredulously. 'My God, those treasures are priceless. They...'

'We have men inside, Mr Nugent,' Sullivan interrupted sharply, 'who may already be dead. The intruders were armed. My first concern is for my men.'

Tom O'Malley stepped up alongside his colleague and smiled at the museum director. 'We've set up garda and army roadblocks on all routes out of the city, Mr Nugent. Airports and harbours are also being watched.'

'In other words,' said Nugent dejectedly, 'you *know* the treasures have been taken.'

'We'll know in a few minutes' time, Mr Nugent. In the meantime, we'd appreciate it if you didn't talk to the Press ...for a variety of reasons.'

The director nodded and walked away. Chief Superintendent Sullivan called to one of the men in the waiting group of detectives. The man, one of the youngest and toughest inspectors in the Garda Siochana, listened to the terse instructions. He was one of the group of forty-two men known officially as the Task Force.

The young inspector briefed his own men first and then said a few words to the captain in charge of the army sharpshooters. All of them put on gas masks and steel helmets and formed up outside the railings. The detectives wearing bullet-proof jackets would lead the assault.

Inside the building, the two security guards and the policeman had given up their attempts to free their wrists and legs from the insulating tape bondage. The material had twisted and narrowed into painful bands which cut into their flesh and muscles, but it would not break. Now the policeman had wriggled and twisted his body down between those of the other men and strained to bring his mouth within range of the groping fingers behind their backs. With one final heave, which brought pained groans from the guards, he forced his face down against the wrists of the older man. He winced as the tape was torn from his mouth and then from across his eyes.

'Right,' he said, wriggling upright again, 'let's get out of here.'

All three began a grotesque, crab-like shuffle along the wooden floor and out through the open doorway onto the marble flooring of the landing, each in turn pushing or pulling the collective body, the security men still blindfolded.

Outside, the detectives ran in pairs up the footpath and crouched, sheltered, against the high stone columns fronting the building. The soldiers moved up behind them, some hugging the wall beyond the pillars, others throwing themselves flat and squirming along the steps to get into firing positions.

The tangled group inside the museum rounded the corner of the entrance hall as the first two detectives ran for cover and threw themselves flat against the door pillars to peer one-eyed through the edges of the glass panels. At first they saw nothing in the gloom. Then they became aware of a movement to one side of the hall and ducked back instinctively.

Garda McIvoy saw the silhouettes of the steel helmets and gas masks and shouted, 'It's all right. They've cleared out. This is Garda McIvoy.'

For a moment the detectives hesitated. The name meant nothing to them. The Task Force inspector had heard the voice also. The tone was not that of a hoaxer, but the intruders had already shown they were no ordinary impersonators. He moved cautiously from behind a pillar and in two strides was pressed tightly alongside the detectives on the right of the double doors.

'Who'd you say you were?' The inspector's voice was muffled by the rubber of the gas mask, but the words were distinguishable.

'Garda John McIvoy, number four-six-nine. Store Street station.'

'Don't move. Not even an inch,' the inspector shouted, and thumbed a direction to the detective opposite him.

The detective braced himself and cleared the first four steps in one leap to reach the sanctuary of the first pillar. He moved quickly down the path and spoke to Chief Superintendent Sullivan. Garda McIvoy's colleague was called from one of the groups of uniformed men behind the police and army vehicles. He confirmed the name, number and the station of his colleague. The detective returned to the inspector and nodded confirmation.

'How many of you are there?' the inspector called.

'Three. Me and two museum staff.'

'Right,' the inspector called. 'When I tell you, walk out slowly, one at a time, hands high.'

'We can't,' the garda answered as the detectives moved back. 'We're tied together. We can't even stand up.'

The inspector paused and then said grimly, 'Well, you'd better be John McIvoy.'

'I am, for God's sake,' the garda snapped, annoyed yet anxious. He knew from reputation the uncompromising methods of the Task Force, and the helmets and gas masks had confirmed that these were the men on the other side of the doors.

The inspector looked behind him and motioned the surrounding group of detectives and troops to move in closer. Then he held his left hand parallel to the ground, clenched his fist and made a single, forward piston stroke with his forearm. The two men with him thumbed acknowledgement and gripped their Uzi submachine guns more tightly.

'NOW!' the inspector shouted.

The men ducked low and threw their shoulders against the doors, bundling onto the marble floor inside and rolling quickly to make difficult targets for the rifle bullets which whined off the plaster and stonework of the high rooms. The fishing line, attached to the handles of the double doors and to the triggers of the FH's across the lofty main hall, had activated the weapons. As the spring-loaded doors swung shut again, the rifles stopped firing.

'Bastards,' hissed the inspector, outside the doors, thinking about the gunmen inside who had lied and led his men into an ambush. He smashed the muzzle of his Uzi against one of the panels but the toughened glass remained intact, the resistance jarring his wrists. His obscenities were lost in the second eruption of firing inside, his men blazing at the spots pinpointed by the flashes at the back of the hall. The detectives stopped to fit fresh magazines to their weapons, one of them calling to the 'gunmen' to surrender. His demand was greeted with silence. Had the inspector waited just one second longer he would have heard the pleading voice of Garda McIvoy from behind the entrance hall corner. But the Task Force officer chose the moment of ceasefire to join his men inside, dropping onto his knees and diving against the doors. Immediately the gunfire re-erupted from the exhibition hall, answered quickly by the stuttering of the submachine guns. The inspector rolled once and squirmed to one side to steady his aim and empty his own gun at the orange-white streaks. The noise was ear-piercing, the different calibre rounds reverberating around the rooms, the singing ricochets smacking off the granite and marble and smashing the glass display cases around the circular balcony. The third ceasefire's silence gradually penetrated their aching eardrums, and with it the terrified voice of Garda McIvoy.

'It's a trick, for Christ's sake,' he howled from between the bodies of the security men taped to him. 'There's no one here except us. They've gone, Stop firing, for God's sake.'

The inspector twisted around to look back at the doors. In the gloom the fishing line was invisible. He slid cautiously towards the doors and reached upwards slowly to the handles until his fingers proved the truth of the young policeman's claim. He tugged sharply on the line and ducked. Nothing. The rifle magazines were empty. The inspector tugged again and this time heard the clicks of the firing mechanisms.

'He's right. Stop firing,' he shouted through his gas mask. The guns went quiet.

'O'Brien.'

'Yes, sir?'

'McIvoy is right. It's a trip wire. Get over to them and cut them loose.'

'Yes, sir.' The detective lifted himself from the floor and walked around the corner to the bundled trio.

'Keating.'

'Yes, sir?'

'Try and get some lights working. The room over on the left, maybe.'

The second detective moved to the room while the inspector pulled off his helmet and mask. The sudden exposure to the drifting haze of gunsmoke made him cough. He rubbed his watering eyes and walked dejectedly towards the exhibition hall. In the gloom he could make out O'Brien working with a penknife on the bound wrists of the three men.

'GO!'

The word spun him around towards the doors, which burst inwards under the weight of an army officer and six soldiers. Instinct made the inspector throw himself sideways onto the four men behind the wall.

'Stand still, or we fire!' the officer barked.

'Jesus wept,' the inspector heard McIvoy ululate, 'here we go again.'

The sound had changed now to a deep and distant rumble akin to a subway train approaching a station. And, like the subway, no certainty as to when the source of the noise would burst into view.

There was less complaining now. The four men had become accustomed to the smell and the slippery floors of the tunnels. Exertion had taken its toll. Speech had become a luxury none could physically afford, especially the out-of-condition Charles Casswell and Simon Coates. Rests had become more frequent despite the urgings of Carl Stolford. They had travelled north-westwards beneath Nassau Street, north under Grafton Street and then eastwards down College Street before turning north again below D'Olier Street to its meeting with O'Connell Bridge. Late-night traffic vibrated the tunnel's ceilings five feet beneath the roadways, adding to the increased rumble ahead.

Now, beneath Burgh Quay and following the flow of the River Liffey towards the sea, they were within a hundred yards of their biggest test and the reason for the tightening of their stomach muscles.

The tunnels through which they had passed had varied in

size. All were ovoid, the greatest width across the roof. Some, such as D'Olier Street, were as low as three feet in height, and slowed the pace to an agonised half-crouch, half-crawl. Their bodies were bruised from the rough brickwork and their arms and legs ached from pulling the equipment and from the awkward movements imposed by the cramped conditions.

Casswell stopped again, sinking to his knees and leaning against the wall. His breathing was tortured, short gasps sucked through his open mouth. He ran a gloved hand across his forehead to divert the salty trickle which stung his eyes. Dufour moved up alongside the actor and placed a hand on his shoulder. The noise ahead obliterated his words. Casswell looked beyond the torchlight to the diver's streaked face and then back to the silhouettes of the other two men, their lights throwing beams around the tunnel as they moved away. He steadied his breathing and gripped the nylon rope more tightly before lurching off the wall to follow. Dufour waited for the actor's froth-covered equipment to clear his own and then moved after his reeling colleague.

In minutes the distant rumble had become a close and deafening roar. A few yards further along the tunnel Stolford brought the procession to a halt. Coates moved to his side and jerked into stillness, stunned by what the flashlight revealed.

Behind them, Casswell on hands and knees in the stream, stared only at the water pouring between his forearms, fighting to regulate his breathing. He knew what was ahead, the knowledge adding to his respiratory difficulty. Dufour pushed past him, pausing only to hand over his nylon towing line, and stepped over the foam-filled plastic bags to reach the other two men and squeeze between their crouching bodies.

For moments he did not move, staring at the turbulent water, rising in waves where the other two streams joined the main flow. Here the entire city's sewage and drainage met to pour eastwards beneath Pigeon House Road to the sewage treatment works and then into the sea. He moved cautiously down the six-foot-high approach tunnel, his legs caught by increasing currents as he neared the point where the three small rivers met to become one. Twice he fell, sliding sideways onto his back, his smooth wetsuit offering no hold on the slimy sludge of the floor, twisting onto his stomach to claw his way back.

Legs spread, he inched towards the black hole in the floor at the end of the tunnel. Three feet from the edge he stopped and shone his light into the gaping darkness beyond the surging water. The light was useless, the black water inpenetrable, the beam reflecting from the spray and foam.

This hole was the mouth of a pipe three and half feet in diameter which plunged vertically for sixteen feet, turned northwards for one hundred and thirty-five feet beneath the River Liffey bed and rose again for nineteen feet where it met the drainage system on the other side of the city. It was this obstacle which would test Dufour's courage and was the reason for his recruitment to the team.

This was the syphon.

Peter Phelan smiled and moved the truck slowly past the police cars parked diagonally across the roadway. The two gardai, wearing orange reflective jackets, had asked him a few routine questions. Adrien D'Albe, in the passenger seat, had remained silent. One of the policemen had climbed up to peer over the tailboard of the truck, then jumped down, satisfied that this vehicle was not the one seen earlier in Leinster Street. Besides, they were looking for a Land-Rover or a Post Office engineer's van, not an open-backed truck owned by Matthews Pressure Cleaners. But the mood at headquarters had been clearly indicated by the radio messages snapped out on the ultra high frequency wavelength. Heads would roll all the way down the line because of this caper. At times like this, fortunately rare, self-preservation shared equal billing with detection initiative. The policeman scribbled the registration number in his notebook, together with a brief description of the occupants, and the name of the firm.

Beyond the checkpoint, a group of armed soldiers stood near a Land-Rover, watching the police activities, their cynicism increasing with each search and passing minute. Cars were searched further along the road at a second checkpoint in case the thieves had changed vehicles en route. But it was a farce, the veteran army sergeant knew. A bloody farce.

Twenty minutes earlier, the 'Post Office van' had driven

from Leinster Street to Hanover Quay, the outlet of the Grand Canal in the south side of the River Liffey. There the canopy of the 'van' was thrown into the deep water of the canal basin. The Land-Rover, with its load of radio and tape equipment, discarded army uniforms and Casswell's pistol, was driven off the truck at grand Canal Quay on the other side of the basin and hidden near a coal distributor's depot. The steel ramps followed the canopy to the muddy bed of the canal. All that remained on the truck now was equipment used by the cover firm of pressure cleaners. The sockets which had been welded to the walls of the truck to hold the canopy now secured the wooden tool boxes. The white adhesive plastic with the black initials PT and the fleet number T284 had been stripped from each door to reveal the painted words 'Matthews Pressure Cleaners'. Finally the number plates were switched to the true registration.

The Post Office engineer's van no longer existed.

Sebastian Stanley, the American art dealer, lay on his hotel bed, pondering the latest telephone call from The Voice. The call, like previous ones, had been taken in a predetermined public booth and was obviously local. But there was no way, or any need, for Stanley to identify the caller.

He had returned to Dublin the previous day to arrange for the first shipment of paintings and sculpture to the Irish-only gallery in San Francisco. Walshe, the Arts Council official, had beamed his customary welcome and confirmed the readiness of the first eighty exhibits for dispatch to the United States. Stanley immediately wired a summons to the seven men and two women in New York who would travel to Ireland to supervise the packing and loading of the art pieces. Three of the 'packers' were expert metal-workers with no police records. Unknown to the others, they would, on a subsequent trip, open steel and bronze statues and place the Irish art treasures inside. But not on this visit, or the next, or the next. Irish police and customs officials would be wary of any shipments after the biggest art theft in history. Checks would be made. X-ray examination of the statues would reveal only that the metal pieces had, not surprisingly, metal fillings. But officials would probably insist on opening one or two of the statues, so two or three shipments must be found to be 'clean'. This type of searching would, in fact, be a bonus: any Irish artist who might visit the art gallery in San Francisco to see his work on display might, despite the workmanship of Stanley's men, notice that his sculpture had been tampered with. A police search during shipment would be sufficient explanation to the artist.

Naturally, during the first searches Sebastian Stanley would be suitably horrified that original works of art should be treated in this way. His protestations would, undoubtedly, be supported by Walshe, the Arts Council and the art world in general. With luck, sufficient pressure would bring a halt to the 'unwarranted and inexcusable' police behaviour. Then the art treasures would be taken from their hiding-place beneath St Michan's Church and shipped to the United States with the next batch of items for the gallery in San Francisco.

Other less complicated arrangements had been considered but abandoned during the planning sessions between The Voice and the New York procurer, Lutz Feldmann: a light aircraft taking off from a field somewhere in a remote part of Ireland and dropping the suitably protected treasures into the sea beside a waiting boat; or taking them directly onto a launch from a deserted beach, as the arms and equipment had been landed by Edouard Dufour at Kilcoole. But the Garda Siochana and coastguard service would be especially vigilant during the next six to twelve months.

He glanced at the bedside clock. One twenty-two. The temptation was great to leave the hotel and walk to the National Museum to see the frantic activity. Fifteen minutes earlier, on his return from supper and drinks with Walshe, the hotel porter had garbled the first news of the operation.

'They've nicked the art treasures, Mr Stanley.'

'Who?'

'Dunno. But they must be some operators. The cops are hoppin', I hear.' The porter chuckled with the glee that only a Dubliner could feel at a time like that.

Sebastian Stanley smiled now at the memory and switched on the radio in the bedside console. At half-past one the disc jockey with the mid-Atlantic accent and sinus affliction interrupted the frenzied periphrases of a third-rate rock group.

'And there we leave out star guests for just a moment to

bring you the latest on the National Museum robbery... It's now been confirmed by a senior Garda officer that the thieves, who were dressed as soldiers, *did* get away with part of the Irish art treasure collection. Exactly how much was taken hasn't been disclosed but according to some sources it was *considerable*. And now back to our musical guests...'

Stanley lay back on the pillows, eyes closed and chest heaving with mirth. Now the rock group distorting the loudspeaker seemed almost musical.

Beneath the single light bulb in the lockup garage in Rathmines, Peter Phelan and Adrien D'Albe huddled over a small transistor radio and smiled mischievously at each other.

The bedside telephone jangled for the third time in the early hours in the suburban house on the south side of the city, this call halting the final showdown between Blackjack Kelly and the hero, Tex Masters.

Deputy Commissioner George Swann placed the book face-down on the bed cover and reached across for the receiver. His wife stirred to register her customary and futile annoyance, burrowing her head more deeply into the pillow. Every night the same, she lamented. Cowboy books and telephone calls.

'Yes,' Swann said quietly into the mouthpiece

'Inspector Mulvihill here again, sir. You asked me to keep you in touch with developments...'

'Yes, go on,' Swann interrupted.

'Well, sir, like I said earlier, it seems the gang practically cleared out the art collection. But our lads've had a break. An eyewitness saw a Land-Rover driving up into the back of a Post Office truck in Lincoln Place. No sign, though, of either since then.'

'And it's taken all this time to find an eyewitness?' Swann asked incredulously.

'Not exactly, sir. You see, the witness had a few drinks on him. He'd been sleeping it off in a doorway when the Land-Rover tried to drive up into the truck and made a ba...made a mess of the first attempt. Woke up our friend.'

'So? That still doesn't explain the delay, does it?'

'The delay, sir, was caused by the fact that the eyewitness

was arrested,' said Mulvihill bleakly.

'Hold it there,' Swann said wearily, placing the telephone on the bedclothes covering his raised, bony knees. He rubbed his eyes slowly with his fingertips, sighed, took a deep breath and lifted the receiver to his ear again. 'Right,' he resumed carefully, 'let me verify our progress so far. We found an eyewitness?'

'Yes, sir,' Mulvihill confirmed happily.

'Who saw an *army* vehicle driving up into the back of a *Post Office* vehicle, right?'

'Correct, sir.'

'And so we promptly arrested that same eyewitness. Right, so far, Inspector?'

'Absolutely right, sir,' Inspector Mulvihill confirmed. Concise and precise reporting had always been his forte. He allowed himself a pleasurable smile.

Swann waited for him to continue. Seconds passed rhythmically to the tempo of breaths exhaled through the nostrils of the inspector. Five seconds evaporated the deputy commissioner's patience.

'WELL?' he bellowed, jerking Mulvihill and Mrs Swann, the latter burrowing protestingly into the pillow again.

'Sir?' Mulvihill clearly did not know what was expected of him.

Swann covered the mouthpiece and hissed, 'Oh, sweet *fuck!*', bringing aggressive moaning from the bedclothes, a registering of disgust at his lamentable lapse into old ways.

Gently, gently, Swann told himself, and uncovered the mouthpiece. With exaggerated mellifluence, he asked, '*Why* was the eyewitness arrested, Inspector?'

''Cause he got sick, sir,' Mulvihill answered simply, then allowed himself a rare elaboration, 'on a young garda's shoes.'

Why Inspector Ulick Cathal Fergus Mulvihill had ever been promoted beyond the rank of recruit and why he had eventually been transferred from Central Stores were questions never satisfactorily answered. The senior officer who had sanctioned the transfer shortly before his own retirement denied emphatically any personal interest in Mulvihill. It was therefore assumed, generally, that it had been the officer's parting shot at the establishment or at certain individuals who had displeased him in some way over the years. The only consolation–and the only reason Swann had not kicked Mulvihill back to Central Stores–was that he was a useful informant, inexplicably loyal to him, and thus vital to the deputy commissioner in his politically sensitive position in the Garda Siochana.

'Go on, Ulick,' Swann encouraged Mulvihill more gently.

'Yes, sir,' Mulvihill snapped obediently, flattered by Swann's use of his first name. 'The eyewitness just doubled over, sir...'

'Doubled over?'

'And threw up, sir. On the garda's shoes.'

'Yes, I get the picture,' said Swann, suddenly very tired. Another tack was needed. 'Where did this happen?'

The tack worked. 'Near Pearse Street Garda Station, sir. The eyewitness went there to report what he'd seen, but threw up before he could say anything...on the garda's shoes, that is. So he was nicked...for drunkenness and damage to...'

'Yes,' Swann cut across hastily. 'So, how did they know he was...?'

'An eyewitness? Well, he eventually managed to tell his story, sir.'

'Oh, good,' Swann enthused, but the sarcasm was lost on the inspector. 'So what's happening now?'

'Frogmen, sir.'

'*Frogmen?*'

'Yes, sir.'

'Alright, tell me,' Swann said resignedly, leaning back against the headboard.

'Apparently there was a manhole near, or underneath, the Post Office truck. Could be, sir, that the gang hid the art treasures in the manhole or in the sewers.'

'So they've called in our underwater lot?'

'Yes, sir. And your Task Force.'

'Yes,' Swann replied, 'I know about that. Headquarters phoned me earlier for permission. And no sign yet of the Land-Rover or truck, I suppose?'

'Not yet, sir.'

'Well, thanks for the information.' said Swann, leaning towards the bedside table. 'And, as I said to you in the earlier call, don't mention that you phoned. They know where I am if they need me.'

'I understand, sir,' Mulvihill confirmed warmly.

Swann moved to replace the receiver but stopped in mid-movement. 'Who's in charge at the scene, by the way?'

'Assistant Commissioner O'Malley, sir.'

'I see,' Swann acknowledged flatly. 'And our rabies scare, any more attacks?'

'Not tonight, sir.'

For some moments after he had terminated the call, Swann sat with his hands clasped behind his head, a grin creasing his normally stern face. Then the rumble of suppressed mirth erupted into laughter, which startled his wife and caused her to burrow again.

'O'Malley,' mused Swann aloud, savouring the image. 'A *right* prick.'

His wife left her burrow in a flurry of sheets and greased face, and jowl-length hair curlers which had always reminded her husband of elephant tusks.

'That's quite enough, George,' she lisped through teethless gums. 'You promised.'

'Yes, dear,' Swann acknowledged automatically, placing the Tex Masters book on the table and switching off the light.

While his wife burrowed, she continued to admonish him, his colleagues and the work he so obviously enjoyed.

'... just no consideration...'

'No, dear,' he recited absently.

'...cowboy books and telephone calls...'

'Yes, dear.'

'... and obscene language...'

But George Swann's thoughts were still on the image of O'Malley and he could contain the laughter no longer.

'*George!*' his wife hissed into the sheets.

Chapter Twelve

The first of the rubber-suited men paused at the open manhole in Lincoln Place and waited for his three companions to join him at the edge of the square opening. Unsure and resentful, they handled the Uzi submachine guns awkwardly. This was the first time that members of the Garda Sub-Aqua Unit had been armed. It showed. Searching sea and river beds for bodies or evidence was their normal function, not chasing thieves through tunnels of diluted urine and excrement.

'Sir,' the leader of the quartet said deferentially to the heavy-jowled figure of Assistant Commissioner Tom O'Malley, standing inside the semi-circle of powerful lamps which had brought premature daylight to the street.

'Yes?'

'I was just wonderin' if it's wise for us to carry these,' the frogman said respectfully, patting the Uzi on his hip. 'We've only used them once, on the range, y'see and..'

'Oh, don't worry, Sergeant,' O'Malley interrupted sarcastically, 'I promise not to tell the robbers.'

'Yes, sir,' the diver murmured blushingly, aware of the snickering among the ranks of the other policemen. 'Come on, lads.'

All four pulled their face masks into position and climbed down into the sewer, their air bottles clanging against the lip of the manhole.

O'Malley turned back to the dishevelled figure at his side. 'Right, Mr Engineer,' he said patronisingly, 'you were saying?'

'I was saying, Assistant Commissioner,' the man replied tolerantly, 'there are one thousand miles of sewers beneath this city, seventy miles of them big enough to take a man.'

'That's not what I asked you,' the policeman barked. 'I asked where the robbers would go from this point.'

The Dublin Corporation engineer had never been spoken to in this way by anyone since his promotion to head of his department. He was now an angry man.

'Take your pick,' the engineer snapped, thrusting the large map towards O'Malley. The assistant commissioner snatched the plans and turned away abruptly, dismissing the engineer and his petulance. The engineer moved across to the dark blue van beyond the cordon of police and leaned against the driver's door, arms folded tightly.

'Are we finished here, sir?' the driver asked.

'Oh, no,' the engineer said with feeling. 'I'm not leaving here until that idiot gets his men out of my tunnels. God knows what he'll do next.'

His face was suddenly illuminated by headlights as a black Ford Granada swept into the street, policemen and soldiers snapping hasty salutes as they identified the hunched and brooding man in the back seat, Commissioner Donoghue.

O'Malley hurried across to welcome the newcomer.

'Well?' the commissioner asked with practised restraint. 'What's the situation, Tom?'

'I have it under control, Commissioner,' O'Malley stated quickly, too confidently–which was reflected in the rising of the other man's eyebrows.

'Have you got the treasures?' the Garda commissioner asked abrasively.

'Eh, not yet, sir. But...'

'Or the thieves?'

'No, sir,' O'Malley answered, confidence crumbling.

'So what have you got, Tom?'

'Well, we have all the possible exits covered. Every manhole and every outlet this side of the Liffey, sir.'

'Hmm,' Donoghue mused, unconvinced, while scanning the army of uniformed men, the clutter, the police and the military vehicles.

'What about the other side of the river?'

'There's no way across the river, sir. So they'll have to come out somewhere on the south side.'

'Just how many manholes and outlets are there?'

'Quite a number, sir,' O'Malley answered hesitantly, hoping the commissioner would not press for elaboration. But the senior man stared hard into his face.

'Well, actually, sir, to be fair about it, there are hundreds of them,' O'Malley admitted uncomfortably. He hurried on to prevent the obvious rebuke. 'But according to our calculations the thieves could only have travelled within a three- to four-mile radius since the robbery. I've spread our men accordingly.'

'And how many miles are there of sewers big enough to take a man?'

'Almost seventy miles under the entire city, sir.'

'So you intend to sit around and wait for someone to stick his little head up out of the ground so you can hit him with your baton, is that it?'

'No, sir,' O'Malley retorted, hurt by his superior's lack of confidence in him. 'I've sent the divers down with walkie-talkies and compasses. They're more used to slippy conditions and I reckoned they could move faster initially. The Army are going down also, to spread out into the various offshoot tunnels.'

The commissioner walked towards the circle of lamps beyond the vehicles. O'Malley tried to fall into step beside him but there was insufficient room and he fell respectfully one pace behind. Soldiers were climbing down into the manhole, breathing heavily into the face-pieces of their gas masks.

'Why the masks?' Donoghue asked over his shoulder.

'In case of CH4, sir,' the assistant commissioner answered, knowledgeably and bumptiously, emphasising the letters.

'Methane?'

'Yes, sir,' O'Malley agreed, further deflated.

The commissioner scanned the scene again, spotting a group of animated senior army officers on the fringe of uniformed figures. He had no desire to become involved with internal politics and recriminations at this hour of the morning and at this stage of the operation. They would catch up with him soon enough. In triplicate.

He turned back towards his car, the assistant commissioner swivelling awkwardly after him.

207

'And you've informed Deputy Commissioner Swann that you're using the Anti-Terrorist Task Force?'

'Yes, sir.'

'Did you ask for his personal assistance?'

The question was for the record. Both knew it had to be asked.

'I felt, sir,' O'Malley answered carefully, 'that Mr Swann had enough problems with the rabies scare and all that. I didn't like to trouble him further just now.'

Damn liar, thought Donoghue, well aware of the animosity between the two men.

At the car door, the commissioner paused to look back at the floodlit area.

'And you're sure there's no way across the river underground?'

'According to the city engineers,' said O'Malley, 'there's only some kind of syphon beneath the river bed that no human could possibly get through unless the water flow was stopped. And that hasn't happened.'

Edouard Dufour checked the retaining straps on his full-face mask for the umpteenth time and inched towards the syphon.

He lay almost completely on his left side, hand and thigh pressing into the slime of the tunnel floor, his right hand clutching the two telescopic steel tubes constructed by Peter Phelan in the Rathmines garage. Around his waist instead of the usual weight belt he wore a length of yellow half-inch climbing rope. He carried a single Spirtechnique air tank. Two would have given him a large margin of safety but the space inside the syphon would be too limited and would present an even greater danger.

The other three watched him ease his body towards the roaring water where the three torrents met and towards the black hole. This was a new kind of fear for them, a fear shared unhappily by the only man in the group who knew all the possibilities of attempting the river crossing. The dangers of the North Sea were known to those who went beneath it. But the syphon was without precedent and with one additional terror: isolation. Once inside, Dufour would be alone and with no hope of rescue if anything went wrong. No paired diving team here with its surface support of scientific and medical manpower and equipment. That it should be so had been his decision. He had discarded the suggestion of a trailing lifeline because he calculated that in the restricted tunnel any attempt to pull him back would add to his peril. Either way, he had thought, it was a lousy choice.

Just before he disappeared into the constant, thundering wave he glanced back into the concentrated beams of the three flashlamps. His face was damp with perspiration yet he shivered. Which was worse, he wondered: to know the hazards as he did or to face them blinkered or imagined?

He turned away and was gone from sight.

Inside the roaring mass of turbulence he was caught by the vicious undertows, each stuggling for supremacy, each gaining control of his body for long seconds until he moved out of grasp. Everything now was done by touch, his hand reaching towards the lip of the inverted waterfall one moment, wrenched back the next to retain his perilous hold on the floor beneath the sludge which oozed through his fingers, the huge feet fins kicking savagely to prevent his body sliding into the main flow towards the sea. Once caught in that, he would be lost, powerless against the enormous weight and volume of the three rivers combined, and he would be swept down into the filtering system of the sewage works.

Several times he saw the faint glimmer of lights through the darkness and knew he had swivelled completely around. The watching trio caught glimpses of the red paint and chrome of the air tanks as it broke the ceiling of surf. Dufour's tough progress gnawed voraciously at their already diminished confidence. Worst affected by the diver's struggle was Simon Coates. The robbery itself and the build-up to it had taken their toll. Now the cacophony around him and the prospect ahead had rendered him immobile, his teeth clenched painfully together, nostrils flaring with the exertion of his breathing. Carl Stolford watched him from the corner of his eye and wondered.

Dufour sensed he was near the entrance now. The flow of water was against his face and chest only, the other two rivers' force behind him and receding with each body movement. His hand touched the edge and held. For a moment he paused, resting, almost luxuriating in the sudden inactivity after the struggle. He reached to his chest to find the pistol grip on the hose attached to the first-stage regulator mechanism of the air tank. Another rubber hose was connected to a gauge calibrated in atmospheres to tell him the amount of pressure remaining in his tank. The sixty cubic feet of air would last an hour if he sat perfectly still with relaxed, steady breathing. But because of the anticipated exertion in the syphon he calculated that he would only have fifteen minutes' supply at most, maybe less, including the reserve in the tank. The odds were ridiculous but, equally ridiculous, he found himself gripped by any excitement so intense, so undeniable, as to equate to a sexual pitch. He had taken risks before, almost gladly, and wondered. Even now he was reluctant to admit the truth.

He fitted the end of the hose to the flanged nipple on one of the steel tubes wedged between his body and the floor of the sewer, then pressed the spring-loaded button on the end of the hose. Immediately he could feel the tube tremble as the compressed air pushed inside. Satisfied, he pulled himself deeper inside the water flow and towards the edge. Because of the exertions he knew lay ahead, he would have to discipline his breathing to preserve the air supply. He inhaled, not too deeply, held the air for five seconds, and then released it slowly. Twice more and the rhythm was established, his lungs locked firmly to the memory cells of his brain. Only an emergency would override the set pattern.

The chrome tipped air tank broke the surface just once as he arched his body over the lip of the syphon outlet. Stolford held the spot in the beam of his flashlamp. An increasing ache in his chest reminded the American that he had been holding his breath, waiting vainly for a reappearance. Coates still stood mesmerised. Beside him, Casswell licked salty perspiration from the false moustache he wore.

For a second Dufour hung suspended in the neck of the syphon, the 120-feet-a-minute water flow holding him like a cork above the vertical drop. He snapped his legs straight and shoved downwards through the darkness, shoulders bouncing from side to side against the walls of the pipe. Once inside the current the feet fins compensated for the reduced gravitational pull and he moved downwards steadily, his free hand guiding the sightless descent. Near the bottom of the sixteen-foot pipe his movements became more difficult, as the turbulence increased because of the whirlpool action of the current at the corner of the pipe. He allowed the pressure to move him back up the pipe a few inches. The buffeting eased. The rhythmic action of the feet fins stabilised his body but his neck and shoulder muscles were now beginning to ache from the strain of the constant dive against the current.

With one sudden movement he pushed the connected steel tube out before him and pressed the air release trigger on the pistol grip. The telescopic tubing expanded quickly, forcing the rubber pads on both ends against the concrete walls of the syphon. He gripped the centre of the expanded tube and allowed the current to pull him upwards and away. His arm snapped straight but the tube held firm. He disconnected the hose from the first tube and gently brought his body forward until the bottom of his rib cage rested on the rigid steel. Then he moved the second tube into position and connected the hose to expand its rubber pads against the syphon walls. Slowly, carefully, he inched forward to grip the tube, reaching behind and releasing the air from the first one by pressing down on the escape nipple. Yard by yard, he moved to, and around, the corner of the syphon. He was now moving horizontally through the 135-foot-long section beneath the bed of the Liffey. He had hoped to conserve his air supply by using the expanding tubes only when necessary, but found he had no alternative but to hand-crawl the entire crossing with them. The current, even beyond the turbulence of the syphon bend, was still strong and, without visual aids, he could not ensure he was making headway without the tubes.

Sixteen feet above the French diver and three quarters of a mile south, the winding procession of police frogmen slid and stumbled through the stinking water and cursed the name of Assistant Commissioner Tom O'Malley. Some distance behind them, and moving off in different directions in the labyrinth, the soldiers wheezed obscenities into their gas masks with every soaking, bone-jarring fall. The last man in each section played out a coil of yellow line to guide them on the return journey to a manhole point. The portable radios crackled and hissed their weak transmissions of positions and progress, each section using its own call sign. In Lincoln Place the assistant commissioner paced up and down beside the communications vehicle, impatient for news. In the dark blue van, the Dublin Corporation engineer glowered darkly at the prancing figure.

In the syphon, Dufour anchored himself against the torrent and lifted the air pressure gauge up to the glass of his mask. The luminous needle and figures read lower than he had expected. He was now near the second bend in the syphon where the pipe would rise vertically to the sewer. At that corner the turbulence would be even greater than on the side of the river he had left. If he moved more quickly to make up time, he would use more air than on a slower journey over the same distance. Either way, he realised, he was going to be dangerously short for the final stretch, the ascent to the sewer.

'What was that?' Charles Casswell mouthed to Carl Stolford, the American seeing the anxiety in the face rather than lip-reading the hushed words. He switched off his torch and followed the actor's strained eyes towards the dark tunnel behind them. He could see nothing. He cursed inwardly at the noise from the syphon mouth. Sight was their only sense now in detecting anyone moving towards them. He looked at the actor and shrugged. Casswell pointed at the lens on his flashlamp and back again into the tunnel. Still nothing. Perhaps it was his imagination, after all. He shone his light on his wrist-watch and licked his lip again. Fifteen minutes, the Frenchman had reckoned. Almost thirteen had passed. Another minute or so and they could assume he had died, or was dying, in the syphon.

Madness. Sheer bloody madness, thought Simon Coates whose eyes never left the black void beyond the roaring and evil-smelling water. Millions of pounds' worth of treasure at their ankles, the greatest art theft in history, and here they were wallowing about in shit and piss instead of admiring the spoils in the comfort of the apartment. The Voice had said this was the only way. But Coates was totally unconvinced that they could not have broken through any cordon that had been thrown around after the raid. He moved a hand to the harness of his air tank and eased the weight. It reminded him of what lay ahead. He sighed, the exhalation changing to an involuntary shudder.

Less than half a mile from the syphon inlet, the sergeant leading the team of Garda divers wiggled his backside towards the men behind him and pushed away the helping hands. He stayed on his hands and knees and felt beneath the surface of the water for the Uzi submachine gun. It had been his third, and heaviest, fall.

'What're ye lookin' for, Sergeant?' the diver nearest him asked by way of offering assistance.

'I'm lookin' for bloody mermaids, ya dummy!' the sergeant roared. 'What d'ya think I'm lookin' for? I'm lookin' for the bloody gun!'

He fumbled for a few more moments, found the weapon and stood up warily.

'Come on,' he growled, pushing his mouthpiece back between his teeth. He snatched it out again and spat, wincing, into the stream of water. He rubbed the mouthpiece with his fingers and, too late, realised his second mistake. He gagged and spat again, more vehemently this time. 'Shag the thing, anyway,' he mumbled, and moved on towards the syphon.

On the far side of the River Liffey, Edouard Dufour wrestled to hold the telescopic tube steady against the current before pressing the air-release trigger. The tube expanded slowly but held against the walls. Now he could feel the tightness in the mouth valve as he sucked air from the tank. He trailed in the pressure-gauge hose to glance at the dial. The needle was deep inside the danger triangle. Gently he reached behind and felt for the reserve rod, the thin steel bar running down the side of the tank. He tugged it forward and felt his throat tightness ease as the air rushed from the tank and into his mouth hose. Now he had two and a half minutes, possibly less, to complete the journey.

The mistake was a momentary loss of concentration. Reaching back and pressing the air release button on the hydraulic tube beneath his ribcage, he allowed himself to twist too far in the current. The pressure on his retaining wrist felt as if someone had placed a vice on it, pulling his fingers from their hold. Instinctively, he kicked savagely with his feet to avoid being pulled back down the tunnel. His left fin kicked the partially depressurised tube from the walls and he was left flailing for long moments, his powerful arms and legs fighting the current, before he wrenched his body broadside to the flow. He was wedged; feet pressed hard againt one side of the tunnel, his head and shoulders against the other. But now he had almost doubled his area, thus increasing the weight of water flowing against him. Like pinching the end of a water hose to increase the force, his whole body was acting as an almost total blockage to a giant jet.

On the other side of the river, Charles Casswell stared hard again into the darkness beyond the sacks of art treasures and equipment. Now he was certain. He had seen the glow of a light, reflected dimly on the walls of the approach sewer.

'There it is again!' he said to himself. Why could he hear his own voice again after so long at the noisy syphon mouth where speech had been possible only by lip-reading?

He turned back to Stolford and Coates. They stood transfixed. The constant wave had died, only a fraction of the former water quantity was now pouring over the lip of the syphon hole. And there, in the beam of Stolford's lamp was one of the steel tubes which the Frenchman had brought into the syphon, caught on the edge by one of its nipples.

Coates looked slowly to Stolford who ignored the implied question. Instead, he handed the young man his flashlamp and waded carefully into the reduced river to retrieve the tube.

'Well,' demanded Coates loudly and impatiently. 'What do we do now?' His voice was tight, verging on hysteria.

Stolford made no reply.

'For God's sake,' Coates urged, 'don't just stand there. Tell us what we're going to do now.'

Casswell's eyes darted from one to the other, like a spectator at a tennis match.

'That's just it,' Stolford said, examining the steel tube, 'we're going to stand here.'

'*What*?' Coates exploded.

Casswell, placing a hand on the American's arm, prevented a reply. 'I don't think we should stand here *too* long, dear boy. I saw the lights again.'

Stolford followed the direction of the actor's thumb. The tunnel was, at the first glance, dark. But, staring hard, he too could now dimly see reflected light. He looked back to the syphon.

'This is madness,' said Coates, uncomprehending. 'Just bloody madness. Dufour's had it. He didn't make it. We won't either if we don't get out of here now. I say we...'

'Shut up and listen,' Stolford barked. 'He mightn't be dead. Just stuck. That would explain the drop in the water flow. We wait a while longer.'

Dufour could feel two of his finger-nails being bent back slowly from their sockets as he dug into the rough concrete of the tunnel wall to pull himself against the current. The weight of water was more painful, compressing his body, compelling him to breathe in short gulps. Inch by inch, he scraped his way towards the remaining tube at the upward bend in the syphon, wriggling his shoulders along the concrete with each new fingertip hold, feet following crabwise along the opposite wall. The tightness had returned to his throat, the air supply running out. Then it was there, the rubber pad of the tube. He reached along it and gripped the steel body. His damaged fingernails throbbed. He eased his feet away from the tunnel wall and let the current straighten his body until he was once again lying horizontally, chest resting on the tube. His breathing had become a chore in itself, sucking long and hard to get even some air into his painful lungs. He wished now he had worn a lifejacket. The attached air bottle would have given him precious extra seconds. He had sacrificed the safety factor to streamline his body as much as possible. He had guessed wrong, he knew now, but only because of the mishap with the tube. He still had a choice: allow the current to take him back to the other side of the river, hoping to avoid injury when he met the first bend in the tunnel, or try to go on. If he went back he knew the operation would have failed. Even with an air tank borrowed from one of the others he would not have sufficient strength to begin the swim again. And if they abandoned the syphon route altogether they would have little hope of escape through a manhole on that side of the river which by now must be teaming with police and troops. Yes, he must try to go on because of that. But really because of himself.

He moved forward into the bend and sucked the last dregs of air from the tank on his back before launching himself away from his foothold on the tube behind. Kicking fiercely with the fins and literally climbing the solid wall of water, he scrambled slowly up through the final nineteen feet of tunnel, gradually allowing his lungs to empty in short exhalations to avoid internal damage. Suddenly his ears were filled with a strange roaring sound as he urged his body upward through the black water, the volume rising from deep rumble to piercing crescendo as he broke clear of the syphon and into the sewer beyond. For a fraction of a second his arms still threshed, fanning the air, before he realised he had broken clear. He pulled himself away from the opening and clawed away the retaining straps of his face mask to gulp agonised lungfuls of sewer air. The roaring had stopped.

It had been his own voice.

The alarms triggered suddenly in the Control Room of Dublin Castle, the pulsing light on the console indicating the location.

The inspector, standing behind the radio operators, stepped forward quickly and placed a hand on his subordinate's shoulder.

'Is that where I think it is?' he asked despairingly.

'Yes, sir,' the operator confirmed with tempered melodrama, 'right beneath us.'

'Better let me do this,' the inspector said, pushing the operator from his seat and sitting down before the microphone. 'You get on to George Swann.'

'Control to Victor One...'

The radio receiver loudspeaker in the communications vehicle in Lincoln Place had been silent for some minutes. The soldiers in the tunnels below were economising on transmissions of their exact positions. In truth, they had become less sure of their geography as they progressed in the sewers, the disorientating sameness of each branch pipe and tunnel sapping their confidence in the compasses they carried.

'Hello Control. This is Victor One,' the operator replied.

'Victor One, Assistant Commissioner O'Malley, please.'

'Yes,' O'Malley snapped, grabbing the microphone. 'This is O'Malley.'

'Hello, sir. We've a showing on the audio panel, I'm afraid.'

'Definite?'

'Absolutely, sir.'

O'Malley screwed his face into an expression of self-pity and then asked the inevitable question.

'And you've informed Deputy Commissioner Swann, I suppose?'

The Control Room inspector sensed the underlying tone in the question and modified his answer.

'Yes, sir... standard... it being the audio panel, y'see... sir.' The voice trailed away.

'Quite right, inspector,' O'Malley interrupted briskly, but the effort was poor. 'Well thank you for... I'll try to sort it from this end. Out.'

He walked away from the vehicle to stand, round-shouldered, near the group of army officers who studied him with sideways glances while maintaining their air of indifference. The most senior of the officers walked unhurriedly to his side and waited for a few moments before interrupting the policeman's thoughts.

'Anything I can do, Mr O'Malley?'

The assistant commissioner turned to face the colonel with barely controlled anger.

'Yes, Colonel,' he answered evenly. 'You can find the idiot of a soldier who strayed off the designated routes.'

The colonel's face stiffened at the words. O'Malley continued, his voice rising, and prevented a retort. 'And when you find him I suggest you put him against a wall and blow out what brain tissue you can find.'

Now both men were angry, but the colonel was more aware of the spectators who had fallen silent to hear the exchange. With some effort he managed to control his voice.

'Perhaps if you explained precisely what has happened I might be able to help, Assistant-Commissioner,' he said, emphasising the word assistant. O'Malley faced the officer squarely, hands clenching and unclenching, and ignored the onlookers.

'You bet your arse I'll tell you what happened,' he bellowed into the colonel's face. 'One of your so-called soldiers has entered the series of tunnels beneath Dublin Castle, ignoring my warning about the microphone-alarm system in that area. *That*, Colonel, is precisely what's happened.'

217

The colonel opened his mouth to speak but O'Malley went on, 'Now we have National Security involved in this thing because that alarm system is under their control.'

He turned to walk back to the communications vehicle but the officer caught his arm and held it firmly.

'May I remind you that each army section has a Special Branch man with it to comply with peacetime regulations which lay down that troops may only be used in *support* of the civil police.'

O'Malley tried to pull away but the colonel held fast. 'And what evidence have you that it was some of our men who activated the alarm? Couldn't it be the men we're searching for?'

For a moment the assistant commissioner seemed trapped by the logic. Then he had it. 'Well if it *is* the thieves, they've certainly taken their time getting to that point, especially as the radio reports show that our men are already in that vicinity.'

He pulled his arm from the officer's grasp and walked back to the communications vehicle.

'Get onto every damn section and get a precise fix on their position. And I mean *precise!*'

'No way,' screamed Simon Coates, pulling away from the rope end extended by Carl Stolford. 'I'm going back. You can keep the damn treasures. I'm not going near that thing.'

He struggled more strongly in the arms of Charles Casswell, straining to get away from the surging torrent and the black hole beyond. Both men fell heavily onto the floor and the youngster wriggled free of the actor's arms and scrambled on hands and knees back along the tunnel. Casswell threw out a hand and caught an ankle, stopping Coates' desperate escape bid. Stolford stepped over Casswell and gripped the other ankle.

'They'll blow your head off, for God's sake,' he roared at the struggling figure. 'They know we were armed at the museum and they won't take chances.'

'Let go,' Coates shouted, his voice breaking in desperation, legs kicking. 'Jesus, let go... please... no...'

His voice was drowned in the staccato, the eight shots reverberating into one deafening thunder peal. The struggling men were frozen into instant immobility, their eyes, wide, fixed on the reflected light at the other end of the tunnel. It was dancing, dimming and brightening and finally steadying to a constant glow.

'Dear God, they're shooting at us,' Casswell whispered, unheard.

But each man was gripped with the same realisation, which broke the spell and sent them sliding and stumbling back towards the sewer syphon, Coates pulling at the bodies of his colleagues to reach the water before imagined bullets reached him. He snatched the rope from Stolford's hand and wrapped it tightly around his own waist, knotting it clumsily, brushing aside helping hands.

Garda Sergeant Kennerly stared at the still smoking muzzle of the Uzi submachine gun in his colleague's hand, the young man's fingers now fanning the fumes as if to remove the stain of his dreadful sin. Kennerly had already lifted himself onto his feet and recovered his lamp from the stream. The other two men lay where they had thrown themselves, reluctant to present themselves as targets should the idiot again slip down onto his backside and trigger another burst of fire.

'Ye dirty gobshite, ye,' was all the shaken sergeant could muster from his numbed brain. With renewed terror, he noticed that the weapon was aimed directly at him. He lunged and pushed it aside. The young man's mouth hung open in the horror of his second sin.

'Sorry, Sergeant,' the diver muttered miserably.

Kennerly, deafened by the recent shots, lip-read the words. 'Sorry?' he wheezed incredulously. 'I'll give ye sorry. If ye kill me with that thing, I'll kick yer arse!'

The other divers now considered it safe to rise from the stream, although they climbed to their feet with noticeable slowness. Kennerly exhaled, signifying the end of his tirade. He turned away to lead the group off again, but shot a glance over his shoulder to ensure he had not crept back into the gunsight. His head shook slowly from side to side as his lamp beam picked up the white horizontal lines torn along the brickwork by the eight bullets. Annie-bloody-Oakley, he seethed inwardly. Then the crackling voice in his walkie-talkie, barely audible through his ringing ears, brought him back from his murderous thoughts.

'Hello, sir... yes, sir. It was our section,' Kennerly confirmed, eyes burning into those of the man who had brought this upon him. 'Accidental discharge, sir. Possibly a faulty safety device on the weapon, sir. We're alright. No casualties. Proceeding towards the Liffey as ordered, sir. Over and out,' he said with deliberate finality. It worked. The receiver remained silent.

'I might kick yer arse, anyway,' he mused at his youthful charge.

The young diver, also temporarily deafened by the shots, misunderstood the lip movements of the sergeant and smiled agreement.

'He *is* a gobshite,' Kennerly muttered, turning away again.

A few feet further along the tunnel they turned right and began the last hundred yards' approach beneath Burgh Quay to the syphon. They moved more quickly now, as had their predecessors, in the relative roominess of the six-foot tunnel. They too heard the increasing rumble of the water's meeting place. Suddenly, Sergeant Kennerly stopped in his tracks, hands tightening on the lamp and the gun grip.

'God,' he whispered.

The other divers crowded behind him to shine their lamps on the black waves and foam. Kennerly moved back a short distance past his colleagues to escape the noise and pressed the transmitter button on his walkie-talkie.

Across the River Liffey, Edouard Dufour extended powerful hands to Charles Casswell. Beneath the actor, and holding his calves, was Carl Stolford, waiting to be pulled clear of the syphon hole. Simon Coates, anchored against the tunnel wall by his feet and shoulders, held the taut nylon rope tied to Casswell's waist. When the struggling and tumbling youth had been pulled through the syphon, there had not been time to allow the rope to flow back twice. One journey had to suffice, Casswell and Stolford being pulled through together by Dufour and Coates. The effort and tension showed in them all. They lay for long minutes, heaving from their exertions, physically and mentally drained, air tanks still strapped to their backs, masks pushed high on their foreheads: Coates and

Casswell were propped against the tunnel walls, Stolford on his side, his face against the actor's thigh. Dufour sat, cross-legged, eyes closed, in the centre of the tunnel, the sewer water flowing around his buttocks and waist.

A slight nudge in the small of the Frenchman's back snapped open his eyes. He turned slowly, reaching behind to touch whatever was persistently tipping the base of his spine. He was tense again now, dreading the anticipated touch of wet fur or sharp claws. Instead, he felt plastic, sliding beneath his fingertips as he stabbed tentatively at the object.

It was the nearest of the treasure-and-foam-filled bags, which had slipped from its temporary mooring.

Stolford saw Dufour's smile of relief, a smile which broadened to joy with the knowledge and satisfaction of what they had accomplished against incredible odds. The two men looked into each others eyes, Stolford's now also twinkling in the lamp light. The chuckle, at first self-conscious, apologetic, came from deep within the diver's heavy chest. Then, encouraged by the grinning American, it burst through his teeth in an explosion of laughter.

The sound jolted Casswell and Coates upright. At first slightly aggrieved at not being privy to the cause of the merriment, they watched Dufour's palm slap the plastic bag rythmically as Stolford's laughter rose in intensity. Casswell's shoulders lifted once, then again, in surrender to the infectious mood of his companions. The resonance of his booming chuckles harmonised with the lighter tones of Simon Coates, who laughed in wave after wave of near-hysteria, his sides aching, eyes streaming.

And the others understood. For he had suffered most.

The policemen and soldiers worked quickly and in silence, their breath, like multiple exhaust pipes, pumping white steam into the damp Saturday dawn as they loaded their vehicles. Back at their base, later, they would spend another two hours hosing down and drying the now evil-smelling equipment.

Sergeant Kennerly lay on his back, shivering, in the back doorway of the diving team's van. The big man's excess stomach fat fluttered with each tug by the young diver trying to free his thighs and calves from the clinging rubber suit.

221

A dull clang diverted Kennerly's attention briefly. The heavy steel manhole cover was back in place. The mechanics unhooked the steel cable and took up the slack on the small crane at the back of the tow truck. One of them glanced briefly across at Kennerly and smirked delightedly at the older man's discomfort, before climbing quickly into the already moving vehicle.

A word, universally known, was formed in exaggerated mime by Kennerly's bluing lips.

To the north-west across the city, the art treasures, in their foam and plastic protective covering, were being stacked and anchored in a sewer tunnel at a point exactly two hundred and fourteen yards from the River Liffey.

The four men had travelled almost a mile since leaving the syphon, moving westwards directly beneath the roadway alongside the sluggish brown river which divided the ancient settlement; then northwards through the smaller feeder sewer underneath Church Street.

Carl Stolford scratched a small cross on the sewer wall, a few inches above water level.

'Now what?' asked a weary and cold Simon Coates.

'Now we wait,' Stolford answered shortly, glancing at his watch. 'For two hours, or a little more.'

He jerked his thumb towards the ceiling of the sewer tunnel.

'When the traffic gets movin' in the mornin' rush hour,' he said. 'Till then, we all get some rest.'

Edouard Dufour, the diver, was already settling against the plastic sacks. The other men sank down tiredly beside him, the sewer water lapping unnoticed over their aching legs.

As time progressed, wakening the city's population, the water level in the sewer would rise.

The tea, foul-tasting and tepid, was the best the duty sergeant was prepared to offer after the night he had endured.

First, the Serious Crime Squad; then the anti-subversive lot, C3, with their long hair and hip holsters. Yes, C3 were the worst: ask a simple question and only get a grunt or averted eyes. Christ almighty, some of them were only wet-arsed recruits when he got his three stripes. Now you'd think they were in a different force.

And to top it all, the smell of vomit. Not from them, mind you, but from him. He should have known. Never wake a wino. Wakes up and pukes all over you. That's just what the little shit, Barney Sullivan, did. Eyewitness, me arse! Wouldn't get sick on the glamour boys, of course, but on him who had given him a bunk in the cell for the night.

Barney Sullivan was now back in that bunk, his suprarenal glands no longer secreting their large volume of adrenalin; his frightened brain succumbing to the still considerable quantity of alcohol in his bloodstream.

He had told his story, if not well at least unvaryingly, seven times since the first group of detectives arrived and barked their questions at him, a discreet distance from his damp and stained person.

'Well, he's stuck to his story, anyway,' said the oldest of the detectives begrudgingly. 'So, that still leaves us with a Post Office engineer's truck that's vanished, a Land-Rover that's vanished, a gang of soldiers that's vanished, and the art collection that's...'

His melancholy and unnecessary diatribe was cut short by the senior of the men present.

'Right, the divers say the gang never went down the sewers or they'd have found them,' he said briskly, trying to inject some enthusiasm into the defeatist ramblings of the other men. 'So, we're still looking for a Land-Rover and a large Dodge van.'

'The Post Office transport section confirm it isn't one of theirs,' another detective reminded him.

'Right,' the senior man acknowledged. 'Where the hell is it, though?'

'We set up road blocks immediately after the raid, sir,' one of the Serious Crime Squad countered gently.

'I know, I know,' the senior man snapped irritably, closing his eyes to emphasise pained tolerance of repetition. They jerked open and he stabbed a finger into the Crime man's chest. 'Now, if *you* had the Irish art treasures in the back of a truck or a Land-Rover, would you make a dash out of the city? No, you'd lie low *inside* Dublin.'

223

'Yes, sir. I'll put more men onto it immediately,' the other man said, striding from the room.

The senior officer rose wearily and walked to the grime-stained window.

'Clueless bastard,' he mumbled sadly to the dull sky.

'Vanished?'

The repetition of the word was a challenge stemming from anger rather than cool courage. The Minister for Justice would not normally risk confrontation. His jaw, beneath the pencil-line grey moustache, jutted aggressively and he placed both hands, palms flat, on the desk top. The eyes, palest blue, were ringed with the pink and shadow of tiredness and stared unblinkingly across the wood-panelled office at the tall policeman. Like an angora rabbit, thought George Swann.

'Yes, Minister,' the deputy commissioner confirmed flatly. 'For the moment, anyway,' he qualified quickly.

Commissioner Donoghue shifted uneasily in the yellow armchair alongside his and cleared his throat as if to speak. But he remained silent.

'We're doing everything we can, Minister,' Swann added then. 'Every available man, uniformed and plain-clothes, is searching for the van. The Land-Rover has been found, as you know, and may produce prints or other clues to establish identity. We know already, from its chassis number, that it was stolen from its owner before last night and reported by him.'

'And the sewers? Will they produce anything for us?'

At another time, Swann would have seen the humour in the last question and also the obvious answer. The commissioner replied, guardedly but correctly.

'I think we may have to rule them out, Minister,' he said. 'Our man at the scene, Assistant Commissioner O'Malley, confirms that opinion. If the raiders went down there at all, they've gone now.'

'Assistant Commissioner O'Malley is confident in that assessment,' added Swann – unnecessarily, thought Donoghue.

The minister turned to Swann again. 'And you, Mr Swann, what do *you* think?'

'I feel, Minister,' he said carefully, 'that we must be guided by Mr O'Malley's opinion. He has assured us that he has searched the sewers thoroughly.'

Too deliberate, thought Donoghue. Swann is sharpening the knife, with O'Malley hanging by a thin cord. The words would probably have little significance for the minister who would, at best, assume the senior police officers were following custom and closing ranks in the face of the common adversary: him. But Donoghue knew the truth. Accounts varied as to what had caused the enmity between Swann and O'Malley. Some maintained it was merely a clash of personalities, others that O'Malley's influence with certain politicians had bought his promotion while Swann pulled his way upwards with efficient detection and dedication. Whatever the reason, the gaping rift was there and he, Donoghue, had to constantly hold the protagonists apart.

The minister looked out over St Stephen's Green park. A dog, unleashed, broke off a vocal attack on the ducks in the artificial lake to lift a rear leg against the shopping bag of an elderly woman dozing on a bench.

'And the rabies outbreak, gentlemen?' he asked warily, feeling the necessity to ask but afraid of what he might hear.

'On that score,' said Donoghue, opening the cardboard folder on his knees, 'it's not too cheerful. It seemed the attacks had fallen off but seven cases were admitted to Cherry Orchard overnight for observation. The army patrols shot three suspected dogs here in the city. One confirmed later as having been rabid.'

'And the new patients?' the minister asked, diverting his eyes from the small pool which had formed around the bottom of the woman's shopping bag.

'No confirmations yet, Minister,' Donoghue said. 'You see, all the bites were on the hands or legs and...'

'Yes, yes,' the minister interrupted impatiently, 'but what are you doing about the cause of the outbreak? The source?'

The commissioner was rattled now, irritated by the sniping interrogation. It was a struggle to keep his voice modulated. 'Everything we can, Minister. We're questioning every patient and trying to trace the owner of every dog suspected of being a carrier. But, with so many strays in the city...'

'And that's the best you can offer?' The question was more

than a challenge. It hung in the silenced air, an ungarnished condemnation which could become accepted thinking among all members of the government unless destroyed now. George Swann knew exactly where to hit the pompous politician.

'We could always round up every dog and cat in the country for mass extermination,' he said evenly.

The minister's eyebrows arched sharply at the horrifying words. He searched the policeman's face for facetiousness or sarcasm but could see only disarming sincerity.

'God, no,' he blustered. 'We couldn't do that to the people of the country. No, no. Out of the question.'

You mean the *voters* of the country, thought Swann delightedly.

'No,' the minister went on, 'I'm sure we can manage without that.'

'If you've any suggestions, Minister,' Swann interrupted amicably. Again the search for sarcasm and again the negative result.

'Yes, well,' the minister stumbled away from the bait, 'I'll be discussing the situation with the Taoiseach and other Cabinet members later today and will keep you informed of any suggestions they may make.'

He rose suddenly from his chair. 'Thank you for coming. Please keep me in touch with developments.'

As they waited for the elevator outside, Donoghue smiled ruefully at his deputy and shook his head slowly from side to side.

'Yeah, I know,' Swann chuckled.

Carl Stolford's eyes were tightly closed. The Phantom jets were laying down their orange carpets of napalm on the thatched roofs and surrounding foliage. Soon the smell of burnt petrol and flesh would drift through the trees, followed by the screams of those still alive filling the vacuum left by the departure of the howling engines. That would be the worst time, moving in on the village through the smoke and stench and with the ache to relieve a bladder already empty; praying to a god forgotten until such times to protect him from Charlies' scything machine gun bullets or the trip-wire explosives which take away manhood and other parts. Shit Charlie's *here*.

226

He could feel the hot breath of the Viet Cong soldier on his face, a face he recognised without looking; feel the fingers touching tentatively at his shoulder before gripping the cloth of his combat tunic. *Now*, Charlie.

Stolford stabbed upwards with extended knuckles: felt bone on bone and heard a muted cry as he opened his eyes to see the face. It moved upwards and back into the gloom, pained and surprised. It was Simon Coates' face. And there were other voices.

'Good Lord, the man's gone mad...'

'He was dreaming...'

'Oh Jesus, he's broken my nose...'

'Let me see... look, dear boy, hold still...'

'It could have been worse, my young friend...'

'Shut your lousy frog mouth...'

'Steady, dear boy, steady now...'

Stolford could see them now, across the tunnel. Coates was against the wall, one blood-soaked hand across his nose, Casswell kneeling beside him, supporting the youngster's head. The burly Dufour crouched above them, a wide grin creasing his face as he held the torchlight's beam on the bloodied centrepiece.

'Sorry,' Stolford mumbled, crawling across to peer at the damage. 'I thought... I'm sorry, kid.'

Coates wanted to retaliate, at least verbally, but he was lulled by the obviously sincere words of the big American. They were the first kind words spoken in all the time they had known each other. He turned aside and spat a mouthful of blood into the sewer stream. Stolford took his face in both hands and studied the damage.

'It's not broken, kid,' he said gently. 'But it'll hurt awhile.'

'Why?' Coates bubbled through his full mouth. He spat again.

'You crept up. Should've talked.'

The rumble of the Phantom jets was still there, directly overhead.

'What time?'

'Almost eight o'clock,' Dufour answered. 'The morning rush-hour has started.' He nodded towards the ceiling of the tunnel.

227

'You OK now?' Stolford asked Coates. The youth sat upright, assisted by Casswell.

'He'll be alright in a moment,' the actor said, and added reproachfully, 'but I do wish you'd learn to control your hands.'

The chuckle brought his attention back to Coates who was wincing from the effort.

'First time you ever said *that* to a man, Charles,' Coates smirked, and winced again. 'Jesus, it hurts...' he whimpered, clutching his nose.

'Perhaps he has said *those* words though, eh?' the Frenchman grinned.

Casswell outwardly ignored the taunts.

'Come on,' Stolford said, smiling. 'We've work to do.'

He moved to the plastic sacks and opened one of the two tied with yellow tape. Dufour opened the other, pulling at the hardened foam to reach the equipment inside. In minutes they had the Fein 2000 stone-cutting tool assembled and fitted to its battery power supply. Dufour made a final check of the atmosphere with the Draeger meter and satisfied, nodded to Stolford.

The American waited for the traffic thunder overhead to reach a sustained level and then switched on the stone-cutter. The carbon cutting wheel whirred up to its full speed of more than five thousand revolutions a minute. Satisfied, Stolford waited while Dufour moved another fifty feet up along the sewer. The diver waited until traffic overhead was sufficiently heavy, and then, moving towards Stolford, he flashed the torchlight. The drill started up again and the wheel began slicing into the concrete wall, the overhead rumble muffling the noise. A second flash of light and Stolford switched off, to wait for another signal. To cut a four-foot circular segment of the wall took almost seventy minutes, Casswell and Coates taking turns with the cutter. Dufour rejoined the group to help jemmy and lift out the complete section. In the gap was a solid wall of dark clay and rough stones of various sizes.

'The Voice better know what he's talkin' about,' said Stolford grimly, eyeing the wall.

'Well, so far he's been bang-on, dear boy,' said Casswell with more conviction than he really felt.

'Yeah, well now would be one arsehole time to ruin a good track record,' Stolford retorted, pulling at the soft clay.

Coates pulled three empty canvas sacks from one of the plastic equipment bags and held one of them open for the handfuls of earth and rubble. Stolford and Casswell hacked and pulled at the soil, working downwards beyond the level of the sewer floor. When one sack had been filled, Dufour and Coates took over while Stolford held a second sack open. Casswell stood behind the group, rubbing his signet ring anxiously and peering at the deepening hole.

They toiled for forty minutes. Suddenly, Stolford, back at the clay face again, fell forward from his kneeling position onto his chest.

'Torch, quick,' he said, reaching back. Dufour handed him the light. The others strained to get a glimpse of what Stolford was seeing, but his shoulders filled the cavity.

Casswell could bear the suspense for only a few moments. 'Well?' he prompted.

Stolford eased himself out of the hole and turned, grinning. 'Like you said, Charles,' he said happily, 'bang-on.'

Stolford moved aside for the actor, handing him the torchlight. Casswell stared down into the hole, sweeping the light slowly from side to side and up and down. What he saw was a picture of time suspended for centuries.

It was a tunnel dressed in giant cobwebs, some hanging in rags, others still perfectly formed and tightly secured to the rough-hewn dark wood beams which supported the roof and walls. It was just over five feet from floor to ceiling and four feet wide. The hole Casswell looked through was just twelve inches beneath the roof of the tunnel.

He handed the light back to Stolford and stood up. Stolford put his feet into the gap and inched his way through to drop down onto the floor of the tunnel. The contrast in ambiance and acoustics was startling. Here the sound of his feet was muted by the walls of clay, even his own breathing was difficult to hear. The air was dry and dusty, and smelt of freshly turned soil. He punched and pulled holes in the cobwebs and examined the wood of the wall props. It was in perfect condition, preserved through the centuries by the constant temperature and damp-free atmosphere. The tunnel ran parallel to the sewer in one direction, down towards the Liffey, and westwards in the other, into the darkness beyond the range of the torchlight beam. It moved towards the river for only a few yards, petering out in a pile of timber and dirt.

A movement at his elbow jolted him. It was Casswell. 'Spooky, isn't it?' the actor said with suitably hushed voice. Stolford ignored him.

'What is this place?' Simon Coates asked, prodding the wood shoring.

'An escape tunnel,' said Stolford. 'Built during the time priests were being hunted and churches and monastries shut down. They could either come down here and lie low, or else move down to the Liffey and get the hell out of the city altogether.'

'How many of these things are there?' asked Casswell.

Stolford shrugged. 'Dunno. No one does for sure. When The Voice mentioned the tunnels in his last message I dug into some old library books. Some said dozens, others said the whole idea was bunkum. There's also another story about a tunnel not far from here, built t'spring revolutionaries who were goin' t'get topped in an old prison. Another story says some monks in a closed order dug one so they could get to the cathedral across the river for services without bein' seen by the public.'

'And this one takes us under St Michan's Church?' said Coates.

'Right,' Stolford confirmed. 'Shit, The Voice knew his stuff, alright.'

'And we leave the treasures here?' Dufour asked.

'Yeah,' said Stolford. 'Then move into the burial chambers under the church tomorrow night. At eleven o'clock Adrien D'Albe comes along, picks the locks on the steel doors of the chamber and lets us out. We lock the doors behind us and nobody knows we've been here. We're safe, the treasures are stashed here, everybody's happy.'

The American had said it all. No one had followed them across the River Liffey. He did not know why the police had come down after them on the other side; maybe a hunch, or suspicion after the raid when someone reported a Post Office van parked over the manhole. Whatever the reason, The Voice had been right: they would not have got far by road after the robbery, and by crossing the river through the syphon they had stopped the searchers in their tracks. The treasures could be left here until such time as it was considered safe to move them to their next destination, presumably the United States. There the final financial transaction would be conducted between buyers and sellers before the treasures found their new homes. He and the others involved in the actual raid would be guaranteed their fees for the job, deposited in their respective Swiss bank accounts. Their knowledge of the whereabouts of the treasures in their temporary hiding place would be their guarantee of payment in full. As an added precaution against doublecross, Stolford had given the Tara Brooch to Peter Phelan for safekeeping. Once payment had been made by The Voice or his associates, then this would be handed over to them.

Dufour and D'Albe would leave the country as they had arrived. Likewise Casswell and Coates. Peter Phelan would remain officially 'unemployed' for some weeks before 'finding it necessary to emigrate to find work abroad'. And he, Carl Stolford, would make one final trip in the black suit and dog collar before Father O'Mahony ceased to exist.

All that remained now was to bring the equipment and treasures into the old tunnel, put the soil and the segment of sewer pipe they had removed back in place with the quick-setting cement, change out of the rubber suits into sweaters, jeans and casual shoes and wait for tomorrow night's appointment with Adrien D'Albe. The small quantity of food and fresh water they had in one of the equipment sacks would be sufficient to sustain them until then.

Peter Phelan had made his decision hours before, a decision born of bitterness and distrust. He would not be a fall guy in anything again. He had lost his business and his freedom through foolish trust and he had lost his wife in the same way. This time he would not be the patsy.

It took forty minutes and two buses to reach the garage in Rathmines from his flat in Monkstown. The main topic of conversation among the passengers on the smoke-filled upper decks was the daring robbery of the Irish art treasures, prompted by the glaring headlines in the morning newspapers. He wiped the fogging from his spectacles and listened to it all. His journey was slowed three times by combined police and army roadblocks, questioning only the drivers of cars and vans and searching the vehicles. Buses were waved through. After all, where would a passenger hide the Ardagh Chalice or Book of Kells on a bus?

He approached the lockup garage carefully and circuitously but, apart from one cruising patrol car, there was no police activity in the immediate area. In less than six minutes he had removed the Tara Brooch from its hiding place behind the dashboard of the lorry and was back on the street again, the cloth-covered treasure in the inside pocket of his dark blue anorak.

At exactly half-past eleven he walked through the entrance to Dean's Grange Cemetery on the south side of the city and began the long walk to his brother's grave. There were few people amongst the huge sprawl of marble and granite markers, but then it was easy to lose a thousand people in the vastness of the cemetery. His brother had been buried in what the gravedigger called a new 'plot', an extension to the grounds at the far side of the complex. Phelan identified the as yet unmarked grave with difficulty. He had to read the cards on almost all the wreaths and plastic flowers in a line of fresh graves before he found the handwriting he recognised: his wife's.

He knelt for some moments beside the grave. Outwardly he seemed to be praying but inwardly he felt nothing except the urgency of the task ahead. His eyes scanned the surrounding graves while his hand moved slowly to his pocket to remove the cloth bundle. His free hand dug the loose soil to a depth of about fifteen inches. Another careful look at his surroundings and the Tara Brooch was placed gently at the bottom of the narrow shaft. He filled in the hole and stood up. He felt he should say something, even a prayer, but the words would not come and the thoughts were contradictory.

Adrien D'Albe paced the floors of Charles Casswell's apartment, wandering with increasing concern from room to room, glancing repeatedly at his wrist-watch and slapping one fist into the palm of the other hand. He could not explain his anxiety. Peter Phelan had said he would call at the apartment early in the morning, but he had not showed. No problem in that, really. Probably slept late after the excitement of last night.

It was more than that. A nagging, gut feeling that made his fingers and pubic hair itch. He rubbed his crotch but the irritation remained. Four times in his life he had had this form of veiled premonition, a foreboding that was unerring. He had last know it the night he had found his sister Léa, aged and broken, among the prostitutes of Toulon.

Suddenly he stopped pacing and stared at the grey day beyond the picture window. He turned quickly and grabbed the keys from the coffee table. The elevator was at the ground floor so he ran down the fire stairs. Now seconds were precious. He climbed into Casswell's hired car, starting the engine even before shutting the door behind him, and reversed savagely out of the parking bay. His geography of the city was still vague but he only made two mistakes in direction and, while ignoring the speed limits, he did not, at least, go through any red traffic lights. He reached Rathmines in twelve minutes and the garage in another three. Four hundred yards down the road the two men in the approaching saloon saw D'Albe's car swerve out of sight into the laneway.

'He's in a bloody hurry, isn't he, now?' The uniformed policeman said to the detective at his side.

'Like he had the shits,' the detective said grimly and reached for the Uzi submachine gun on the back seat.

The simple lock presented no problem to D'Albe and he was already inside the garage and climbing into the cab of the truck when the policemen pulled up quietly behind the car outside. The uniformed man stepped out from behind the wheel and tugged his peaked cap straight as he approached the open doors of the garage. His colleague walked slowly around D'Albe's car, peering inside, the Uzi held loosley at his side.

D'Albe was too impatient to hunt for a screwdriver and grabbed a tyre lever from the cab floor, jamming the end into the crack between the panel and the dashboard. The screws held despite the vicious levering but the panel buckled outwards. It was sufficient to see that the space behind it was empty. His pubic hair was itching madly.

'Bastard,' he roared in English and smashed the lever into the glass face of the speedometer.

'Who is?'

The voice startled him, whirling him around to stare into the enquiring face beneath the peaked cap. The fright, in effect, killed him, jolting him into a frenzied attempt to escape. Had he heard the policeman's approach he might have had a precious second to rationalise and to talk his way through some kind of excuse for his seemingly demented behaviour. Instead, he instinctively lashed out with the tyre lever, the blow catching the policeman on the head just above the temple. The officer fell backwards, dazed but not seriously injured. The rim and crown of the cap had absorbed most of the impact. He tried to hold himself upright but D'Albe lashed out with his foot, the toe crunching into the upper lip and teeth. D'Albe jumped down and tried to step over the fallen man. The detective outside had heard the first cry of pain and reached the door as the second, more muffled, cry reverberated around the interior. He ran up the wrong side of the truck, realised his mistake and rounded the rear of the vehicle as D'Albe raised the tyre lever to smash down on the uniformed policeman who was blindly gripping his ankle.

Twenty-four round-nosed bullets, loosed in one burst, punched neat oblique holes in the steel side of the truck, passing effortlessly through the Frenchman's chest and upper stomach and shoving him against the vehicle. D'Albe died instantly, but he stayed upright for several seconds as though the rounds had stitched him to the truck. Then his legs quivered as the brain released its control of the nerve ends and muscles, and he sagged to his knees, his torso remaining upright, his chin sagging onto his chest. A grumbling sigh gurgled from deep inside as the remaining air in his lungs escaped through the holes. His eyes stayed open but the face around them began to turn purple.

'Sweet Jesus,' the detective shuddered, and lowered the gun.

An hour after the staring face had been held up into the lens of the police photographer from the Technical Bureau, the records section of Interpol provisionally identified the wired

234

picture as that of Adrien D'Albe, restaurant owner and safebreaker. They also listed his convictions, known associates and general background. In addition, they wired photographs of his fingerprints for comparison and positive identification in Dublin.

Deputy Commissioner George Swann took sole charge at this stage.

The French Embassy in Dublin was notified, as were the crime investigation units of the police in Marseilles and Toulon, and the French secret service, the Service de Documentation Extérieure et de Contre-Espionage. Each was asked to withhold the information from all, including next-of-kin, until cleared by the Irish Special Branch. The one word which featured in all the messages was *délicat*.

The greatest threat to keeping secret the death of Adrien D'Albe would be the Press. Minutes after the shooting, the area around the Rathmines garage was sealed. After D'Albe's face and the scene had been photographed the body was taken in an unmarked police van to St Bricin's Military Hospital near the Phoenix Park. The inevitable enquiries about the condition of the patient and his identity were referred by the hospital authorities to the Garda Press Office. The Press Office was told that a man, as yet unidentified, had been shot and a policeman badly injured during a break-in in the Rathmines area. His condition was 'not good'. Later the Press would be told truthfully that his condition was 'unchanged'.

No fingerprints had been found on the truck or anywhere in the garage. The motor taxation office computer, linked to the Garda information circuit, showed the truck was the property of a Mr Malachi Doran, a scrap-metal merchant, with an address near Birr in County Offaly. The local police winced when the name was passed on to them for checking. Doran was well known to them and to many district courts in that county and its neighbours. In half an hour, roused from a drunken stupor in a cottage surrounded by pieces of cars and trucks, he was giving his usual 'co-operation' to the local police. Yes, he had sold a Dodge truck a while back. But no, he couldn't remember the name of the fella. Something like Stapelton or Stokes or the like. It was a cash deal, you see, and well, he saw so many people in his line of business that he couldn't possibly remember names or faces.

The Companies Registration Officer could only produce the Rathmines address of Matthews Pressure Cleaners. The directors, according to the records, were Brian O'Rourke, Graham Stanton and George Matthews. The private addresses were subsequently established as being false.

Newspaper advertisements for Matthews Pressure Cleaners had not listed a telephone number, only the Rathmines address. The man who gave his name as Brian O'Rourke, had paid for the newspaper space with cash.

The printer of the letterheads for the company told a similar story.

It was not a great day for the police.

Chapter Thirteen

Throughout the morning and afternoon, the four men in the dark tunnel leading to the burial vaults beneath St Michan's Church heard the voice of the sexton at regular intervals as he conducted parties of visitors through the historic chambers. The voice was barely audible through the wall of clay and debris, and none of the words was discernible. But the repetitious rhythm of the patter never varied.

The warning light on the Draeger meter had first flickered shortly after two o'clock when the afternoon's guided tours were about to begin. Now, an hour and half after the last time they had heard the sexton's voice, the light was flickering again. The smell confirmed the meter's warning.

Like a bad fart, was how Stolford aptly described the odour of the methane gas. The reason for the build-up had become obvious now: the tunnel in which the four men waited was not completely airtight and this had been warned of by The Voice when the final message had been delivered to Stolford. For this reason, air tanks were considered unnecessary. This was, however, only true when the tours were in progress, the draught from the outside steel doors of the vaults sucking and blowing fresh air through the tiny gaps in the clay barrier between the vault and the man-made tunnel where Stolford and the others waited.

Filtered, the quantity of methane from the sewers was harmless. But, with the doors shut for any length of time and the natural filtration process reduced, the methane built up to danger level in the tunnel.

'Not bang-on this time, eh?' Charles Casswell whispered to

237

Stolford as he watched the flickering warning light.

'The Voice still has it right, though,' said Stolford in admiration. 'He knew the longest we'd be in here without air would be about an hour. Not enough to build up the methane to intolerable levels.'

Dufour smiled comprehension. 'And the man, The Voice, knew that as soon as the tours of the vaults ended for the day we would break out into the burial chambers where the gas cannot gather, huh?'

The American ignored the question. 'Right, let's get out of here,' he said. 'Edouard, you and me dig first. Charles and Simon take over in fifteen minutes.'

Assistant Commissioner Tom O'Malley was greatly surprised and not a little relieved at the attitude of the Minister for Justice when he telephoned with his latest report on the police search and investigation. He had expected, at least, an outburst of exasperation about the lack of real progress. Instead, he had received understanding, even sympathy, from the minister and a gentle summons to his office in St Stephen's Green. The leader of the Task Force, Chief Superintendent Dan Sullivan, had also been asked to attend.

A porter brought the two men to the fourth floor and led them along the corridor to one of the two entrances to the minister's office. Being Saturday morning, the building was eerily quiet except for their padded footsteps on the carpeted floor. They went through the empty outer office, normally occupied by the minister's personal secretary, and waited while the porter announced them and showed them in, shutting the door silently behind them.

The surprise showed on O'Malley's face. Lifting himself out of a chair to extend a hand was Chief Superintendent Bob MacIntyre, Deputy Head of New Scotland Yard's Anti-Terrorist Squad. Also rising was the Porton Down scientist, Doctor Timothy Dunstan. Sitting to one side and slightly embarrassed was Garda Commissioner Donoghue. A stoney-faced Deputy Commissioner George Swann sat beside the commissioner.

O'Malley shook MacIntyre's hand briefly and muttered distrustfully, 'Back again, Bob?'

It was courtesy for a visiting officer to inform the local police of his intentions, especially so for senior officers who might hold sensitive positions and would require discreet protection. MacIntyre knew this system and had operated it unfailingly, until now, on visits to Dublin. There was something ugly in the air and they knew O'Malley sensed it. His instinct was heightened by the over-friendliness of everyone so far that morning.

The minister beckoned O'Malley and Sullivan to empty chairs and then leaned forward, interlacing his fingers and speaking for the first time.

'Gentlemen,' he began evenly, his tone measured to the point of melodrama, 'what I am about to say and what others here will say must not go outside this room. For that reason, I have not summoned any of my immediate subordinates here this morning. There will be no record of this meeting having taken place. In short, gentlemen, it never happened.'

Only O'Malley and Sullivan shifted uncomfortably in their chairs. The other men stared intently and without surprise at the minister.

'Assistant Commissioner,' the minister went on, studying his own hands, 'have you any idea of the whereabouts of the treasures or the gang responsible for their theft?'

O'Malley cleared his throat, embarrassed by the presence of his own more senior officers and the visitors.

'At this precise moment, sir?' He was hedging like a schoolboy caught smoking in the lavatory.

The minister nodded tolerantly.

'Not at this precise...'

'Right,' the minister interrupted.

'Have you any suspects, any definite leads?'

'Well, sir,' the unhappy O'Malley began again, 'we are, we have been...'

This time he was interrupted by the Task Force leader, at his side. 'We hope to trace the truck used by the thieves in the vicinity of the sewer entrance during...'

The minister waved him silent.

'But as of this moment you do not know the identity of the men involved in this robbery, apart from this Frenchman, Adrien D'Albe, who was... who died this morning at the

239

garage in Rathmines?'

'No, sir.' The reply was abrupt but did not belie the underlying defeat.

'Good.'

O'Malley's jaw slackened in disbelief and the minister smiled immediate reassurance.

'Let me explain, Mr O'Malley,' he said calmly. 'These men from England, and indeed your own colleagues here, believe the rabies outbreak here was deliberate, part of the operation to steal the art treasures.'

Chief Superintendent Sullivan broke in. 'That is, of course, something we had considered ourselves, sir. However, at this moment, there is no proof of that theory. Until we apprehend the...'

'Precisely,' the minister silenced him. 'And if that proof comes our way, we want to keep it from the public. We cannot afford to have this information leaked officially or unofficially.'

'Sir,' O'Malley protested, 'we have a city out there rampant with rabies. Hospital beds and mortuaries are filling up with victims. And if we catch those responsible and they confess, we're not to inform the public?'

The minister nodded.

'And how can we keep that secret?' O'Malley protested. 'Even if we kept it out of the trial, one or two of them might sell their story to the newspapers.'

'There will be no trial,' the minister said simply.

For the first time, the enormity of what was proposed and what had obviously been already agreed among the other men present hit the two late arrivals at the meeting. For seconds they could only stare mutely at the minister who was again studying his interlaced fingers. The silence was oppressive but words would not come from the assistant commissioner and the chief superintendent.

'With your permission, Minister,' Doctor Dunstan said, eyebrows raised in an expression of formal request.

The minister dipped his head in approval.

Doctor Dunstan turned to the still dumbstruck men. 'Until now, the potential of rabies as a weapon had remained, mercifully, unnoticed. While we haven't any conclusive proof that it has been used in this case, the scales seem heavily weighted in that direction. Now, if its use becomes public knowledge, the terrorist organisations will be queuing up to get supplies. This outbreak would become a blueprint for them.'

'So, what are you suggesting we do?' asked O'Malley suspiciously.

'Exactly what we have decided to do,' the minister answered flatly.

'Sir…?'

The minister sat back in his armchair, elbows on the arms, his fingertips touching.

'If anyone is…to use your word, Chief Superintendent…*apprehended*, the interviews will be conducted only by Deputy Commissioner Swann. No *official* record will be kept of that interview and no one will subsequently be charged with the theft of the art treasures.'

'They just go free?'

The minister looked very briefly at the English policeman, Chief Superintendent Bob MacIntyre, who met his gaze and then looked away.

'They will just go,' the minister said slowly, his delivery measured.

'They will just go,' O'Malley repeated, his tongue dry, the words hanging in the heavy atmosphere of the room.

'Yes,' the minister repeated, his eyes closed, a thumb and finger pinching the bridge of his nose. 'They will be released after they have given us all the information they have. Officially they will merely be numbered among the many people brought in for questioning and subsequently released.'

'Is that an order, sir?' O'Malley asked starchily, glancing across at the commissioner and his deputy. The senior men ignored the question.

'I see,' O'Malley muttered.

'I'm glad you understand the delicate nature of this business, Mr O'Malley,' the minister said with affected warmth. 'The security of this country and others throughout Europe could be at stake.' The politician rose to signify the end of the conversation. O'Malley and Sullivan stood but the others remained seated.

'Thank you for coming in, gentlemen, and for your understanding,' the minister said, shaking their hands.

When they had left the room, the minister placed the palms of his hands flat on the desk top and, with deliberate clarity, said to MacIntyre, 'If we do catch any of those involved, Chief Superintendent, nothing must happen to them on *Irish* soil.'

The Englishman matched the minister's frank expression. 'Our people will make absolutely sure of that, Minister.'

Outside the building, O'Malley and Sullivan stood for a moment in silence, drawing heavily on cigarettes.

'The man behind this whole caper, sir,' Sullivan said with an air of confidentiality, 'any idea who he might be?'

For just a fleeting moment, a knowing, comprehending, smile touched O'Malley's face. Then it was gone.

'How the hell would *I* know,' he rasped, and walked quickly to his car.

Charles Casswell has just completed a second stint at the clay and rubble wall separating the escape tunnel from the burial vaults. He and Coates lay now at the other end of the tunnel while Stolford and Dufour laboured at what they had nicknamed 'the pitface'. They worked in silence and in darkness. Stolford had advised against using electric torches in case even the tiny spark from the switch ignited the methane gas.

All of them wore Siebe Gorman gas masks linked by rubber breathing tubes to gas-absorbent canisters strapped to their chests. Each canister had a working life of about thirty minutes and every man had two. As they had put them on only when the gas warning light on the Draeger meter had begun emitting a constant beam, they were well within the safety limits for the length of time they would be confined in the escape tunnel.

They were all sweating now, from their exertions and because air no longer blew through the tunnel. There was only one small draught, from a hole the size of a thumb in the clay wall where Casswell and Coates lay.

The actor kept his face close to the hole, luxuriating in the tiny current of air playing on the side of his head. For some reason he could not understand, the flow was not constant, stopping for several seconds and then resuming. He swivelled onto his side and began poking at the hole to increase the draught. His hand, ungloved for his rest period, hit a sharp stone, his gold signet ring scraping along its edge. He changed hands and resumed the scooping action. The hole was now big enough to take his entire hand and wrist. The clay suddenly felt warm. Then the pain. Deep and searing like a cut from a jagged and rusty bread knife. He pulled his hand back sharply and the brown rat came with it, teeth still embedded in the soft flesh between his index finger and thumb.

Casswell was on his knees now, swinging his arm and the rat from side to side. 'Dirty bastard,' he screamed in pain and fear. The rat released its hold and scampered across Coates' legs. The youngster squirmed and fled along the tunnel away, he thought, from the rat. Stolford and Dufour had stopped working now, peering uselessly into the gloom to try to see the cause of the commotion.

'What's happenin'?' Stolford demanded.

'A rat,' Coates yelled, now suddenly beside him.

'No, no,' the Frenchman moaned. 'Keep it away, keep it away...'

'Stay still, Edouard,' Stolford barked. 'Don't move. Just listen for it... we'll find it.'

Dufour fell silent, listening, terrified, holding his breath. He could hear nothing except the breathing of the other two men. Coates had frozen in an all-fours position. His arms began to tremble from the strain of supporting the weight of his body. He moved slowly and gently to one side, easing himself down onto one buttock. His backside brushed Dufour's leg and foot as he lowered it to the floor and the effect on the Frenchman was like a detonation.

With an ear-splitting scream, Dufour threw himself across Coates and grabbed for the spot where he had left his torchlight. Stolford knew the danger. He screamed at the diver, a long, piercing word which melted into, and became part of, the vortex which followed. And the light of the torch became part of the light of death when Dufour found and pressed the switch. A huge blue-tinted whiteness filled the mens eyes before they were pushed back into the sockets and the brains beyond. In the confined space it was as if they were inside a giant reactor, part of the implosive detonation of an atom bomb. The massive compressive force of the blast waves effortlessly burst through the flesh and bones of their chests, destroying tissue and organs and flattening skulls and bodies to a depth of only three and a half inches, front to back.

Only Charles Casswell was alive, saved by the proximity of the clay obstruction beside him. He had been thrown through the clay into the old tunnel beyond, the ceiling above the obstruction caving in and sealing again the escape route. Both legs had compound fractures and one hand was bent and twisted into a mass of blood and bone fragments. The gas mask, which had otherwise saved his face, had been torn off, and with it his right ear. His hair, what was left of it, stood in tiny tufts on his scorched scalp. His sight was blurred when he tested it on the luminous dial of his watch.

Slowly, very slowly, he began the tortuous journey towards the river Liffey, pulling his broken body with the one useful arm. Perhaps there would be an opening. The cold air lapped over his face like the waves of consciousness and pain. The tunnel sloped slightly as it dropped towards the river and here the clay became damp to the touch. The river, tidal, flowed up to this point, a little higher during storm flooding. Now he could see tiny rays of light. It was street lighting, reflecting through the rat holes in the quay wall. Just below the stone he could feel the flowing water passing the cracks between the granite blocks. Oh God, so close. He tried to shout but the effort only produced a faint croak and a mouthful of blood from his internal injuries.

All this time they had watched and waited. At first, dazed and terrified by the deafening blast, they had worked deep into their homes in the clay walls of the tunnel. But now, sensing his defencelessness, they approached to within a few feet of the injured human. Normally, even in the greatest of numbers, rats would not attack a man except when cornered or provoked savagely. But their temperament had changed in the last week, since the first of their breed had been attacked by the mad dogs scavenging in the alleyways. Fighting among themselves had increased, and those still unaffected by the madness were afraid to venture far for food. They were very hungry.

Casswell heard them, vaguely, scurrying around his feet, sniffing and moving back again quickly, stumbling into each other, squealing in fright and anger, getting bolder with the passing seconds. He felt, or thought he did, the first tentative nibbles at the broken flesh where his splintered leg bones protruded. He tried to shake off the vermin but his legs could not respond.

His lips moved, but the words were only in his mind. 'God, oh Jesus, please help me.'

They chewed everything: his clothes, his shoes, even his hair. Later they would squirm into the empty eye sockets to savour the succulent tissue beyond. It would take less than one day to reduce Charles Casswell to his basic frame. And for days after that they would enjoy the marrow in the broken bones.

Only the signet ring would remain untouched.

Chapter Fourteen

Monday morning hung like dark canvas over the huddling city of Dublin, early lowering skies quickly losing contrast and turning deepest grey, people and vehicles moving dispiritedly through the layers of drizzle – unrelated, removed, as ghost ships and their souls from generations apart.

Peter Phelan, stooped deep in the shoulders of his anorak, drove Charles Casswell's hired car the mile from his apartment in Monkstown to Dean's Grange Cemetery, the windscreen wipers thumping their lazy tattoo, smearing the glass with the street's diluted dirt. He did not notice the black car which followed at a discreet distance.

Like others that morning, others in their centrally heated offices around the city, he wondered about the whereabouts of Ireland's art treasures and those who had taken them. Phelan had read the newspaper reports of the shooting at the lockup garage in Rathmines, and a slow-motoring drive past the premises yesterday, with their guard of two uniformed policemen, confirmed the address. The same reports told of the fruitless search for the treasures and the thieves. So, what had happened? Where were Stolford, Casswell, Dufour and Coates? Exactly what was the plan of escape for the men and their haul? Only one man knew the overall plan, but who the hell was The Voice?

He parked the car close to the gates of the cemetery extension, unaware of the other vehicle and its driver a short distance down the road. For once in the past five years, Phelan knew he had protected himself against the scheming and weaknesses of others who had used him and his skills: the Tara

247

Brooch was lying in its cloth protection under the surface of his brother's grave.

But as he neared the area, his eyes widened in disbelief, his fingers impatiently wiping the droplets of drizzle from the lenses of his glasses. He stopped at the foot of the grave, or what had been a grave. It was now just an empty hole. Maybe his memory was playing tricks? He counted the graves in the row. The number tallied. He looked down again: no coffin and no soil.

On the grave alongside were several wreaths and dome-covered plastic flowers. He scrabbled frantically among them, discarding each carelessly and roughly as he moved to the next. Then there it was, his wife's handwriting on one of the cards. He counted again. Eleven, same as before.

'Somethin' wrong, mate?'

The voice jack-knifed him straight. He turned to look into the bristled face of the man in the waterproof overalls. The man was leaning on a shovel, his expression anxious, accent Dublin.

'I was watchin' ye from over there,' he said, jerking a thumb, 'and reckoned somethin' was up.'

Phelan pulled himself to his feet, wincing. The gravedigger reached over and helped him up.

'My brother...,' Phelan began awkwardly, 'his grave, that is...'

'What's his name, mate?' the gravedigger asked.

'Phelan, John Phelan.'

The gravedigger reached inside his overalls and brought out two sheets of folded paper, grubby from handling.

'This is the new graves list,' he explained, reaching inside again for his spectacles. He peered down through the thick lenses at the sheets. 'Phelan.. Phelan... ah, here it is. Let's see now...'

The gravedigger squinted over the top of his spectacles at the row of graves, his mouth silently moving as he counted, his head turning slowly until it came in line with the flower-be-decked grave.

'There y'are, that's the one,' he said positively, pointing at the flowers.

Now Phelan countered. He turned accusingly to the grave-digger. 'Are you sure about that? I was here just the other day and that was my brother's grave,' he said, nodding towards the open hole. 'The flowers were on that one.'

'Ah, God,' said the gravedigger, 'not another one.' The last words had a ring of kindly if patronising understanding.

'What do you mean?' Phelan demanded.

'Well,' said the gravedigger with the patience of one imparting knowledge to an imbecile, 'ye picked it out by the names on the flowers, right?'

Phelan nodded.

'Mistake, mistake,' said the gravedigger in a tone of gentle admonishment. 'Only go by the number. Every grave is numbered and every plot is named. Like St Ann's or St Ita's, ye see. So ye get the number from the office and ask one of us here to help ye find it if ye don't understand the system.'

'But there are no numbers on these graves,' Phelan said sharply, sweeping his hand along the row.

'Ah, ye see,' said the gravedigger, 'that's where yer wrong. All right, there might not be numbers to see, but they're there all the same. We know them,' he thumbed his chest importantly.

'But the flowers...'

'Yeah, well, that's a different story,' the man acknowledged. 'Y'see in the past few weeks we've had a clutch of young brats comin' in here after school and causin' all kinds o' trouble. Knockin, over vases, throwin' marble chippin's around the place. And their latest gag is takin' flowers from one grave and puttin' 'em on another. Causes no end o' problems for the relatives. And for us. Little bastards.'

'So that means...' Phelan began, his face filling with comprehension.

'Exactly,' the gravedigger interrupted. 'What I've been tellin' ye for the last five minutes. The other day when ye came, ye musta gone to the wrong grave. That one.' He pointed at the hole.

'But there was a... it was filled in the other day,' Phelan protested.

'It was filled in until early this mornin' even,' the gravedigger confirmed.

'So what happened?'

'Ah, now there's a funny thing,' the gravedigger said, a smile twinkling the eyes behind the thick lenses. 'Yer man there was an Irish-American, if ye know what I mean. Name of Tobin. Michael Tobin. Over here to visit cousins or somethin'. Anyway, he ups and dies. Heart. So he's buried here 'cause his will said he wanted to be buried in Irish soil.'

Phelan nodded unnecessary encouragement. The gravedigger was warming to his tale.

'But the wife now, she thinks different. She's in America and she wants yer man buried over there. So they've got a problem, ye'd think, wouldn't ye? But no. Some whizzkid of a Yankee lawyer comes up with the perfect answer: take the whole thing to Los Angeles, coffin, body and even the bloody soil. Everyone's happy.'

'Jesus,' said Phelan, with more feeling than the gravedigger realised.

'Bloody Yanks,' the gravedigger chuckled, folding his glasses and putting them back inside his overalls. 'They think of every shaggin' trick, don't they?'

The question was unanswered. The young engineer had turned away, his stomach knotted in the face of this final, merciless twist of fate. His entire body was numb, hands hanging loosely by his side, his gait a shuffling and unco-ordinated momentum. The drizzle was heavier now, blowing in swirls around the marble and stone slabs and crosses, whipping its needle points across his unfeeling face.

The gravedigger watched him for a few moments, then shrugged dismissively and turned away to find shelter in the workers' building across the cemetery.

Through the gates now, Peter Phelan turned towards the hired car at the kerbside. Only then did he hesitate in his stumbling stride, the small paper package under the windscreen wiper sharply focusing his attention.

He looked around but there was no one on the road except for an elderly man huddled in a raincoat and pushing laboriously on the pedals of his bicycle to make slow headway into the wind. The old man ignored Phelan, the only sound as he passed being his heavy breaths and the rhythmic squeak of one wheel.

Phelan took the package and sat in the car. He peeled the damp, brown paper from the rectangular plastic container and stared intently at the C-60 cassette tape. Too much had happened today and he was having difficulty in concentrating his mind on the simplest tasks. He shook himself from the trance and put the tape into the radio cassette player in the dashboard. When he switched it on, the sound was the same as all the previous tapes, metallic and distorted.

Mr Phelan, I believe we have some unfinished business. The art treasures did not come out of the sewers, as planned, and the police have tried unsuccessfully to find them there. Therefore, they must still be in the old tunnel leading to the vaults beneath St Michan's Church.

We have all done too much in this operation to abandon it now. It deserves – you deserve – to see it completed. The transportation plans are still operative, the buyers still anxious to purchase: the only task remaining is to see that the treasures are removed safely from the tunnel and sent on their way. Your knowledge of the tunnel and the vaults is vital. For that knowledge and your assistance, a sum of two million United States dollars will be deposited in a Swiss bank account for you.

In a few days from now, Mr Phelan, a further tape will be despatched, with dates, times and other details, including the names of some men who will be sent to assist you. Goodbye for now.

For long seconds, Phelan listened to the hiss of the tape in the loudspeaker before he reached forward and switched off the machine. Again the inevitable and unanswerable: who *was* The Voice, this faceless man who seemed to know him as well as he knew himself and who knew his every movement. The knowing and shadowy being was haunting, even frightening, yet, strangely, reassuring in such moments of indecision and loneliness.

For a moment, Phelan thought he imagined what he now saw approaching through the heavy rain. He switched on the wipers and wiped the inside of the glass with the back of his hand. The image was suddenly clear.

He stepped quickly from the car and blurted, 'Hello, Betty.'

The girl stopped in the gateway of the cemetery and turned

to face him, wiping a strand of hair from her forehead. She wore a white raincoat and floppy-rimmed waterproof hat.

'Hello, Peter,' she replied, her reflex smile disappearing in her sudden uncertainty.

He walked towards her and stopped a few feet away. 'What are you...?'

'I come here every day,' she interrupted – too hastily, she realised. Then the smile again, this time of apology, reassurance. 'It was the only place I could think of that you might visit.'

She searched his face for some sign. 'I didn't know where you lived and I wanted... I thought, you know...' She shrugged, leaving the sentence incomplete.

Again the scanning of his thin face for some indication of his mood, his feelings. His eyes, behind the rain-splashed spectacles, were a blur.

'I was just thinking,' he began, his tone seemingly measured.

'Yes,' she prompted in an eagerness which embarrassed her instantly.

'I was just thinking,' he began again, 'that that is the silliest hat I've ever seen.'

She snatched her hat, reflexively, from her head, her hair falling to her shoulders, the rain forgotten.

'Yes,' she said quietly, studying the hat, held now at her waist. 'I suppose it is, really. Just with the rain and everything...'

Betty looked up into his face again. He was grinning broadly, enjoying her shyness and her vulnerability. She was, as she always had been, the most complete, the most consumingly beautiful woman ever created.

'Oh, God,' she whispered, and threw herself forward into his arms.

His lips were everywhere, on her mouth, her forehead, her nose, her eyes, her neck. Her hands gripped his wet hair, pulling his face onto hers, their bodies tight together in a frenzied release of long captive emotions. The water on their faces tasted salty now, tears mingling with the raindrops, and still they embraced and explored.

When finally they stood quietly for a few moments in each

others arms, Betty gently chuckled, 'You'll have no battery left.'

'Huh?' Phelan followed her gaze. The windscreen wipers were still sweeping across the glass but more slowly than before. He remembered the tape that had been placed there.

'I've eh, something to do... in the next few days, so...' he began. He felt her stiffening. 'Relax,' he soothed. 'Just a little unfinished business.' He kissed her forehead. 'Then, I'll be around so much I'll bore the pants off you.'

'Yes?' she grinned mischievously.

His laughter welled up from deep inside, a long, gurgling infectious sound which Betty had not heard for so long but which she had never forgotten. Suddenly, she was laughing too, her forehead pressed into his shoulder, her body trembling with the delicious joy of their unity.

Inside the cemetery, at a grave not far from the gates, the tall man in the black raincoat and hat stood reverently, his head bowed and hands joined before him. His eyes, however, never left the embracing couple in the gateway.

The laughter, eddying in the rain and wind, washed over him at short intervals. He found the sound irresistible. His chuckle, when it came, was more subdued but no less enjoyable.

Deputy Commissioner George Swann gave the couple a last look and pulled his hat brim further down his forehead before he turned, smiling, onto the path which led across the burial ground. He was still smiling long after the sounds were but a memory.

It had been a good day for The Voice.

Eight miles distant, the elderly woman with the shopping bags huddled into the inadequate collar of her saturated overcoat and tried to increase her pace. Her frail legs, tired and chilled by the biting rain, would not respond. No matter, she consoled herself, it was now only a few hundred yards to her grandchildren's home in this concrete maze of housing.

The cross-bred, alsatian-type dog watched the old woman's swaying approach and, despite the hunger and more strongly felt anger, checked his impatience. Once, then again, he shook the slimy, white trail from his slobbering jaws and braced himself, ears flattened, teeth bared...